GATEKEEPERS

GATEKEEPERS

For: Russell Burwell

Ace Texas Attorney

James E. Merriman

J. Merriman

iUniverse, Inc.

New York Lincoln Shanghai

GateKeepers

Copyright © 2007 by James E. Merriman

iUniverse books may be ordered through booksellers or by contacting:

iUniverse
2021 Pine Lake Road, Suite 100
Lincoln, NE 68512
www.iuniverse.com
1-800-Authors (1-800-288-4677)

ISBN-13: 978-0-595-40788-0 (pbk)
ISBN-13: 978-0-595-85153-9 (cloth)
ISBN-13: 978-0-595-85152-2 (ebk)
ISBN-10: 0-595-40788-9 (pbk)
ISBN-10: 0-595-85153-3 (cloth)
ISBN-10: 0-595-85152-5 (ebk)

Printed in the United States of America

Fay, without your love and encouragement
this book would not have been possible.

PROLOGUE

▼

Ricky Meredith was happily tapping the steering wheel of his new Cadillac Escalade as he sang "My Maria" along with Brooks & Dunn. It was another day in an endless string of sunny days in Scottsdale, Arizona, as he pulled up for the stoplight at Ninety-sixth Street and Shea Boulevard. Today, for the first time in a very long time, his knee was pain free. More importantly, he was on a mission; he had things to do.

He glanced over as a black Mercedes eased up on his left side. The driver had long, blonde hair and was wearing big sunglasses. A large diamond on the third finger of her right hand reflected the sunlight.

As Ricky stared at the woman, the Mercedes' window slid downward, and the blonde leaned toward him across her front seat, saying something he couldn't hear with his window up.

With a big smile, he pushed the button and lowered his window. The woman smiled in return and calmly raised a Beretta from the seat next to her. The last thing he saw was the silencer affixed to the Beretta—just before his brains were plastered all over the inside of the Escalade.

As the light turned green, the Mercedes eased away and left the Escalade blocking traffic.

Vince Jones was stuck behind Ricky's Escalade. The cars that were left from the morning rush hour whizzed by, refusing to let him change lanes. It was already ninety-five degrees, and the air conditioner in his car wasn't working. He was sweating like a pig. He wiped a drop of sweat from his nose with the back of his hand, knowing he was going to be late for work again. His horn was having no effect. When the light turned red and the lanes around him filled with cars, his patience snapped. He leaned forward, peeling his shirt off the car seat, and pulled his obese body out of his old Pontiac. Vince lumbered toward the Escalade, ready to read the idiot driver the riot act.

As Vince was approaching the Escalade, the black Mercedes turned left at One-hundredth Street. Two blocks up, it pulled into a Lucky's Supermarket parking lot.

Careful to avoid being hit by the cars rushing past him, Vince approached the Escalade from which some idiot country song was blaring on the radio. He hated country music. Vince took a deep breath and prepared to give the driver a piece of his mind. When he looked inside the Escalade, what came out of his mouth was not a string of invective but his breakfast.

As Vince was depositing his breakfast all over the side of the SUV, the blonde, wearing a white sundress, exited her Mercedes and went into the Lucky's store, carrying a big straw handbag. A few minutes later, the same woman, now with dark hair and dressed in jeans and a dark blouse, emerged from Lucky's, carrying the same straw handbag. She crossed the parking lot to a nondescript Toyota sedan.

Twenty minutes later, the Toyota pulled into the parking lot at the Kierland Shops. The dark-haired woman left the car unlocked and casually window-shopped along the narrow street. At mid-block, she put a wad of white fabric into a trash container and crossed the street, entering the gift shop of the Kierland Hotel. A few minutes later, she emerged from the front door and took a taxi to the airport.

CHAPTER 1

▼

My ranch, the Durango Land & Cattle Company, was nestled in the Pine River Valley near Durango, Colorado. Four thousand acres ran for almost five miles along both sides of the Pine River. Beside the river toward the south end of the ranch, set among a stand of pine trees, sat a rambling, old, two-story house. A twelve-stall horse barn was situated about fifty yards from the house, and a set of corrals and a two-hundred-by-four-hundred-foot riding arena could be seen beyond the barn.

The sun was setting behind the pine forest that rose upon the western perimeter of the ranch as I followed two Corriente steers out of the shadows and headed down the hill toward the barn. It had been a long day, and I was lazily spinning a rope above the backs of the steers as they moved toward the corrals. One of the steers made a move to turn back toward the pines, and my horse effortlessly stepped sideways and blocked its path.

After putting the steers in the near corral, I headed toward the barn from which a mournful tune blended in with the darkening shadows.

"Hello, Tommy, you here?" I asked, entering the barn.

A short, bowlegged man, wearing a grimy, sweat-stained Stetson of indeterminate color, emerged from the feed room, holding four feed buckets. He spit a stream of brown tobacco juice in the general direction of a sleeping barn cat and said, "Sure, Grant, did you find those steers?"

"Yeah, they were down by the pond. What song is that?"

"'Blues at Sunrise'—Albert King, Jimi Hendrix, and Janis Joplin at the Filmore West in 1968."

The flash of blinking red and white lights cut through the darkness, preceding the arrival of a La Plata County sheriff's jeep at the barn entrance. Deputy Sheriff Larry Walker slowly climbed out. He was normally a happy-go-lucky, beer-drinking buddy of Tommy's. Today, he trudged slowly into the barn, looking like a very unhappy man.

"Grant, I've got some really bad news." He stopped and looked at the ground.

"Come on, Larry, out with it."

Larry took a deep breath, and the words spilled out. "We got a call from the Scottsdale police. They said your brother has been murdered." He handed me a card with a name and phone number written on it.

CHAPTER 2

▼

I caught the 7:00 AM flight to Phoenix and spent the next hour staring out the window at miles and miles of high desert with nothing there. I didn't know whether to be angry or sad. What I could feel was a sense that part of my life was gone forever. Ricky had been a scrawny, little kid that I had protected from school-yard bullies. At fourteen, he filled out, grew to over six feet, and discovered basketball. We spent countless hours playing one-on-one in the backyard. I was in college, and Ricky was a high-school, all-American basketball player when our parents died in an automobile crash. We helped each other overcome that tragedy and had been very close over the years. With his death, I had no more family. I had friends, of course, but at this moment I felt alone, all alone.

What had happened? I was to contact a Detective Dolan but had no information other than the address of the police station.

In the lobby of the police station, I asked the receptionist for Detective Dolan. A young, female, uniformed officer was passing by and said, "Come on, I'll take you to his office. It's like a maze back there. What brings you to see Dan?"

"I'm here about Ricky ... I mean ... Richard Meredith. I'm his brother."

"Oh, I'm so sorry, Mr. Meredith."

"Thank you." This young woman was in her late twenties, trim, and attractive. She didn't know me from Adam; yet, from her expression and the tone of her voice, she seemed genuinely concerned. Not the usual "I'm-sorry-for-your-loss" mantra.

"Here we are, Mr. Meredith. If there is something we can do, just let us know."

"Thank you, that's very kind, Officer—"

"Gonzales. Lisa Gonzales."

I took the wooden chair Detective Dan Dolan offered across from his desk and put my cowboy hat in my lap. Dolan was middle-aged and skinny, and his pot belly protruded over wrinkled gray slacks.

"I'm sorry for your loss, Mr. Meredith. We're doing everything we can to find the killer, but these things take time."

"What have you found out?"

"Very little. This may be a random drive-by shooting, but at this stage, we can't be sure. Do you know of anyone who might have had it in for your brother—an ex-wife, bookie—anyone like that?"

"No, Ricky was a very easy-going guy. He never married. He had a lot of girl-friends, but he always left them smiling. He was a sports nut, but I know he wasn't into gambling."

Dolan tore a sheet of paper off the pad on his desk, picked up his pen, and said, "I have a few routine background questions, if you don't mind."

"No, go ahead."

"Did your brother have any history of drug use?"

I didn't hesitate. "He hated drugs. His best friend in high school died of an accidental drug overdose, and on top of that, Ricky had a problem getting off pain killers after his knee surgery. He couldn't stand being around the stuff."

"Does he have any relatives besides you?"

"No, our parents are dead. We have a couple of distant cousins, but we have no contact with them."

"Can you think of anyone who might benefit from your brother's death?"

"No."

"Where did your brother work?"

"I don't think he did. He didn't need money." That answer got Dolan's attention, and, for the first time, he seemed interested in my answers.

"Really, how did he support himself?"

"He played with the Knicks for a few years before his knee gave out. I under-stand that his contract had a lot of deferred compensation or some kind of an annuity connected with it."

With this answer, Dolan stopped writing and leaned back in his chair. "I see. Other than this contract, did he have any other source of income?"

"I really don't know. We never talked about money. He lived in an apartment and got a new car every few years—nothing really special. He tended to hang out with women who had a lot of money. I don't think he had much beyond the con-tract payout."

"Did he have any life insurance?"

"I don't know."

Dolan leaned back into his desk and made a few notes. He looked directly into my eyes and asked, "Where were you Wednesday afternoon?"

"At my ranch in Colorado."

Dolan made another note, folded his hands on the desk, and gave me a sincere look. "Mr. Meredith, at this point, we don't have any leads. This could have been a drive-by shooting, possibly a gang initiation. Unfortunately, drive-bys happen all the time. But they don't happen in North Scottsdale in broad daylight with a Beretta. We'll talk to your brother's friends and see if anything turns up. We're under a lot of pressure to solve this case quickly. The mayor called. This is a tourist town, and the season is getting ready to start. You can be sure that finding your brother's killer has top priority."

He took a pack of Camels out of his desk drawer, shook one out, and lit it. "Let me tell you what we do know. We have one witness. He was behind your brother at the stoplight. Your brother's SUV didn't move when the light turned green, so he got out and looked in the window and saw your brother. He said he thinks there was a black sedan next to your brother at the light.

"We found an abandoned black Mercedes in a nearby supermarket parking lot but no usable prints or fibers. There was some gunpowder residue, but that may not be related, and even if it is, it doesn't take us anywhere without something else. The car had been stolen that morning from the underground garage in a downtown-Phoenix office building. It may be the car our witness described, but we can't be sure.

"I have two men interviewing store employees where the car was found to see if they noticed anything, but I'm not hopeful. That's all we have."

What they had was nothing. While I didn't want to be cynical, it was clear to me that this investigation needed a major breakthrough, or else, it was going nowhere.

"I'll do my best to keep you informed, but feel free to call me or stop in from time to time. You'll have to excuse me now. I have a squad meeting." Dolan rose to his feet.

"I'll be at the Boulders Hotel until they release Ricky's body," I said.

As I headed up Scottsdale Road toward the Boulders Hotel in Carefree, I thought about Ricky. I was a decent athlete and serious about school. Ricky, on the other hand, had never been serious about anything *except* basketball. He was a white guy that could fly like Michael Jordan. School was something to endure until he could get to the NBA. After our parents died, he lived with his coach until he finished high school.

By the time Ricky was playing college hoops for Gonzaga, I was flying Apache attack helicopters for the army. He was drafted by the Knicks, and the army sent me to Georgetown for a degree in Arabic studies.

Although we were apart most of the time, we stayed in contact by phone and e-mail. We shared our successes, failures, hopes, and dreams. When Ricky blew out his knee, I got emergency leave and stayed in the hospital with him. I think that when we lost both parents so unexpectedly at our relatively young ages, it bonded us even more closely.

I agreed with Dolan. It seemed highly unlikely that Ricky's murder had been a random drive-by shooting. But if it weren't, why would someone murder him?

For the next three days, I couldn't read or watch TV. I just couldn't focus. I felt helpless and alone. To clear my head, I ran aimlessly for miles and miles. It didn't help. One moment I grieved for Ricky, another moment I felt sorry for myself. No family, no one to confide in or share my grief with. Once, when I couldn't put one foot in front of the other, I looked around and had no idea where I was. Fortunately, another jogger pointed me in the right direction, and I walked back to the Boulders.

Ricky's apartment remained off limits as part of the investigation, but they finally released his body. I had him cremated and returned to Durango with the ashes.

CHAPTER 3

▼

The last light of the October day faded in the western sky. A muted television set and a single lamp lit the ranch library as I sat smoking my favorite pipe. The pipe smoke curled toward the ceiling, giving the room a hazy glow. Ricky's ashes were on the desk in front of me. Two weeks and I still couldn't figure out what to do with the ashes. They just sat there, waiting.

I loved Ricky. He was always upbeat. At six foot four and with the lean, athletic build of a basketball player, dark, wavy hair, and an infectious smile, women loved being around him. He was not opinionated, minded his own business, and just went with the flow. For the past few years, he had squired a succession of women around Scottsdale, who couldn't get enough of him.

I had been after him to do something with his life after his basketball career had ended but had not had any success. He kept telling me not to worry and that everything was cool, but there was an aimlessness about him that bothered me. He had so much to offer, but the motivation was missing. A shrink friend of mine told me that the premature loss of our parents and the unexpected end of his basketball career had set him adrift in life without an anchor.

I wasn't sure I agreed with that, but I *was* sure that I loved him, that I missed him, and that I was angry, lonely, and frustrated that his murder seemed senseless and that there was no progress in catching his killer. Why would anyone want to murder Ricky? I wanted to know why someone would do this.

I looked up, and the ashes were still there.

Once, soon after I had bought the ranch, Ricky had come to Colorado for his only visit. We had trailered horses around Vallecito Lake to the Pine River trail head. After riding up the trail a few miles, we had ridden into the river. A passing backpacker had taken our picture on horseback in the middle of the river. The picture was on the wall, lit by the lamp.

About midnight, it hit me. I got up, turned out the light, and went to bed.

At dawn, I was in the barn, saddling the gray gelding, Cloud, that Ricky had ridden on his visit. After hitching a horse trailer to my pickup and loading up my gear and the horse, I headed for Vallecito with Ricky's ashes on the seat next to me.

At the Pine River trailhead, I poured the ashes into the right side of old leather saddlebags and set off up the trail. Passing through the pine forest along the fence line of Granite Peaks Ranch, Ricky and I had crossed two small creeks that were virtually dry this time of year but would be rushing with water during the spring snowmelt.

At the two-mile point, the trail entered the Weimenuche Wilderness—four hundred thirty thousand acres of pristine wilderness intersected by only a few trails. Here, the mountains closed in on the trail, and it began to run alongside the river, rushing clear and cold from its headwaters far above.

I eased Cloud into the river which, at that point, was about thirty yards wide and eighteen inches deep. The Pine River valley had narrowed to no more than a half mile. Large swaths of aspens grew among the pines that covered the mountains. The golden color of the aspen leaves sparkled in the autumn sunlight and was highlighted by the green of the surrounding pines.

Pulling a hunting knife from my belt, I lifted the right saddlebag and made a hole the size of a quarter in the bottom of the leather bag. As Cloud meandered up the middle of the river, Ricky's ashes slowly drifted out of the saddlebag and into the shimmering water.

I knew that the Pine emptied into the Animas River above Farmington, New Mexico, and that the Animas emptied into the San Juan, which leads to the Rio Grande. The Rio Grande divides Texas and Mexico and finally runs into the Gulf of Mexico. It would be a beautiful journey.

A lonely bald eagle soared in circles high above.

Sometime later, I left the river and returned to the trail. About a mile later, the river narrowed into a gorge almost one hundred feet deep. There was a fixed suspension bridge across the gorge, which Cloud gingerly crossed. Another mile and we came into a large clearing where the mountains receded and the valley opened. I hobbled Cloud and made a fire in a ring of stones. When the fire was blazing, I put the saddlebags in the fire and waited until there was nothing left.

I took each stone to the river and dropped them in. After dousing the fire with water, Cloud and I headed back down the mountain trail.

I got back to the ranch long after dark. I left my frustration in the mountains. It was replaced with a determination to find out who murdered Ricky and why.

CHAPTER 4

▼

I spent the next few days doing busy work around the ranch—cleaning tack, mending fences, and straightening the workshop. How was I going to find out about Ricky's murder without the police getting all over me? I was stuck just trying to figure out where to start.

My answer came that evening with a phone call from Rose Donnelley who, through her tears, told me that she and Ricky had been seeing one another for about six months. The police had been there and had told her about Ricky. She hadn't been able to help them but had felt the need to reach out to someone. My number was listed.

Rose told me that Ricky had talked about me often. She talked about Ricky for a while, and we agreed to meet when I came to Phoenix to dispose of Ricky's effects.

The thirty-six-seat Mesa Air airplane from Durango finished its heat-induced bumpy descent into Phoenix. As the attendant opened the door, a wave of heat turned the inside of the small plane into a sauna. Welcome to Phoenix in October—105 degrees at 11:00 AM.

I met the Goodwill truck at Ricky's apartment and let them have the furniture and clothes. I bagged the dishes, kitchen utensils, and some other junk to throw out. All that was left were a dozen basketball trophies and assorted plaques and awards from his playing days. That was it? Thirty-four years on this earth and all he left behind was basketball memorabilia? There had to be more meaning to his life than his brief basketball career.

I bagged the trophies and dropped them with the other junk in the dumpster behind the apartment building. I went about ten feet when I stopped, turned around, and went back to the dumpster to retrieve the trophies and the other memorabilia. I realized that I had thrown them away in a fit of anger directed at Ricky because he was dead and I was alone. That was foolish. I was proud of my brother and of what he had accomplished with the talent God had given him. I decided to create a special place at the ranch for his memorabilia.

I drove up the 101 freeway toward North Scottsdale, debating with myself. I was no detective; shouldn't I just let the police do the investigating? I finally decided to go one step at a time. Getting started was the hard part.

Rose Donnelley lived in Estancia, an exclusive golf-course community about thirty minutes from the airport. I pulled up to the front gate and was confronted by a guardhouse connected to a massive arched entryway made of stone.

"Can I help you, sir?" asked a uniformed, no-nonsense-looking woman.

"Grant Meredith to see Rose Donnelley. She's expecting me."

"One moment, sir." She examined a clipboard and apparently found my name.

"Go on in, sir. Take the second left. It's the third house on the right—number 206."

The earth-toned house was Santa Fe pueblo style and blended perfectly into the mountain that rose sharply behind it. I approached the door, wondering how Ricky found these women or, rather, how they found him.

The door opened, and I was engulfed in a cloud of cloying perfume. I thought I was going to gag. There stood a forty-something woman with too much bottle-blonde, teased hair. Artificial boobs were bursting from a too-tight, purple tank top. White short-shorts and sandals completed an ensemble that should have been on Pamela Anderson but, instead, was squeezed onto a body that was at least twenty pounds overweight.

She extended a hand with long, fire-engine red fingernails. "Hello, Grant, I'm Rose. Sorry to meet you under these circumstances. Come in."

"Likewise." I entered the cloud of perfume and followed her down a long, marble-floored hallway into an enormous room with a twenty-foot ceiling. The far wall was entirely glass. Outside, a negative-edge pool seemed to disappear into the mountain. A bar with a mirror behind it was positioned on the left side of the room. Mounted on the wall beyond the bar were stuffed heads of elk, prong horn antelope, and a big horn sheep. The middle of the room was home to a pool table. Off to the right, I saw a seating area positioned around a huge flat-panel TV. This was a macho, jock, guy room if I ever saw one, and it sure didn't fit Rose Donnelley.

As if reading my mind, Rose waived her arm around and said, "My ex-husband was really into guy things. This is his idea of decorating. One of these days, I'll get around to changing it. Can I get you a drink? I'm having a martini."

"Sounds good to me."

Rose poured straight vodka into a silver shaker, which she handled like a pro. She filled two chilled glasses and dropped an olive in each one. "Please sit," she directed, handing me my frosted glass. She kicked off her sandals and settled on the leather sofa with her legs curled under her. I sat on the adjacent club chair.

"Here's to Ricky," she said, raising her glass to lips that matched her fingernails. She inhaled a large portion of her drink. I sipped mine, and the vodka burned all the way down.

As we talked about Ricky, her eyes got misty, and then tears washed mascara from under her eyes. Rose seemed to have been genuinely fond of him. What he saw in her, beyond the obvious, was a mystery to me. As we exchanged some memories of Ricky, she settled down, and by the middle of the second martini, I figured it was time to get to the point of my visit before she got into a third.

"Rose, do you know of anyone Ricky was having trouble with or anything that might shed some light on why he was murdered?"

"The police asked me that," Rose answered. "We had only been seeing each other for about six months. Ricky didn't talk about much except sports, sometimes politics, but that was so boring."

"Did you notice any change in his behavior recently?" I prodded. "Was he moody or withdrawn? Did anything about him seem different? Maybe he talked about something besides sports and politics?"

"Well, it didn't occur to me when the police were here, I was so upset. But now that I think about it, he started talking about kids and drugs. He rambled on and on about how politicians and judges had just opened the school doors to drug dealers. I didn't pay much attention. My kids are grown, and, thank God, they didn't have drug problems. Booze problems, maybe, but not drugs—at least none that I knew about."

She got up and weaved toward the bar and the martini shaker. "Ready for a refill, Grant?"

"Sure." While she looked down to make the drinks, I dumped my half-full glass in the plant next to the chair. I was running out of time to get anything useful out of her.

"Did Ricky say anything about why he was so interested in kids and drugs?"

She spat. "That bitch!"

"What are you talking about?"

"I had put it out of my mind, but that bitch Anna had been talking to him about her son."

I forced myself to keep from showing any surprise at this news. "Apparently, you don't care for Anna?"

"Ricky was dating her before we met, and she just didn't want to let go. She kept calling him. I told Ricky he should tell her to stop bugging him, but he said that her son was having problems and that she needed someone to talk to. The kid's father wasn't around. Personally, I think she was just trying to get Ricky back."

Finally, I had a lead—something to work with. If I could fish some more out of her about Anna, I might have the next person to talk to about Ricky.

Rose took a long swallow of her martini and handed me a fresh frosted glass. She had forgotten the olive. "Say, Grant, would you like to stay for dinner? I'm really a great cook." As she said this, her red fingernails reached over and gently squeezed my thigh. I could feel the warmth of her hand through my jeans.

"Rose, I really would like to, but I have a 6:00 PM flight back to Durango. How about a rain check?"

She pouted and said in a little-girl voice, "But we could have such a good time."

I didn't doubt that for a minute. "I'm sure we could." I smiled. "Oh, by the way, Rose, what is Anna's last name?"

She stood up on somewhat wobbly legs and replied, "Garcia. Let me show you out."

Rose Donnelley said good-bye and closed the door behind me. Nothing about keeping in touch or seeing me again. I guess the moment had passed. Thank God! I needed a shower. Her perfume hung on me like smoke from a bar.

CHAPTER 5

▼

With time to kill before my departure, I stopped in to see Detective Dolan. Luck intervened, and I ran into Lisa Gonzales, who led me to Dolan's office. This time, she was with another officer, and I followed them. As she undulated down the hall toward Dolan's office, I paid very close attention, appreciating life's simple pleasures.

Lisa knocked and opened the door for me. I was assaulted by the smell of cigarette fumes. Lisa wrinkled her nose and left.

Dolan was sitting with his feet up on the window sill, looking out the window. He turned and put his feet down, but he didn't get up or offer any greeting.

"Sit down, Mr. Meredith. I'm glad you came."

I sat and waited. He shook out a Camel from the pack and lit up, filling his lungs and exhaling a stream of smoke toward me.

"You told me you were at your ranch the day your brother was murdered. Did anyone see you there?"

I paused and thought about it. What was going on? Tommy was the only one besides me at the ranch that day, and I hadn't gone anywhere. "The guy who works for me."

"Do you know anything about your brother's contract with the Knicks?"

"Just what I told you."

"You sure?"

"Of course, I'm sure. What are you driving at, Detective?"

"It seems the contract has a two-million-dollar death benefit associated with it."

"No."

"Yes. Do you have any idea who the beneficiary is?"

"I have no idea."

"Well, Mr. Meredith, it's you. I find it hard to believe you didn't know that. It seems to me that that's the kind of thing your brother would have told you. After all, you're the only family he had." Dolan sat quietly, staring at me.

Two million bucks! That was serious money. I didn't know what to say. My brother gets murdered, and I get two million dollars. I didn't feel anything. Not sad or happy. How is one supposed to feel?

Dolan sat back, tapped another Camel out of a pack, and lit it with the butt of the one he had going. He sat and smoked, watching me. I looked at his eyes through the smoke that drifted upward from his cigarette. They didn't blink, they squinted, studying me. He was waiting for my reaction. Oh Jesus Christ, the money was a motive to kill Ricky!

I leaned forward with a straight back and said with as much force as I could muster, "I didn't kill Ricky."

"I didn't say you did. Is there anything you would like to tell me?"

"I didn't kill Ricky. He was my brother. I was in Colorado. You can ask the guy who works for me."

Dolan just sat there, looking at me.

Talk about being blind-sided. Ricky is murdered for no apparent reason, and I inherit two million dollars. In Dolan's mind, that gave me a motive. I was a suspect.

The door opened, and Lisa Gonzales came in and handed Dolan a sheet of paper. Dolan watched her hips with more than casual interest as she moved out of the room.

Dolan inhaled deeply and studied the paper. "At the moment, Mr. Meredith, my only lead is the death benefit.

Most murders aren't very complicated. Assuming this wasn't a drive-by—and I don't think it was—motive will lead to the killer."

"If this is your idea of an investigation, you're wasting your time," I said with as much authority as I could muster.

"Perhaps, but following up leads is what I get the big bucks to do. Do you own any handguns?"

"Yes, I live on a ranch, remember?"

"How many?"

"I don't know. Maybe a dozen if you count the antiques."

"Is one of them a Beretta?"

"No."

"Have you ever owned a Beretta?"

"No."

"Do you know anyone who does?"

"No."

"Do you mind if we take a look around your ranch?"

I had nothing to hide, but I didn't like the way this conversation was going. Innocent people ended up in jail all the time.

"Am I a suspect?" I knew damn well I was.

"Of course not. If you were, I'd have to give you Miranda warnings. I was just wondering if you would cooperate with the investigation."

I liked to think of myself as worldly and reasonably sophisticated, but I had no experience with being a murder suspect, other than seeing one occasionally on television. What should I do? If I had a choice, would I enter enemy territory without understanding the terrain? Of course not.

"I'll consult with my attorney and let you know."

"Come on, Meredith. If you have nothing to hide, what's the big deal?"

"The big deal, Detective, is that I'm in your ball park, playing a game with unfamiliar rules. I'll get back to you as soon as possible," I said, standing.

"This isn't a game, Mr. Meredith. You'll be hearing from me." His words followed me down the hall.

I left Dolan's office with mixed emotions. Two million tax-free dollars was a lot of money—only a fool wouldn't be glad to get it—but it was going to cause Dolan to start poking around in my life, and I liked my privacy. That was the whole point of my buying a ranch in southwest Colorado. I loved the isolation.

However, I wasn't a hermit, and I often emerged from the Colorado mountains for business and the occasional social event. I needed a break. My former boss, Rex Lyons, was getting married in Santa Fe, New Mexico, next week. After the last few weeks, I could certainly use a diversion, and, knowing Rex, his wedding would be just the ticket.

CHAPTER 6

▼

When Rex Lyons graduated from New York University in 1950, no one would have thought him most likely to succeed, but succeed he did. He had enlisted in the army and had served with distinction in Korea as an infantry company commander and, later, as an aide to General Bill Withers, commander of the First Cavalry Division.

After Rex was discharged, General Withers put him in touch with "Curly" Bill Jackson, who, at that time, was the head of Merritt Jackson, a major Wall Street investment firm.

Rex had successfully threaded his way through the corporate labyrinth, becoming an immensely successful investment banker before leaving to become chairman of Tatum & Hallis, the premier investment-banking firm. It was said that Rex had the biggest rolodex on Wall Street. He was a major contributor to both political parties but kept a very low political profile himself.

Tatum & Hallis had recruited me when I graduated from Georgetown University with a masters degree in Arabic studies. Rex, always a patriot, had wholeheartedly supported me when I had stayed in the army reserves.

Rex had taken me under his wing and had given me the opportunity to learn and earn, and I had done both. My specialty was gathering Saudi money for Tatum's private equity-investment funds. Tatum got a 2 percent management fee and 20 percent of the profits. Tatum earned many millions of dollars, and I got my share.

Rex had retired a few years ago and had devoted himself to building what he euphemistically called his "casita" a few miles west of Santa Fe. Only Rex could get away with referring to a thirty-thousand-square-foot mansion on a hill overlooking two hundred acres as a casita.

Rex's casita was home to one of the most extensive collections of Western and Spanish American art and memorabilia east of the Autry Museum in Los Angeles. On display throughout the casita, one could find unique treasures, ranging from a classic Spanish Colonial back-edged sword from the late eighteenth century to a Mexican sombrero from the 1870s to antique saddles, tack, and chaps. The casita housed a small arsenal of antique weapons, several original Remington bronzes, and works by Charlie Russell and other well-known Western artists. Rex had told me the casita was really a museum waiting for his death, which he intended to put off as long as possible.

After what he called a five-year free home trial, Rex was marrying his longtime girlfriend, Valerie Kaminski, a thirty-five-year-old Romanian beauty. The wedding was a three-day command performance for seven hundred of the most influential people in America. Not even Herb Allen's Sun Valley conference of glitterati could match Rex's guest list.

Since I hadn't had a regular lady for a long time and since none of the women I had been seeing around Durango would feel comfortable at such a gathering, I decided to go alone. Rex assured me that would be no problem because he had an unattached female guest he was sure I would find most interesting. That, I doubted.

I pulled out of the ranch Thursday morning in my GMC pickup and headed east on Highway 160 toward Pagosa Springs. My plan was to make the three-hour drive to Santa Fe in time for a leisurely lunch and a little window-shopping before the festivities got under way.

The two-lane road to Pagosa Springs had the usual late-fall compliment of RVs, pickup trucks, and sedans with bicycles on the back end. The road wound through the mountains, and pine trees spilled down the slopes almost to the highway.

Just east of Pagosa Springs, I left the road that went over Wolf Creek Pass and headed south toward Chama, New Mexico. This was my favorite part of the drive. The two-lane road wound up through the mountains to the border of New Mexico and into the Chama Valley. Along the road, cattle and horses grazed peacefully in lush green pastures against a backdrop of snow-covered mountains. I descended from the Chama Valley into red-mesa country. This was the place where a recent automobile commercial showed a dream car, zooming alone along the open highway with high mesas in the background. Maybe in the commercials. In the real world, the New Mexico state troopers did not have "warning" in their vocabulary. The drive was the highlight of my trip, and I arrived in Santa Fe refreshed despite three hours behind the wheel.

The party on Thursday night was to be held at Eames Ranch—a Western-themed town, which, in the old days, had been the site of many Western films but which, these days, was rented out for charity functions, weddings, and the like.

Rex's wedding planner had thought of everything. There were motor coaches to take guests from the hotel to the party. No one would get lost, be fashionably late, or get cited for DUI. As I exited the coach, I could hear country-swing music from a live band in the saloon. The rich, smoky smell of barbeque was in the air, and the sun was setting. Even the weather cooperated with Rex.

Most of the guests were from New York City and Washington DC. Except for a few transplanted Texans, country-western was not in their repertoire; however, looking around, I had to hand it to them. Almost everybody looked like they had stepped out of the pages of *Cowboys and Indians* magazine. There was a kaleidoscope of colorful, full skirts circled with belts of silver and turquoise. Blouses, vests, hats, and boots. There were a few stubborn holdouts, but at least, they had left their ties behind.

"Hey, Grant!" hollered Rex Lyons, walking up to me with an outstretched hand. "How are you?"

Rex was still ramrod straight. His close-cropped, gray hair framed a tanned face with surprisingly few wrinkles for his age. Could he have had a face lift? In any event, Rex still exuded the kind of confidence that could control a board room full of self-important bigwigs.

"Fine, Rex, good to see you. Looks like a great party. So you're finally giving in. Why ruin a good thing?"

"When Momma ain't happy, ain't nobody happy. Say, have you met Stephanie yet?"

"No, just got here."

"Grant, this is some gal—smart, single, no kids, and a successful PR executive in the city. Knows everybody."

"Sounds too expensive for me, but I look forward to meeting her."

"Well, Grant, Valerie and I are counting on you to resolve a bet we have."

"If I can. What's the bet?"

"Stephanie is in her midthirties, tall, athletic, good-looking, successful, and has never been married. I mean, it's hard to believe this gal is still single. She dates some, but she doesn't seem interested in men. It just seems a little queer—no pun intended."

Rex was too old and too rich for political correctness. I had a feeling that the outcome of the bet was of interest to a lot more people than Rex and Valerie. "Listen, Rex, I've got no interest in a lesbian and less in being part of some kind of outing. We've been out of junior high school for a long time."

Before Rex could respond, Tammy Walsh, the Washington DC hostess of the moment, costumed like a Spanish grand dame, pulled him away to meet her new beau—the owner of the New Jersey Jaguars—who was dressed like Hopalong Cassidy, all in black with white trim.

For the next hour or so I wandered around, chatting with some old friends and catching up on the New York gossip. It was funny how some things can be so important at one point in your life and of absolutely no interest at another point.

CHAPTER 7

▼

Stephanie Chambers walked down the dusty street of the Western-themed town, which looked just like a Western-movie set, which it should have since it had been the set for movies by Randolph Scott, John Wayne, and other old-time Western movie stars. The crowd became denser as she approached the barbeque, which was set up outside the restaurant across the street from the saloon. Young women in low-cut Western tops, miniskirts, cowboy hats, and boots and young men in cowboy hats, boots, and tight jeans, showing off packages that would make ballet stars drool, circulated among the crowd, taking drink orders. Across a sea of people dressed in denim, turquoise, leather, and lace, Stephanie spotted the bride to be and made a beeline for her.

As Stephanie arrived, Valerie had just turned from a group of women who seemed to be wearing the entire Double D Ranchwear collection.

"Hello, Valerie," said Stephanie. "It's so good of you to include me. You look fabulous. What a party."

"Three hours with a make-up artist and a hairdresser can do wonders. Thanks so much for coming. A friend of mine who has a women's Western-wear store in town told me she has virtually no Double D or Patricia Wolf clothes left and has put in an emergency reorder. Say, have you met Grant Meredith, yet?"

"No, I just got here. What does he look like?"

The crowd seemed to be closing in around them as Valerie took two glasses of champagne from a passing waiter and handed one to Stephanie. They were interrupted while Valerie received a kiss on the cheek and congratulations from Val Kilmer. She took a sip of champagne and said to Stephanie, "A real hunk. Late forties. About six feet tall and one hundred eighty pounds. Bushy black mustache. Just think of a cross between Omar Sharif and the Marlboro Man, and you'll get the picture."

"Sounds interesting. How do you know him?"

"Grant used to work with Rex at Tatum & Hallis in the late 1980s. A real go-getter. Made partner in record time. He was in the army reserves, and his unit got called up for the Gulf War. He ended up in the Defense Intelligence Agency, you know—the DIA—as a foreign-area officer. He was inserted into Iraq and expected to gather intelligence to help the army figure out what was really going on inside the civilian population. He told me once it was his job to span the cultural divide. He never came back to Tatum.

"Rex and Grant hooked up again in 1998 when Grant left the service. Rex and some of his friends raised venture capital for Grant to start a private-security company called BlackRock USA."

"Rent-a-cops?"

"Hardly. A private army, really. The company provides military training and security services around the world. Full of ex-military types—you know, Green Berets, Seals, Deltas. Remember Paul Bremmer, the guy President Bush put in charge of Iraq reconstruction? BlackRock provided his bodyguards."

"Fascinating. I never heard of such a company. Rex didn't say anything about the military stuff. He said Grant was a cowboy with a big ranch somewhere in Colorado."

"That's true. Grant dumped Jessica Lynch—the TV newswoman—and went west to play cowboy. Men. Go figure."

"Not me. It's just not worth the effort."

"You're right. Guess we'd better mingle."

"Congratulations, Valerie."

CHAPTER 8

▼

As I headed for the bar, I couldn't help but notice a tall woman with short, black hair and tight blue jeans with her back to the bar, leaning on her elbows. A soft-white blouse set off a triple-strand Navajo necklace of green turquoise. With one boot on the bar foot rail, she was casually surveying the crowded dance floor.

Striking, though not beautiful, she looked completely at ease with herself and the surroundings. I walked up next to her to get a drink. The best line I could come up with was, "Hello, having a good time?"

"Absolutely. I wouldn't miss one of Rex's parties."

She had a soft North Carolina accent, which caressed me like a soft summer breeze. I turned and assumed the same position at the bar as she had and asked, "So … how do you know Rex and Valerie?"

She turned her head toward me, and I noticed she had the biggest, most beautiful green eyes I had ever seen. "I did some business with Rex when he was at Tatum & Hallis," she said, "and I see him and Valerie socially from time to time."

Before I could say anything else, a guy who looked surprisingly like Bill Clinton interrupted us and asked her to dance. They joined the dancers, who were diligently turning the two-step into the toe-step but having a great time doing it.

Around 11:00 PM, people started to head for the parking lot to the buses to take them back to Santa Fe. Most of the guests had flown in that afternoon from New York, and it was 1:00 AM by their body clock. A big day of sightseeing was planned for tomorrow.

I climbed onto one of the coaches and took an aisle seat near the front. A minute later, "Green Eyes" came up the steps, chatting over her shoulder with

Jack Lieberman, chairman and CEO of General Electric. They sat opposite me, "Green Eyes" on the aisle. When there was a pause in their conversation, I leaned across the aisle and touched her arm. "Did you enjoy yourself?" I asked.

She swiveled toward me with a movie-star smile and looked directly into my eyes for a moment before saying, "Of course." Then she turned back to Lieberman.

All the way back to the hotel, I thought about those green eyes. Original issue or contacts, one can't tell these days. "Green Eyes" and Jack were first off the bus and were deep in conversation. Tammy Walsh grabbed my arm to introduce Hopalong, and by the time I turned around, "Green Eyes" was gone.

CHAPTER 9

▼

On Friday morning, I met Jason Hilberger for breakfast in the sunlit patio of our hotel. Jason had been secretary of the navy during most of the Reagan years and had been one of the original venture-capital investors in BlackRock. He was still on the board of directors. Jason was the quintessential big-city guy: short; dark, kinky hair; dark eyes; and a big hook nose. He did not look comfortable in jeans and a golf shirt.

"Well, Jason, how is Linda?" I asked. "Sleeping in?"

"A little too much to drink. She's getting a slow start today. Are you here with anyone?"

"No," I answered, "Rex and Valerie are trying to fix me up with someone. Do you know anything about a Stephanie Chambers?"

"If you mean Stephanie Chambers of the Laughlin Group, I haven't met her, but I know she's the go-to girl if you've got a PR issue or problem. I didn't think a guy like you would need a blind date," Jason said, chuckling.

"I need this like a hole in the head. Rex and Valerie want me to find out if she's gay. Those two are something else," I said, shaking my head.

"Well, these days you can't tell. Maybe she swings both ways," he said with a lascivious grin.

"Okay, okay, what did you want to see me about?"

"Last week, I was approached by a lawyer I know from Nathan, Zachary & Allen. He said he represents a group that wants to hire BlackRock to train personnel for a company in Mexico, which provides security to a number of businesses along the border. Apparently, his client read about the work we did with the Croats in Bosnia and is willing to pay top dollar. I asked him how much that is, and he said 'whatever we want.' He wouldn't give me any more details until we tell him we're interested in the job. I told him I'd get back to him. I spoke to Reggie, and Reggie thought we should pursue it. What do you think?"

I never should have let them hire Reggie Johnson as chief operating officer of BlackRock. A former colonel in the army's Delta Force, he had argued against a daytime operation in Somalia and been overruled. He had quit in frustration after that disaster. He was a tactical genius but lacked the real-world judgment to see the danger of doing business with the wrong people.

Most of BlackRock's business fell into three categories: (1) training military and police forces for foreign governments under permits from the State and Defense departments; since the end of the Cold War, our armed forces did not have the manpower to do this, and we made good money at it; (2) training SWAT teams for the FBI and local police forces; and (3) providing security in highly dangerous situations, most recently, in Iraq. All of the companies trying to rebuild that country needed security. There was no way the military could provide the thousands of security personnel necessary to do that job. We had competition, but we recruited the best our military had to offer. A top-notch Delta or Special-Forces guy could earn one hundred thousand dollars a year or more with us. The U.S. military did all of the training and the adverse selection. When one of these guys wanted out of the service, we were the market for their skills.

Training other security companies in foreign countries was not going to be our line of work. The South Africans and Russians did that sort of thing. They were really mercenaries. It was a strange world. In South Africa, all of these ex-military guys lived together near military bases. If you needed security for a diamond mine in Angola, you could call a certain South African company, and these quasi-military settlements became ghost towns. The guys got paid in diamonds. Sometimes, they got hired by a warlord to seize a diamond mine. The warlords and the governments fought back and forth over control of diamond mines and other minerals. BlackRock was not in the mercenary business.

"Tell Reggie we are not interested in that kind of work. For all we know, BlackRock could end up training security for some drug lord."

"I told Reggie you'd say that, but he wanted to be sure."

"We have all the legitimate work we can handle. Tell that lawyer to buy a copy of *Soldier of Fortune* magazine," I said dismissively.

Jason quickly changed the subject. "What are you up to today, sightseeing?"

"No, I've been to Santa Fe lots of times, and I've seen the sights. I think I'll wander through some galleries and hit the Lucchese store and look at their boots."

As we were leaving, I brushed against a woman who was waiting to be seated. I turned to excuse myself, and there were those green eyes, sparkling in the dappled patio sunlight.

"Pardon me," I stammered.

"No problem," she said and continued her conversation with a fiftyish, blond woman who looked like Carly Taylor, former chairperson and CEO of Hewlett-Packard. Who didn't Rex invite?

I spent the rest of the morning wandering among the art galleries around the square. After lunch, I headed to Canyon Road to see what was new up there. The paintings and sculpture were excellent, but the prices made me wince. I spent a lot of time looking at an exquisite Two Grey Hills Navajo rug but finally decided that I could probably get a better deal at the Crownpoint rug auction next month.

CHAPTER 10

▼

Friday night was a buffet at the casita. The enormous, west-facing patio was awash with round tables covered in white-linen table cloths. As the sun set, a Spanish guitarist played, and the guests wandered in and out of the casita, marveling at the setting, the architecture, and the art collection. Torches were lit among the tables, and despite the seven hundred people milling around, it was hard to imagine a more romantic setting.

Once again, the guests were decked out in their newly acquired Western finery. Tonight was show time. The women were in their element. Instead of turquoise, silver, and other Indian jewelry, which a few of the ex-Texans still sported, it was the night for gold and diamonds. Given all of the jewelry on display tonight, it was hard to imagine Tiffany's having anything left.

"Hello, Grant."

It was Dillon Dunigan, secretary of defense during part of the Reagan administration and now a principal in the Plaza Group—a merchant banking firm, specializing in the defense industry. I had met Dillon during the road show to raise financing for BlackRock. He was taller than me and had long, thick, gray hair that covered his ears like an aging rock star. Today, with his Savile Row suit, striped shirt, and matching tie, he qualified for the cover of *GQ* magazine.

"Hello, Mr. Dunigan, how's Joan?"

"Joan's doing fine. She's inside with Valerie, getting a tour of the house, and it's really something. How's my favorite cowboy? Actually you're the only cowboy I know."

"Well, sir, my roping is getting a little better. At my age, it's nice to get better at something rather than get worse slowly."

"I know what you mean, Grant. Thank God for Viagra." He laughed. I almost spit out my drink. "So, Grant, who is the lucky lady this weekend?"

"I came alone. Rex has me sitting next to Stephanie Chambers tonight, but I don't know if that makes her lucky."

"Really, how do you know her?"

"Actually, I don't. When I asked Rex if it was okay to come alone, he said he had an extra woman, so it would be no problem. Do you know her?"

Dunigan paused for a moment as if deciding what to say. "No, she and my daughter were friends in high school, so I know about her. I knew her father quite well. When I was with the Defense Department, Tony Chambers was my principal liaison with the Joint Chiefs. He was a combat soldier's soldier. Two Silver Stars in Vietnam. One hell of a guy.

"He was on assignment in Beirut in 1988 when he was assassinated by terrorists. It was unbelievable. Stephanie was in the car with him when it happened. On top of that, her mother was on the Israeli Olympic team at Munich in 1972 and was killed by those PLO terrorists.

"Stephanie was Tony's only child, and he never remarried. They were inseparable, incredibly close. It was devastating. Stephanie was on the short list for the Olympic heptathlon team and had a track scholarship to USC. My daughter, Julie, said that Stephanie was not the same person after her father was killed."

"How could you be?" I asked. "I can't imagine what that would do to a young person, sitting next to her father when he was assassinated."

"Julie said Stephanie became very bitter and withdrew from everyone. She got the army's five-thousand-dollar death benefit, and that was it. After about six months, she stopped returning Julie's phone calls."

We were interrupted by Rex's voice booming over the musician's speaker system. "Ladies and gentlemen, the buffet is open. Please remember that tonight, we have assigned seating, so please cooperate, or our Navajo medicine man will put a curse on you."

After filling my plate, I wandered around, looking for my place. I walked along a huge negative-edge pool and past a massive stone fireplace. I should have located my seat earlier. Finally, I found it and said hello to my tablemates. The chair next to me was empty, and the place card read "Stephanie Chambers." The empty chair was pulled out, and I looked over and up into the green eyes. "You're … Stephanie Chambers?" I stuttered.

"Yes, you can ask Bill and Mary here to confirm it if you were expecting someone else."

"No no, please sit. It's just you don't look at all like your advance billing," I said, trying to recover some semblance of savoir faire.

Stephanie laughed and sat down. She raised her wine glass and offered a toast, saying, "Here's to Rex and Valerie and the triumph of hope over experience."

As the others were laughing, she leaned over and whispered in my ear, "You were probably expecting a short, wide-bodied bull dyke."

Before I could say anything, she turned to the man on the other side and was lost in conversation with him for some time. The rest of dinner was consumed with genial conversation about Rex and Valerie, the casita, the elaborate wedding festivities, and the usual social pleasantries. Despite several attempts, I was unable to engage Stephanie's attention for more than a moment as everyone wanted her opinion on everything.

Interestingly, she never really answered the questions. She usually turned it around and asked them what they thought. By the time the other six people at the table chimed in, everyone seemed to forget that although the initial question was aimed at her, she hadn't answered it. The interesting thing about this group was their fascination with their own opinions. At one point, the conversation was about the merits of the South Beach Diet, and a guest asked, "What do you think about it, Grant?"

"Well, I've got an opinion, but that doesn't mean I know anything about the subject?" There was some nervous laughter around the table. I glanced at Stephanie, who had a mischievous grin on her face as she winked at me.

The after-dinner entertainment was a Navajo dance group in full, traditional regalia. It was magnificent. As the performance concluded, Stephanie and I headed to the bar for a drink.

"Club soda, please," she said.

"Brandy for me. You're not much of a drinker."

"Oh, I drink my share, just not when I'm working."

"You call this work?"

"Grant, I'm in the public-relations business, and many of these people are, or may become, clients. A tipsy single woman is great gossip material."

"I guess you're right. Say, how about a nightcap when we get back to the hotel," I asked.

"Sure, I'd like that very much. I won't be working then." She gave me that mischievous smile again and turned to speak with a man I didn't recognize.

After being bused back to the hotel, Stephanie and I settled in at a booth in the bar with brandies and chatted awhile about the various guests and the likelihood of success for Rex and Valerie's marriage. The dim bar lighting and the brandy combined to create a comfortable, relaxed glow.

"Valerie tells me you gave up a partner position at Tatum & Hallis to stay in the military after the Gulf War. Would it be prying to ask why?"

"No, I wanted to do something else with my life rather than work twelve hours a day and make more money than I could spend. After all, what was the point? Actually, I really liked what I was doing for the DIA. My job was to accumulate historical, political, and cultural knowledge about the country or area in a country to which I was assigned and to figure out how to promote American policy there. For example, when I was assigned to Yemen, I advised the army brass on how to get Yemen's tribal culture to go along with a fledgling democracy. Things went pretty well there—not so well in Bosnia."

"What happened in Bosnia?"

"Well, the culture wasn't so—how shall I put it—primitive. It was very social. I entertained a lot in this huge rented villa: cigars and brandy in the library with governmental officials and, the next day, coffee with the opposition. By then, I was reporting directly to the secretary of defense. My conclusion was that the situation was intractable unless we could get rid of Milosevic, but the secretary couldn't get the politicians to go along. Bottom line, I got frustrated and left the army."

"I know what you mean. My dad was in the military, and he said the politicians were turning soldiers into policemen. He was really frustrated about that."

"I was told your dad was a general."

"Yes, well, anyway, what's it like to be a cowboy?"

If she didn't want to talk about her father, I wasn't going to push it. We chatted awhile about dude ranches and the transition from New York to Colorado. The bar closed at 1:00 AM, and we took the elevator together. I said good night as I stepped off the elevator at my floor.

As the elevator door was closing, she asked, "Grant, do you still think I'm gay?"

This woman was fun to be with, gay or not.

CHAPTER 11

▼

The wedding ceremony was like no other. Rex and the male wedding party were dressed in cavalry uniforms, and the bridesmaids were outfitted like Indian princesses. Valerie arrived for the ceremony sitting bareback on a white horse.

Stephanie continued to work the guests, but we sat together after the ceremony. "Do you travel much out West?" I asked her.

"Not that much," she said, "but I have a meeting with a client in Scottsdale at the end of next week."

"Really, I'll be down there on some business as well. How about dinner?"

"I won't have time for dinner, but breakfast Friday morning would work."

"It's a date," I said.

Back at the hotel, as I got off the elevator and the door was closing, I turned to Stephanie and asked, "You aren't gay, are you?" Her green eyes sparkled as she raised her eyebrows and grinned, saying nothing.

I was sure she was just jerking me around. That thought occupied my mind on the drive back to Durango.

CHAPTER 12

▼

At 7:30 AM Friday morning, I was on the patio at the Four Seasons in North Scottsdale, gazing out over the Valley of the Sun. A few brown clouds of smog were hanging in the air but seemed far enough away not to be health threatening.

"Hello, Grant," said Stephanie, startling me out of my reverie.

"Do you always sneak up on a guy from behind?"

"Only when they're not looking."

Stephanie looked fantastic in white running shorts and shoes, a navy blue, form-fitting tank top with white trim, and a Yankees baseball cap. She had the long, lean build of an athlete and sported a light tan and red fingernails. Quite the picture.

"Sorry to be so casual, but I got in late last night and really needed a run to clear my head before a long day of sitting on my backside."

"What client are you meeting with?"

"Sorry, Grant. Client confidentiality and all that."

"Sure, I understand."

"What brings you to Scottsdale?" she asked.

"A board of directors meeting for BlackRock USA. Keeps me busy between rodeos."

"Valerie told me a little about BlackRock. Do you ever go in the field?"

"I'm a little too old for most of that stuff. My job is to prepare the retired generals and politicos who are our business-development people on how to deal with the culture of the country or group that wants to hire us. If we get hired, I set up the training program for the people we send. The whole idea is to blend in to the best extent possible and to avoid the "ugly American" tag. To put a PC spin on it, we want our people to be culturally sensitive.

"We aren't mercenaries, and we work with Washington's approval. Anyway, these days, I just give advice. The fun was seeing the opportunity, bringing in the right people, and getting the business off the ground. Guys like your father are what make the business work now. I don't do much these days."

I was curious about her father and wanted to know more about him, but Stephanie didn't take the bait. She deftly changed the subject. "You said that BlackRock kept you busy between rodeos. Do you compete in rodeos?"

"Yes, I do. Whether I win anything is a different subject, but it's a lot of fun."

"Excuse me, but what's fun about getting bucked off horses and bulls and getting gored and stepped on?"

"You have a point there, but that isn't what I do. I'm a team roper. It's much more civilized. Generally, we stay on top of our horses."

"I saw that on ESPN once. Pretty amazing stuff."

"Well, if you ever get to Durango, there is a rodeo on Tuesday nights. It's really for tourists, but it's a kick for us to perform for a crowd."

"Must be a great way to impress us Eastern girls." Stephanie put her forearms on the table and leaned forward, watching me very closely. "Tell me, what's a handsome guy like you doing running around loose?"

"I almost married once. Fortunately, it didn't work out."

Stephanie raised her eyebrows and gave me a look that told me she wasn't going to accept that answer. "Come on, Grant, I know you had a life before meeting me. What happened?"

I thought about my answer while I took a sip of coffee. How much did I want to share with this woman? I liked her. And my theory about relationships was that you generally got what you gave, so I went for it. "When I was getting Black-Rock up and running, I spent a lot of time in New York, meeting with investors and potential clients. I spent a lot of time with Jessica Lynch."

Stephanie did not seem surprised. She probably knew about the relationship from Rex and Valerie. "Valerie told me about her," she said. "Didn't she make the cover of *People* magazine with the line, 'The Most Beautiful Woman on Television'?"

"That's the one. She listened wide-eyed when I talked about the life we could have on a Colorado ranch, but the day she realized I was serious, she told me I had lost my mind. She had no intention of giving up her career and the city for flyover country.

"Jessica did her best to persuade me that New York was the place to be. A ranch to visit once or twice a year was okay, but the idea of actually living there didn't compute for her. In any event, her efforts at persuasion convinced me that we were headed in opposite directions. She kissed me good-bye. I haven't seen her since."

Now it was my turn. "What about you, Miss Chambers? Boyfriends … girl-friends?"

"I love Rex, but he's a dinosaur. If I don't have a man in my bed, he thinks I must be gay. I don't have anything against men—just the kind who think sex comes with a dinner date. My daddy warned me about that. I didn't believe him, but he understated the problem. I actually enjoy spending time with witty and charming men. Unfortunately, the only single ones I meet are gay." She looked at her watch and jumped. "Jeez, Grant, this was great fun, but I've got to get a shower and get going. We should see each other again."

"My sentiments exactly." Before I could say anything else, she was off at a trot.

CHAPTER 13

▼

It was time to follow up on Rose Donnelly's lead. I found Anna Garcia's phone number through Information. She had a tired voice and showed little enthusiasm but agreed to meet me at her home in South Scottsdale. After my encounter with the Dolly Parton wannabe, I had no idea what to expect.

It took me awhile to find Anna's house on Rimsey Lane, not far from Scottsdale High. At some point in the past, this had probably been a neighborhood of comfortable, middle-class families with kids playing baseball in the street. I could imagine kids walking or riding bicycles to the nearby schools. Where were Ozzie and Harriet when we needed them?

The 1950s, middle-class days of Rimsey Lane were long gone, however. Small block houses with dirt front yards needed paint. A few homes had trees and bushes but no flowers. The only things missing were rusted washing machines in the yards. Bars covered the windows of several homes. These people had to be more afraid of what was outside than being trapped inside the house.

There was one exception in the middle of the block. The small block house had a fresh coat of white paint and deep green shutters. There were two large shade trees in the front yard, which sheltered the house from the brutal desert sun. I parked at the curb and walked up the short, petunia-lined walk toward the front door. A black wreath hung on the door.

A small, thin woman in a black dress opened the door. She could have been pretty, but with dark circles under her tired, brown eyes, a pale complexion, and lifeless hair hanging to her slumped shoulders, she looked to be an emotional wreck. Ricky's death must have been very hard on her.

"Hello, Grant, I'm Anna. Come in."

The small living room was clean and neat with a well-worn fabric sofa and two matching club chairs surrounding a wooden coffee table. A cotton-knit rug gave the room a homey feeling. Anna looked so devastated that I was unsure what to say.

"Anna, have I come at the wrong time. Perhaps tomorrow would be better?"

"No, that's all right. I don't know if I'll be any better tomorrow," she said, sighing.

"What happened? Can I help with anything?"

"Only if you can bring my son back to life," she said softly with a wan smile.

Oh my God, I had walked in on this woman's grief. With as much sympathy as I could muster, I asked, "When did he die?"

"Last week. I guess Ricky's death was too much for him."

"Please tell me about it."

"Sit down, Grant. It's a long story. Can I get you a glass of water?"

"No, thank you."

Anna Garcia sat across from me and spent a moment collecting herself.

"I met your brother about a year ago at the Salty Señorita, a restaurant and bar up on Scottsdale Road where I'm a cocktail waitress. We dated a few times but became friends rather than lovers. Ricky was the nicest man I have ever known. He made me feel good about myself and made me laugh like a girl. He also took a special interest in my son, Tomas."

Anna took a tissue from the box on the coffee table and dabbed at her eyes. For the next half hour, with frequent breaks to wipe her eyes and blow her nose, Anna told me about her son. Tomas had been a promising student and an outstanding baseball player until his father abandoned them. As a tenth grader, Tomas had started having disciplinary problems and had experimented with drugs. He had become hooked on crack cocaine, which had been readily available at Scottsdale High. Then along came Ricky.

"Ricky got Tomas playing whiffle ball in the backyard," Anna remembered. "That broke the ice between them. Whenever Ricky beat him, Tomas demanded a new game. Ricky took us to spring-training baseball games at Scottsdale Stadium. We ate hot dogs, laughed, kidded, and had a great time.

"When Ricky found out about the drugs, he offered Tomas a trip to Dodger Stadium in Los Angeles if he could go without drugs for a month. If he failed, Tomas had to wash his car every week for three months. Tomas made the month, and the two of them went to see the Dodgers play the Mets. Little by little, Tomas opened up to Ricky about drugs at the high school.

"Ricky told me he was looking into what was going on over there," Anna said. "He didn't really tell me anything. He was pretty mysterious about the whole thing. He said what I didn't know couldn't hurt me. Well, he was wrong. I grieved for Ricky, but Tomas took it so hard. His father had left us, and with Ricky's murder, I guess maybe it was too much for him."

"What happened?"

"Tomas died of a cocaine overdose all alone down by the Salt River. I still can't believe he went back to drugs. He didn't seem depressed to me. Actually he seemed more angry than anything else about Ricky's murder. But you know, Grant, to the cops, it was just another Mexican kid with a drug problem who overdosed. When they found out about his using, they called it a self-inflicted OD and closed the case."

"Did Tomas say anything about Ricky's murder being connected to drugs?"

"No, all he would say was that it didn't pay to mess with the Deuce."

"Who or what is 'the Deuce'?"

"Tomas would not say."

We chatted for another half hour about Ricky and her son before I headed back to North Scottsdale and the casita at the Boulders. I felt so sorry for her. It seemed to me that she was going to have a very hard time putting Tomas's death behind her and moving on. I wanted to help her, but I didn't know how.

CHAPTER 14

▼

The next day I stopped by the police department at the request of Detective Dolan. I thought that if I had the opportunity, I would ask about Tomas. Maybe the police had closed the investigation too quickly simply because he was Mexican. I didn't see Lisa Gonzales this time, but by now, I could find my way to his office. As I opened the door to Dolan's office, I was again assaulted by the stench of cigarette smoke. Detective Dolan was tilted back in his chair, feet on the desk, staring at the wall.

"Good morning, Detective. You wanted to see me?"

Dolan turned his head and squinted at me through a haze of smoke. "Since you stopped answering my questions, I have been doing some checking around. The DA up in Durango was very talkative."

Oh Christ! Not long after I moved to Durango, I was having a beer in the Billy Goat Saloon when a drunk lurched into me. As I slid off the stool to get out of the way, I knocked over the beer of a big construction worker. This enraged the guy, and he took a swing at me.

"I also spoke to a bartender at the Billy Goat, who said he had never seen anything like it. A guy takes a swing at you, and you grab his hand and slam your other hand palm-up into his nose. The guy was dead before he hit the floor."

I leaned forward, pointing at Dolan, and said as forcefully as possible, "Look, Dolan, the district attorney and everybody else said it was an accident—an involuntary reaction—self-defense."

Dolan wasn't fazed. He gave me a tired-cop look like he didn't believe a word I said. "Maybe so, but the move was a result of training. Where did you learn hand-to-hand combat?"

With increasing frustration, I said, "I was in the army, first as a helicopter pilot and later in the DIA. Everybody gets hand-to-hand training. The whole thing took me by surprise, and I just reacted. Are you accusing me of something?"

Dolan didn't flinch. He looked at me with expressionless eyes and said in a neutral tone, "Not yet. I wanted your confirmation of the Billy Goat incident. You're a smart guy. Put yourself in my place. Your brother's death could be a random drive-by shooting. It could be a case of mistaken identity. If it's neither of those, someone had a motive for killing your brother. Unless someone comes forward with evidence of a random or mistaken killing, I've got to look for a person with a motive to kill your brother. Your brother's death gets you two million dollars. Your alibi is weak. You have the capability to kill someone. Money's the only motive for this murder so far."

It was time to get control of my temper and calm things down. I didn't kill Ricky, so I shouldn't be upset. If I started yelling at Dolan, he might think I had something to hide. He was not a friend, but that didn't make him an enemy.

"All right, Dolan, I respect that you're just doing your job, but you're wasting your time. On a different subject, I spoke to Anna Garcia, a friend of Ricky's. Her son went to Scottsdale High School and died of a drug overdose. I want to talk to the detective on the case."

"Talk to Lisa Gonzales down the hall. I've got work to do."

I left Dolan's office in search of Lisa. If I were unemotional about it, the life insurance proceeds were a possible motive, so Dolan wasn't totally off track. Still, I didn't like the idea that he was looking at me as a suspect.

CHAPTER 15

▼

Lisa Gonzales headed the juvenile drug and gang unit of the Scottsdale police department. "Mr. Meredith, sit down. How can I help you?"

Her office was completely organized. Nothing was out of place. Family pictures, pictures with fellow officers, her degree, and several certificates of merit hung neatly on the walls. Lisa sat down behind a gray, metal desk, upon which were placed three neat stacks of files, a telephone, a pad and pen, and nothing else. As she sat there with a straight back, I couldn't help but notice the way her breasts pushed against her uniform shirt.

"Thanks for giving me some time. I wanted to ask you about Tomas Garcia, the kid who died of a drug overdose. His mother was a friend of my brother's."

Lisa sat there for a moment, considering her answer. "This isn't your business; however, I will tell you he was depressed, not doing well in school, and OD'd. Sad case."

"Are you sure he did it to himself?"

"Do you mean did he intentionally take an overdose, a suicide?" she asked incredulously.

"I'm thinking about suicide. His mother told me he was off drugs; it seems strange he would kill himself that way."

"The medical examiner's report was clear. He died from an overdose of crack. Did he set out to kill himself? I have no idea. The odds are it was an accident. Either way, he's dead. What we know is that he was alone and that there was no sign of a struggle. He had a history of drug use. Does it really matter whether he OD'd accidentally or on purpose?"

"Probably not. Could someone have done it to him?"

"Murder?" Now she was getting exasperated. "There is not even a wisp of a motive for that. Mrs. Garcia is a nice lady, and I feel for her, but she can't accept the fact that her kid was a druggie. We have to deal with real crimes." Lisa's professional demeanor was cracking a little. It was time to change the subject before she threw me out.

"I understand. Are drugs much of a problem in the schools here?"

"This is Arizona, Grant. The Mexican border is two hours from here. Pick your poison. It's available in any high school and in most middle schools." Frustration had replaced exasperation in her voice. Lisa leaned back, turned sideways, and crossed her legs. I couldn't help but wish she were wearing a skirt. I bet she had great legs.

"The Feds sent us a study that says 29 percent of all students in grades nine through twelve have been offered illegal drugs on school property. This study also says that drug use is down. I think the numbers are higher, and at least here, I see no evidence that drug use is declining. If you read the papers, you can see that the sheriff has started an investigation concerning heroin in some county high schools.

"The pushers catch these kids in eighth or ninth grade when they start questioning everything and are so concerned about fitting in with the crowd. We can't even get a drug-testing policy for participation in extracurricular activities. The school board says it violates the students' right to privacy." Lisa's monologue of frustration went on for another five minutes before she wound down. I listened patiently.

"It must be frustrating for you."

"Sorry, when I talk about saving kids' lives, the do-gooders talk about their rights. Anyway, enough of that. Have I answered your questions?"

"One more. Have you heard of someone or something called the Deuce?"

"Why are you asking?" she asked suspiciously.

"Anna Garcia said Tomas mentioned something about the Deuce not long before her son died."

Lisa uncrossed her legs and turned back to the desk before answering. "Deuce is a nineteen-year-old Scottsdale High School student. He runs with a gang called the Mara Salvatrucha, or MS-13. It is an incredibly violent gang that started in Los Angeles in the early 1990s made up of mostly Central American immigrant kids. Deuce is Guatemalan. MS-13 is very heavy into drugs. Rumor has it that the drug cartels hire them as assassins and for security. Very bad people.

"Deuce's mother died of AIDS, and he lives with his grandmother. No idea who his father is. Another urban tragedy. It's public information that I busted him last year with half a pound of marijuana, but he lawyered up with a suit from Wells & Bunch, who got him off because of a bad warrant," Lisa said disgustedly.

"Wells & Bunch. Is that a big firm?" I asked.

"The biggest. Central Avenue high-rise downtown. Three hundred an hour at least."

This was really surprising. "How does a Hispanic kid get that kind of legal firepower?"

"I don't know. They said it was just another pro bono case. Attorney—client privileged information. Drives me nuts. Deuce is probably dealing at Scottsdale High, but we can't catch him. The kids are really scared of him."

"How about an undercover operation?"

Lisa sighed and started in a patient voice. "Two basic reasons: First, we don't have anyone dumb enough to volunteer for that assignment. Drug dealing is a violent business everywhere but, particularly, here. Do you know that our cops kill more suspects here than anywhere else in the country? Want to know why? Because the suspects are more likely to attack us here than anywhere else in the country. Do you know why? Drugs. Around here, drug dealers answer questions with guns.

"Second, once you get beyond the street dealers and enforcers, most of the leaders are related to each other in one way or another. When you cut to the chase, it's a family affair, and that's almost impossible to penetrate. Bottom line—it's too much risk for too little potential reward. Look, Grant, tell Mrs. Garcia that we have no reason to believe her son's death was anything but an accidental overdose. She needs to let it go and move on."

"Thanks for your help, Lisa." Since it was almost noon, I took a chance. "Can I buy you lunch? I'd like to learn some more about Scottsdale."

She looked at her watch. "Okay, but we have to make it quick; I've got a one o'clock with my squad."

Lunch was at a little storefront Mexican restaurant on Scottsdale Road. Formica-topped tables and a linoleum-tiled floor offered little ambience, but the blue-corn enchiladas were excellent.

While we were eating, Lisa told me she had been recruited by the Scottsdale police force right out of Arizona State University. She was intelligent, fluent in Spanish, and dedicated to getting drugs out of schools. She had been involved in Operation Trifecta, which had been a nineteen-month-long investigation into drug trafficking that had included the Drug Enforcement Administration (DEA), the FBI, the IRS, and a host of other federal and local agencies and police departments. The operation had resulted in the indictment of Ismael Zambada-Garcia and two of his top lieutenants for smuggling fifty-million-dollars worth of cocaine into the United States.

"My goal is to become an FBI agent," Lisa said. "I'm the first in my family to go to college, and I want to have a career and make something of myself. But sometimes, it's so frustrating. We have so many rules, and the bad guys have no rules. We got the indictment against Zambada-Garcia, but he's never been arrested. In fact, no one can find him."

"Is he hiding in Mexico?"

"Who knows? There is a rumor that he had major plastic surgery. The feds put up a five-million-dollar reward for information, but we have zip. I guess you can't spend the reward if you're dead."

"Lisa, I'm curious. If you could change something to help you with your job, what would it be?"

She didn't hesitate. "Public attitude. To be crude about it, dealers are like flies on shit. You are going to have flies until you get rid of the shit. Change the perception that users are victims. Revive personal responsibility. No excuses. Without users, there is no problem. Educate them, punish them, and, if necessary, jail them."

I started it, and it was very interesting, but it was time to get things back on my track. "What do you know about my brother's murder?"

"Sorry to carry on so, but you got me going." Lisa's body relaxed, and her eyes softened. "Dolan says it may be a drive-by. It could be, but that doesn't happen in Scottsdale. Frankly, we don't know anything. Dolan is very good; he used to be with the Chicago PD before the winters got to him. We're shorthanded; the story is already out of the papers and, with it, the political pressure to solve the crime. I'm sorry to say that if we can't get it solved in the next thirty days, the only way it will get resolved is for someone to come forward with information."

While I appreciated her candor, the reality of the situation was instantly depressing. We said little on the way back to the police station.

CHAPTER 16

▼

My investigation was leading to Scottsdale High and the drug scene; however, I had absolutely no idea whether it was the beginning of finding Ricky's killer or a dead end. In any event, the next step was to find Deuce.

I called Anna Garcia and asked her if she could set me up with a friend of Tomas's who might know something about Deuce. She set up a meeting at her house.

Enrique Hernandez was slightly over six feet tall with the long, lean muscles of an athlete. With black hair cut short, jeans, and a T-shirt, he looked like the athlete he was. Anna told me he was the captain of the Scottsdale High School baseball team and had remained Tomas's friend even after Tomas had left the team.

Anna made the introductions and asked Enrique to help me if he could. She left the room.

"Enrique, do you know a kid at Scottsdale High called the Deuce?"

"What do you want to know for?" asked Enrique, instantly on guard.

"I'd like to meet him."

"Mister, the Deuce is bad news. He'd as soon punch out a white guy as talk to him … unless you want to get high. Is that what this is about?" he asked disgustedly.

"Take it easy, son. I just want to find him. What does he look like?"

Enrique silently considered his answer. "Latino, maybe five foot ten, tattoos on both arms. He usually wears a Diamondbacks baseball cap on backward, a white muscle shirt, jeans, and combat boots. He has a scar on his right cheek."

"Could you point him out to me?"

"I could, but I won't. There's a park down on McDowell and Seventy-eighth streets with a basketball court. He's there most afternoons. You can't miss him."

It was evident that Enrique didn't want to get involved. Best to let him go and not push too hard. If I couldn't find the Deuce, I could try again.

I was at the park that afternoon. There was no doubt who the Deuce was. I sat in my car across the street from the basketball court, watching him. Three on three games were in progress on both ends of the court.

A red-haired, freckle-faced boy of about fifteen approached Deuce. They talked briefly, and the two of them headed behind a restroom building. I exited my car and walked nonchalantly toward the restrooms. As I approached the corner of the building, the red-haired boy hurriedly brushed past me, stuffing something in the pocket of his jacket. As I turned the corner, Deuce was putting some money in his pocket. His eyes narrowed as he looked me over from head to toe. He stood up straight, swelling his chest. "What's your problem, dude?"

"Actually, young man, the problem is yours," I said, moving toward him, smiling.

"Fuck you, mother fucka!"

As Deuce moved toward the corner of the building, he reached out with his left hand to push me out of the way. I stuck out my left foot, pivoted, and pushed him hard between the shoulder blades. His feet went out from under him, and he hit the ground before his arms could cushion the fall.

Deuce was up in a flash with a roundhouse right, headed for the general vicinity of my head. I stepped inside the wild swing, caught his right arm with my left hand, pivoted, and drove my right fist into his solar plexus. He dropped to his knees, gasping for breath. I watched him until he almost had his breath back.

"Now, young man, it's time to talk about solving your problem."

"Man, you're an asshole. I don't have any problems."

I reached down, drew him slowly to his feet, put him in a wrist lock, and bent his wrist back, forcing him to his knees again. "By now, young man, it should have dawned on you that I'm your problem." I bent his wrist back further.

Beads of sweat were breaking out on his forehead. "All right, all right, what do you want?"

"Remember the white guy who got popped at the light up on Shea a few weeks ago?"

"No, I don't know nothin' about that."

I took his right little finger and bent it back hard. Snap! The finger protruded from his hand at an odd angle.

"Ahhhhh!" Deuce screamed and started to cry. "Oh Jesus, mister, give me a break. Please, I'll get killed."

"Jesus has nothing to do with it, young man. You're going to tell me what I want to know—now or a few minutes from now. The only difference will be how many broken bones you have."

"You don't understand, mister—" Snap! The third finger of his right hand now lay almost to the back of his hand. "Ahhhheeee!" Deuce screamed, and his body convulsed as he tried uncontrollably to breathe in and out at the same time. Tears streamed down his face.

"I understand perfectly, young man. You didn't tell me what I wanted to know. Let's start over. Do you remember the guy who got popped at the stoplight up on Shea a few weeks ago?"

"Yeah."

"Did he talk to you?"

"Yeah."

"What did you tell him?"

"Nothin'."

"Who killed him?"

"Jesus, I don't know."

I pushed back on his wrist, hard. His knees gave out, and he fell forward. I let go and stepped on the hand with the broken finger. He shrieked in a high-pitched voice. I reached down and grabbed a hand full of hair and pulled his head out of the dirt.

In a quiet voice, I said, "Tell me who knows or your balls are next."

"Honest, I don't know," he gasped, trying to catch his breath between sobs. "Maybe Jorge Torres knows."

"Who's that?"

"The *presidente* of MS-13."

"Where do I find him?"

"Most nights he's at Axis late."

I let go of his wrist and stepped back. Deuce struggled to his knees. With his hand cradled, his shoulders heaving, sobbing uncontrollably, he was a pitiful sight.

"Time to quit dealing, or we may have another conversation."

I walked around the building, bent to pick up a basketball that was rolling toward me, and tossed it back to a tall, gangly kid, who looked to be about fourteen. I headed toward my car. I took no particular pleasure in torturing a high-school kid even if he was a drug dealer, but Ricky was dead, and I was going to find out who did it and why.

CHAPTER 17

▼

The city of Nogales straddled the Arizona-Mexico border. It was not a pretty place. Every year, over three million vehicles and containers crossed from Mexico into Arizona at its port of entry. The passage of NAFTA had increased the commercial traffic at the border crossing, but that was not how the real money was made in Nogales.

Nogales was the "coyote" kingdom—home to those who trafficked in humans and drugs. The coyotes were in a violent business, and Nogales was a violent place.

When darkness settled on the Mexican side, day-tripping tourists scurried back across the border. Night in Nogales belonged to the coyotes and to those for whom they worked.

Two men sat at a corner table on the patio of La Mujer Roja cantina on the Mexican side of the border. The glow from torches created a semidarkness that an alert tourist would find uncomfortable.

"Why did you bring me out here tonight, Esteban?" asked Carlos Sanchez. Carlos was dressed in a blue blazer; gray slacks; an open-necked, white, silk shirt; and black loafers polished to a high gloss. Esteban, on the other hand, was dressed in rumpled tan slacks, a faded Tommy Bahama shirt, and a new pair of Nikes.

"Señor Sanchez, we may have a problem, and I wanted to get your advice."

"What is it?" snapped Carlos.

"A gringo roughed up one of our MS-13 dealers, trying to find out who killed some other gringo named Ricky Meredith. I have no idea who this Ricky Meredith is ... er, was, but I am still very concerned. The kid denies having told him anything about drug dealing, but my sources have grave doubts about that, and so do I."

Carlos's dead black eyes bored into Esteban. In a soft voice, he said, "Give me the details."

Esteban was plainly nervous. "Monday afternoon, the gringo approached this kid up in Scottsdale and asked him questions about the Meredith killing. The kid has two badly broken fingers. The gringo left unharmed. If this gringo was able to break two of our man's fingers, why not keep going until he got the information he was after? I believe our man talked."

Carlos just stared at Enrique. Again, in a quiet voice, Carlos asked, "What could he have told the gringo?"

Esteban fidgeted in his chair and looked away from the unblinking, expressionless, black eyes. "Like I said, I don't know anything about the Meredith killing, but MS-13 sells a good portion of our product in the Phoenix area schools. This kid would know other gang members who sell, their territory, and that Jorge Torres runs things. If the gringo got this information, he could go after Jorge and cause problems."

Carlos sat silently for a while and sipped his iced tea. Esteban knew from long experience to keep quiet while his boss was thinking.

"You are right to be concerned. The gringo was obviously not from the police. American police are not allowed to interrogate people in such an efficient fashion. All is quiet with our competitors, and there is no reason for any of them to involve a gringo. This man has some private agenda pertaining to the Meredith killing. We need to find out who he is and what he is up to." Carlos's voice remained quiet, but the intensity was increasing. "However, one thing is clear— the kid talked. A kid who talks once will talk again, more easily the second time. We cannot tolerate such behavior. I want to turn this problem into an opportunity. Tell me about this kid."

Esteban looked around before replying, "This kid is nineteen years old and has Scottsdale High as his territory. I have learned that he will be given a social graduation by the school to get rid of him. Jorge says he isn't too bright and will probably move him to the muscle side of the business once he is out of school."

"What about his family?" queried Carlos.

"He lives with his grandmother. His mother is dead, and his father is unknown. He may have brothers and sisters, but we don't know about them. No one but his grandmother would miss him."

Carlos's voice was quiet, flat, and without emotion. "Good. This will be a perfect opportunity to demonstrate to MS-13 and the other dealers that we will not tolerate talking to outsiders about our business. I want this kid to disappear permanently without a trace, along with his grandmother. Then have Jorge spread the word that if you talk, you and your family die. I want you to send a couple of the Zetas."

Esteban was stunned. He expected the kid to die. But the grandmother? Sending a couple of the Zetas meant Carlos was really serious. The Zetas were former Mexican soldiers trained by U.S. Special Forces to fight the drug organizations; once their training was complete, however, about one hundred of them deserted and sold their services to the drug lords for top dollar.

"Esteban, get a description of the gringo from this kid and alert your people that he is dangerous. You are to be advised immediately if he surfaces. I want to find out who this person is."

"*Sí*, Señor Sanchez."

CHAPTER 18

▼

There was a message at the Boulders that Detective Dolan wanted to see me. He was in his office. He didn't stand when I walked in. "Hello, Detective. I got a message that you wanted to see me."

"Sit down, Mr. Meredith. We need to talk." I couldn't read anything into his tone of voice. It was flat. Out came the cigarette pack, and he lit up another cancer stick. "You were with the DIA?" he asked.

"What in the hell are you up to, Dolan?" Anger exploded out of me without passing my brain. I knew better. I folded my hands and squeezed hard to focus on something other than Dolan and his cigarette.

"I can understand why you don't want me poking around," Dolan said in a voice filled with fake concern.

"What are you talking about?"

"We checked with the Defense Department. You were with DIA for eight years. You got an honorable discharge. The rest of your file is classified. Why?"

"Why is it classified?"

"Yes."

"Obviously, that wasn't my decision."

"Answer the question."

"I can't."

"Can't … or won't?"

"Both. It's none of your business."

"Meredith, you've got a motive. Now with this DIA business, I'm convinced you have the ability to have popped your brother. We are going to press hard on your flimsy alibi and establish opportunity. When your alibi disappears, you won't be a suspect any longer. You'll be a defendant."

I stood up, leaned forward, and put my hands on his desk. "I'm out of here, Dolan. From now on, you'll have to talk to my lawyer."

"Lawyering up? That's a convincing sign of innocence," smirked Dolan. I straightened and started to turn for the door. "Hold it, Meredith. Lisa tells me you were asking about a kid called Deuce. Why?"

I took a deep breath to regain my composure. "Anna Garcia is a friend of mine. Her son is dead from a drug overdose. You guys think he did it to himself. She doesn't. His name came up. I was curious, that's all."

Dolan's voice cracked like a whip. "Where is he, cowboy?"

"I don't know what you're talking about."

"The school reported him truant. We can't find him or his grandmother. My gut tells me you're involved."

"I told you I don't know what you're talking about. Good-bye." Deuce and his grandmother were missing. Why? As I left, I wondered whether my session with Deuce had anything to do with it.

CHAPTER 19

▼

I saw Lisa walking down the hall on my way out. "Hey, Lisa." She turned and gave me questioning look. "Have you got a minute to talk?"

"Sure, come to my office. You're on my call list, anyway."

I settled into her guest chair and asked, "Dolan told me Deuce has disappeared. Even his grandmother is gone. Do you have any idea what's up?"

Lisa's face showed no expression as she looked at me with flat, brown eyes. It was the first time that she seemed like a cop to me.

"Grant, I think you need to answer that question first. You ask me about him one day, and a week later, he and his grandmother disappear. I'm not a big believer in coincidences."

I could play rope-a-dope with Dolan for a while, but Lisa was different. First of all, I liked her, and, more importantly, if I alienated her, I would be completely on the wrong side of the police.

I tried to sound as forthcoming and sincere as possible. "I talked to Deuce a few days ago, and he told me Jorge Torres, *presidente* of MS-13, might know something about Ricky's killer. I haven't seen Deuce since."

Lisa put her forearms on the desk and leaned forward. In a skeptical tone, she asked, "Are you telling me you just asked him who killed your brother and he told you?"

"Not ... not exactly," I stammered.

Lisa held up both hands in front of her. "Wait! For now I don't want to know why he told you. That probably explains the word on the street that Deuce got sideways with someone big and was eliminated. They took his grandmother to underscore their point that if you screw up, your family will be at risk." She wagged her right index finger at me. "Grant, if you're responsible for this—and I'll bet you are—you set us way back. You have no idea how hard it is to get someone to talk to us. With this, we will have no chance to get cooperation. Christ!"

"I don't have any idea what happened. Maybe they just left town. If something happened to them, I'm really sorry." And then it occurred to me. With Lisa's knowledge of the Scottsdale gang scene, she would be the perfect person to help me find Jorge Torres—if I could persuade her. That was a big if. "Lisa, help me find Jorge Torres. If he's Deuce's supplier, he may know what happened to him and his grandmother. He may even have some information about Ricky's murder."

Frankly, I didn't give a damn about Deuce, and I didn't want to waste a lot of time trying to find Jorge. With Lisa's help, I could find him quickly. It took me a half hour to persuade her that she should help me find him.

"All right, Grant, I'll go with you Friday night and see if we can find Jorge, but you must do two things: First, there are no cowboys where we're going, so you've got to dress the part. If you don't, you'll look like my father. I want you in expensive black slacks; a white, silk shirt open at the neck; and black loafers with no socks. You'll need a fake Rolex and a couple of gold chains around your neck. We'll go in my car. Second, I am a police officer, and we have rules. I expect you to behave. Do you understand?"

I understood that this was my only lead and that I needed her help. "Sure, I'll be in uniform and be a good boy."

Lisa and I decided to meet for dinner at Houston's, a high-class burger place in McCormick Village near the Scottsdale nightlife.

I was standing at the bar, surrounded by a bunch of young people, when a low-cut, white peasant blouse caught my attention. The blouse emphasized some seriously great boobs. Next, my eyes went to the short, tight, black skirt and high heels. Next, my gaze went to the black hair that was swept up in a fancy hairdo. The woman walked directly up to me and spoke. "Hello, Grant, don't you recognize me?"

Truth be told, I had to look at her twice. Without the police uniform, this was one beautiful woman. The only problem was that she was clearly young enough to be my daughter, and I looked like some idiot going through a midlife crisis with my silk shirt and gold jewelry.

"Well, I almost didn't recognize you," she said, giggling.

"Same here. Wow, you sure don't look like a cop."

"We cops like Friday nights, too, you know."

After dinner, we headed for Axis, a downtown-Scottsdale nightclub frequented by yuppies. When we got inside, I could see why Lisa had demanded my appearance in costume. I was at least twenty years older than anyone else there except a half dozen or so guys dressed like me, who were in their mid- to late forties and ogling the young girls in short skirts with bare midriffs. I looked the same, but with Lisa by my side, it looked like I had gotten lucky.

Axis was a high-tech disco—dark walls and ceiling, purple and gold fluorescent lighting, and throbbing music. We found an empty table on an elevated platform with a good view of the club and settled in with a couple of beers.

About an hour later, Lisa poked me in the ribs and said, "There he is, heading toward the bar."

Jorge didn't look much like a gang leader. His height was average, and his black hair was closely cropped. He sported a thin mustache. He wore black slacks and a Tommy Bahama print shirt that was not tucked into his pants. If it weren't for the tattoos that covered his muscular arms and the slight bulge at the back of his belt, he was just another yuppie, cruising for girls on a Friday night.

"Lisa, notice anything special about our friend?"

"Do you mean the two-hundred-dollar shirt or the gun it's covering?"

This woman was sharper than I had expected.

Jorge got himself a drink and looked around. He apparently saw what he was looking for and headed toward a Mexican woman, who looked to be in her midtwenties. She was talking to a slight, waspish woman with straight blonde hair. I had noticed them earlier on the dance floor. The Mexican woman was absolutely gorgeous—about five foot eight with wavy, shoulder-length, black hair and big, gold hoop earrings. Tight, white jeans, a red tank top, and high heels showed off her long legs and a body that could get work as a model. The blonde was a little shorter, wearing khaki pants, a loose-fitting blouse, and no makeup. They had been dancing very close and very personal.

As Jorge approached, the Mexican woman put her lips against the blonde's ear and said something. The blonde walked away toward the restroom. Jorge and the Mexican woman obviously knew each other. After a couple of minutes of conversation with Jorge, the Mexican woman followed the blonde to the restroom. Jorge headed for the door, and Lisa and I followed.

A Jeep Cherokee was waiting for Jorge at the door. We got a quick glimpse of the guy driving: a rough-looking character who seemed too big for a Jeep. Fortunately, Lisa's car was parked right across the street in the same direction as the Jeep, and Lisa and I moved quickly to it.

As we followed, Jorge and his driver went to the Burger Delight drive-through on McDowell Street. Then they drove about a mile north and pulled into another Burger Delight on Hayden Street. Finally, they stopped at a third Burger Delight at Scottsdale Road and Shea. Each time, they entered the drive-through and got a big bag of food. These guys had to be really hungry.

At a discrete distance, we followed Jorge up Scottsdale Road and east on Dynamite toward Rio Verde. Out here, there were no streetlights and few houses. This late at night, there weren't many cars on the road, either. When Jorge turned off on a dirt road heading north, we doused our headlights and just tried to keep his taillights in sight. We saw Jorge's headlights turn left and go out, so we pulled to the side of the road and stopped.

"Where in the world are we?" I asked.

"I think this road dead-ends at the Tonto National Forest, just beyond where he turned in."

"What's out there?"

"Three million acres of nothing. There are more national forests to the north, two Indian reservations to the east, and a few man-made lakes. Out here, there are only a few paved roads and not many dirt ones. If you ask me, it's a giant cactus plantation."

"Why would this gang leader live out here?"

"We don't know that he lives here," said Lisa. "All we know is that he's here now. Since we're acting on the assumption that his gang is dealing drugs, this place may have something to do with drugs. Maybe they bring in the drugs across the reservations and the national forest to this house?"

"Could you stake this out for a few days and see what goes on?"

"I'll put somebody on it for a couple of days," said Lisa. "Let's go. I've got to work tomorrow."

"Okay, I've got to go back to Durango for a few days. I'll give you a call and see how it's going."

CHAPTER 20

▼

Clang! The metal gates of the chute opened and released a four-hundred-pound Corriente steer.

I pushed Paint's reins forward, and he broke after the steer from the left side of the chute. The reins and four coils of my rope were in my left hand; the loop was in my right. As soon as we cleared the chute, I moved my right arm forward and up over my head, moving the loop in a circular motion. Simultaneously, Tommy Taylor's horse broke from the right side of the chute, and his rope came up in a similar motion.

About one hundred feet down the arena, Paint's nose was six feet to the left and even with the steer's churning back legs. I released my loop, and it sailed smoothly over the steer's horns. I dallied the rope around the saddle horn, and as the rope came tight, I eased Paint off to the left. The steer fell in behind, hopping with its back legs together.

Tommy moved in behind the steer, and his loop caught the back legs. As Tommy's horse slid to a stop, I turned Paint and faced Tommy. A 7.8-second run. If the next team didn't do better, we would pick up a first-place check.

"Nice spin, Grant," said Tommy, spitting a stream of brown tobacco juice toward the ground as we left the arena.

The Durango Pro Rodeo wasn't the national finals, but the tourists, many of them foreigners, loved it.

"Hey, Grant! Grant, over here!"

I couldn't believe my eyes. There stood Stephanie Chambers in jeans, boots, and a black-leather, fringed jacket.

"Well, this is quite a surprise, Stephanie. It's great to see you. What brings you to town?"

"At the last minute, a client asked me to speak at an executive retreat here at Tammaron."

"Let me put my horse up, and I'll buy you a drink."

"I'd love to, but I'm here with my client. I'll be finished after lunch tomorrow, and my plane doesn't leave until 8:00 PM. What about something in the afternoon?"

We decided she would come out to the ranch for the grand tour. I gave her directions and headed after Tommy, who was at the trailer, taking the splint boots off his horse.

"Hey, Tommy, I got a good-looking gal coming to watch us rope tomorrow."

"Who?"

"Stephanie Chambers. I met her at that wedding in Santa Fe."

"Oh Christ, Grant, when are you gonna learn? You bring a city girl out there, and we'll hear no end of 'doesn't that hurt the poor steers? You're being mean to the animals, making them run like that.' Next thing you know, she'll have ASPCA or, worse, PETA out there. She'll be tip-toeing around the cow pies and driving us nuts. Shit." A stream of tobacco juice hit an empty beer can lying on the ground.

Tommy grabbed his saddle horn, gave a little hop off his right leg, and his left foot was in the stirrup, right leg up and over. He was so fluid; it never ceased to amaze me. He rode off to collect our check at the pay window, muttering to himself.

The next afternoon, we were halfway through the pen of steers when Stephanie showed up, wearing jeans, boots, and a light brown leather jacket. Maybe Tommy was right.

"Stephanie, come on over here and meet Tommy Taylor, the best heeler in the county."

Stephanie walked over, and, to my utter amazement, Tommy dismounted, took off his grimy, sweat-stained cowboy hat with a flourish, and bowed. "Pleased to meet you, Miss Stephanie," he said.

"Well, Mr. Taylor, I'm impressed. Such manners."

"Ma'am, I'm from South Texas, and my momma brought us up civil-like."

I was still sitting there on my horse like a jerk.

After a quick lesson, Stephanie was loading and releasing the steers. Riding back up to the arena, we saw that she was having a problem getting a brown steer to load into the chute. It was kneeling on its front legs with its head down and its tail end up, like a Muslim praying. She was slapping the steer on its upturned rump to no effect. As we got closer, she kicked the steer, and it stood up but refused to move forward.

Stephanie grabbed the manure-covered tail and lifted it up and forward. The steer moved into the chute. She leaned over and wiped her hand in the sand, stood up, and smiled at us.

Tommy unleashed a stream of tobacco juice, saying, "Grant, this gal might just turn out to be useful after all."

We turned a few more steers and headed for the barn.

"Tell me, Tommy," asked Stephanie as we were sitting around the tack room, sipping Coors Light, "do you have a girlfriend?"

"Well, darlin'," he drawled, "it was like this." He picked up a feed bucket and began thumping out a tune:

Stephanie started clapping. "What song is that?"

"'Livin' it Down,' by Delbert McClinton," answered Tommy.

"Fantastic."

Tommy pulled a tin of Skoal from the back left pocket of his dirty jeans and put a pinch between his cheek and gum.

"Well, that's right nice of you, Miss Stephanie."

"Grant, where did this cowboy learn to sing? He made that feed bucket sound like a musical instrument."

"You can't judge a book by its cover," I quipped.

"Tommy?"

"Well, ma'am, I did spend a little time with Stevie Ray Vaughan when I was a might younger."

"Incredible! Did you sing or play an instrument?"

"Well, ma'am, I was a picker but it didn't last too long."

Tommy held up his right hand with half of its thumb missing. "Lost that at the Houston rodeo; kind of hard to pick without it."

"How did you lose it?"

"Jake and I needed a 5.5-second run to win. We got it, but my thumb got caught in the dally. We won forty-five hundred dollars, and the medical bill was seventy-five hundred dollars. Not my luckiest day but, hey, life's a curve ball. You got to keep swingin'. Anyhow, I can still rope pretty good."

"You should have your head examined. A musician roping!"

"Well, I did that once but they couldn't find anything in there," Tommy said, chuckling.

We talked about life on the ranch for a while and then decided to take target practice with an old army forty-five that we had in the tack room for emergencies. Tommy set up some cans in front of a low hill behind the steer pen. He and I took turns from thirty feet. Tommy was one for five. I was three for five.

I handed the forty-five to Stephanie and with great care, showed her how to hold it and aim. She didn't say anything. When I stepped away, she lowered the gun to her side and then raised it and cupped the butt with her left hand. Bang, bang, bang, bang, bang. The can barely moved as each of the five shots hit on top of the other, leaving only a large hole.

I just stood there. Tommy walked over, looked at the can, and shook his head.

"Well, Grant, I'm thinkin' we ought to be takin' lessons from Miss Stephanie here."

"Where on Earth did you learn to shoot like that?" I asked.

"Remember, I'm an army brat. Firearms were a big part of my life when I was a kid."

While Grant and Tommy set up some more targets, Stephanie's thoughts drifted to her father. He had set up a Junior Ranger program for the eight-to-twelve-year-old children of officers, which met three times a week. During the week, they had classes on the role of the military in American history. On Saturday mornings, they had field exercises to deal with tactics and firearms. The kids got to fire real weapons, not only to learn how to use them, but to learn how dangerous they could be. It had been such fun. By the time she was twelve, Stephanie could outshoot all of the children and some of the instructors. Her father never said much, but she knew he was proud of her. She went to the firing range several times a week with her father's aide or with one of the drill sergeants until she was sixteen.

She remembered this one drill sergeant, Art Branch. On Fridays when he needed beer money, he would razz a trainee that little girls could outshoot him. They would end up making a bet, and Sergeant Branch would match her against the guy. The sergeant always got to drink for free.

Grant and Tommy would not believe the weapons she had fired besides handguns. M16s, AK-47s, Russian sniper rifles, even machine guns. Several times she got to fire an RPG. Stephanie smiled to herself. Some young girls get hung up on horses, clothes, or boys. Me, I got hung up on guns. I'm sure Freud would love it, she thought to herself and almost laughed out loud.

"Well, now, Miss Stephanie," said Tommy, "have you got some tips for me?"

"Okay, Tommy, step over here," she said, ejecting the clip and the round in the chamber and handing him the forty-five.

"Put your trigger finger along the barrel. Put your left foot forward, right foot back, and get comfortable. Raise your right arm and cup the bottom of the gun butt with your left hand. Good. Now, look down the barrel and put the target on top of the front sight. Now focus on the target, not on the front sight. Got it?"

"Yeah, I think so," said Tommy uneasily, "but ifin' you don't mind my sayin' so, ain't the bullet gonna go below the target?"

"Just trust me, Tommy. Now, put the pad of your index finger on the trigger and slowly squeeze."

Within ten minutes, Tommy was hitting the can 80 percent of the time. Back in the tack room, Stephanie quickly disassembled the forty-five, cleaned it, and put it back together.

"Miss Stephanie," drawled Tommy, "I'm mighty grateful for the lesson. If you'll excuse me, I believe I'm gonna ponder my inadequacy over a pitcher of margaritas."

"Come on, Stephanie, I'll grill a couple of steaks before you have to head to the airport," I said.

After Stephanie left to catch her flight, I sat on the porch with a cigar and a glass of port wine, listening to the night sounds and looking at the stars splashed across the dark country sky. Stephanie was an extraordinary woman. Good-looking, physically fit, educated, and professionally successful. She could shoot better than I could and took that forty-five apart like she did it every day. Why hadn't she ever married? She would probably intimidate many men but, certainly, not all. There was much more to know about her, and I was looking forward to the education.

CHAPTER 21

▼

As Stephanie's plane lifted off, she looked out the window and drifted back in time.

May 15, 1987 was a clear, bright morning full of sunshine. She was seventeen years old and visiting Beirut before starting college at the University of Southern California on a track-and-field scholarship. A short sightseeing tour from the American embassy to the center of Beirut was the order of the day.

General Chambers's bodyguard opened the rear door of the sedan for Stephanie and her father and then climbed into the front seat beside the driver.

Beirut was not a friendly place then, and the men in the front seat were heavily armed. General Chambers carried his regular 45-caliber sidearm. An open jeep, containing four heavily armed soldiers, was positioned closely behind them.

As the vehicles left the embassy and turned left onto the narrow street that served as a shortcut to Central Avenue, a huge trash truck blocked their path. A deafening explosion, followed immediately by a wave of heat, engulfed the sedan. The jeep behind the sedan was a mass of twisted, burning metal from which black smoke plumed into the sky.

With the trash truck in front and the wreckage behind, the driver of the sedan could not maneuver the vehicle. He had no choice. He floored the sedan in reverse, hoping to knock the jeep out of the way. The sedan slammed into the jeep but only moved it a few feet. The front-seat-passenger window shattered, and the bodyguard's body was forced to the left and disappeared below the seat. The driver moved the sedan forward and again floored it in reverse. On the third try, he floored it and spun the wheel viciously to the left. They missed the jeep entirely. Before the surprised driver could get his foot off the accelerator, the sedan slammed into a lamppost.

The impact left the driver and General Chambers stunned. Stephanie took the forty-five from her father's hand.

Stephanie's door was torn open from the outside, and a robed man pointed an AK-47 inside. Too late for him. Stephanie squeezed the trigger to her father's forty-five, and a bullet entered the middle of the robed man's forehead.

The chaos continued—small-arms fire, thick smoke. Stephanie couldn't see outside the car. Her father revived, put his hand on her forearm, and told her to stay put. He yanked open his door and rolled out onto the street. She couldn't see what was happening, but the gunfire seemed to be moving farther away from the car.

Several minutes later, as Stephanie glanced warily from her open door, a voice from behind her said, "Easy, girl, it's all over now. You're safe." It was Master Sergeant Randall Johnson. Stephanie expelled a long breath. Randall Johnson was a career enlisted-man—a "lifer" in military parlance—who had been awarded the Congressional Medal of Honor for service in Vietnam. He had been an aide to her father for as long as she could remember. His face and clothes were covered with dirt and soot. As he helped her from the car, they were surrounded by soldiers from the embassy. Johnson hustled her into an armor-plated limo that roared back to the embassy.

"Where's Dad?"

Johnson said nothing. He turned away from her and looked behind them.

"Where's Dad?" Stephanie reached up, took Johnson by the chin, and turned his face toward her.

Tears were running down his face, leaving tracks in the grime. He took a deep breath and took hold of Stephanie's hands. "He didn't make it."

Stephanie just stared at him. She said nothing. She was frozen.

"He ran from the car and away from the embassy. He got about half a block before they zeroed in on him. He managed to duck into a doorway, but by the time we got there, he was dead."

"I had his gun," said Stephanie woodenly. "He had no chance."

Johnson was still holding her hands. "He did it to draw them away from you," he said. "They followed him and ignored the car. It gave us time to get there."

Stephanie said nothing. In fact, she said little for weeks. There were a few relatives but no friends with her when General Anthony Chambers was buried with full military honors at Arlington National Cemetery.

She never enrolled at USC and abandoned her track-and-field career. Instead, she enrolled at the Sorbonne and majored in Spanish literature and romance languages. Her circle of friends included other foreign students, including some from the best families in Mexico and Spain.

Men. She couldn't help but compare them to her father, and when she did, they had no chance of measuring up. The boys she met in France, particularly Hector, were useful in a sexual sense. Hector didn't claim to be in love with her or try to take over her life; it was just good, clean sex, like, a workout at the gym with a little more pleasure involved.

She had no idea why Grant Meredith interested her. She was attracted to him in a way she didn't understand. He wasn't like her father. That surely wasn't it. He seemed like a man that a woman could trust. She had not trusted anyone since her father's death. It was a totally new emotion for her, and she liked it.

Oh, well, enough of that. He sure was easy on the eyes.

CHAPTER 22

▼

Detective Dan Dolan wanted to check Grant Meredith's alibi in person. He didn't trust some redneck sheriff to do it, and it was too easy to lie on the telephone. Since this was a murder investigation, he had enough money in the budget for a ticket to Durango.

Dolan flew to Durango and arranged for Deputy Sheriff Larry Walker to drive him out to the ranch to question Tommy Taylor. As the deputy pulled off the county road and under the massive wooden arch that framed the entry to the Durango Land & Cattle Company, Dolan knew he was a long way from Chicago and Scottsdale. The land sloped down gently toward a river about half a mile away that wound from right to left across his line of sight. As they approached the river, the ranch road turned past a stand of pine and aspen trees.

When they came to the ranch headquarters, Dolan let out a low whistle. "Impressive," he said as he surveyed the freshly painted ranch house, which was at least five thousand square feet, good-sized barns, and what appeared to be a workshop. The corrals and arena were made from metal pipe rather than wood. The grass was trimmed—even under the fences. To Dolan, the whole place looked like a magazine cover. Meredith must have some serious money to own a place like this, he thought. Maybe he needed the insurance money to keep it up.

They found Tommy out by the cattle pen, cutting open a bale of hay. "Tommy," said the deputy, "this is Detective Dan Dolan from the Scottsdale police department. He wants to ask you some questions."

Tommy nodded, and Dolan held out his hand, which Tommy ignored. He moved away from them up the side of the pen and began tossing portions of hay to the steers.

"Mr. Taylor, how long have you worked for Meredith?"

Tommy reached in the back left pocket of his jeans and took out his tin of Skoal, carefully putting a pinch between cheek and gum.

"Never have."

"Who *do* you work for, Mr. Taylor?"

"I don't work for nobody, Detective. From time to time, I work *with* people, Grant being one of them. Tell me, what are you detectin', Detective?"

"I'm just making some general inquiries about Meredith."

"Do you like blues music, Mr. Detective?"

"No."

"Too bad. You know, you remind me of an old Albert King song where he sings 'ask me no questions, and I will tell you no lies.'"

"What on Earth are you talking about?"

"Well, Mr. Detective, I sure ain't the sharpest knife in the drawer, but seeing as how you're a detective and got on a suit and all and came up here from Arizona, even one of these steers here could figure it isn't to make general inquires about Grant Meredith." Tommy spit a stream of tobacco juice, which landed about three feet from Dolan's shoe.

"Mr. Taylor, if you don't cooperate with me, there will be serious consequences."

"Well, now, Mr. Detective, it seems plain that someone is lyin', and I don't reckon it's me." Another stream of tobacco juice landed about two feet from Dolan's shoe.

"Taylor, you can be charged with obstructing justice."

Tommy looked over at Larry, who had been his drinking buddy for years. Larry just raised his eyebrows and shrugged. Tommy pitched hay into the pen and handed a fork to Dolan.

"All right, Mr. Detective, help me finish my chores and you can detect away."

Dolan pitched the hay into the pen but did not take into account the breeze. Loose hay flew back into his face and hair and down his shirt collar. While he was sputtering, Tommy looked at Larry and grinned.

"Taylor, let's cut to the chase," said Dolan, fuming mad. "Was Meredith here three weeks ago Wednesday?"

"I reckon he was."

"How can you be so sure?"

"'Cause I is."

"Why?"

"Is this detectin' you're doing now, Mr. Detective?"

"Just answer the question."

"'Cause I was here."

"That doesn't answer the question."

"Well, I reckon it does, 'cause if I wasn't here, no way I'd know if Grant was here. All this detectin' is makin' me a bit thirsty. You about done?"

Dolan turned around and stomped off without looking where he was going. His right foot came down in a fresh cow pie, and the manure oozed over his shoe and down inside it.

"I can detect somebody just stepped in it," said Tommy, sending them on their way with a stream of tobacco juice.

CHAPTER 23

▼

I hadn't heard from Lisa concerning the surveillance on Jorge, so I called her at the Scottsdale police department.

"Grant, I can't begin to tell you how pissed I am. I got a reprimand and have been ordered to stick to my juvenile gang and drug responsibilities and leave Jorge Torres alone. I just don't believe it."

Being this upset seemed out of character for her. "I'm sorry to hear that. Tell me about it."

"I put my best undercover guy on the stakeout. He hiked into the area and was able to set up an observation post that was only about fifty yards from the house. On the second day, Jorge shows up around noon by himself. About an hour later, two Suburbans pull up, and ten goons with guns get out. A couple of them go inside, and the others set up a perimeter around the house.

"About ten minutes later, an Escalade pulls up, and a woman gets out and goes into the house. My guy got a couple of pictures of her. He says that maybe ten minutes later, Jorge and the woman come out and that she seems really angry. She is screaming at him and poking him in the chest with her index finger. Jorge just stands there, hanging his head and taking it. Now, get this, my guy says she is screaming something, like, 'You work for us. You will do what I tell you when I tell you. Is there anything about this you don't understand?' My guy got a couple more pictures. The pictures weren't great, but it looks to me like the woman reading Jorge the riot act was the same woman he was talking to at Axis the other night. I put the picture into our system but didn't get a match.

"Later that day, Chief Ramirez comes into my office, closes the door, and asks me what I'm up to. I tell him about following Jorge, the stakeout, and trying to identify the woman. He launches into a lecture about unauthorized use of department personnel, wasting time and money, and so forth. Bottom line—he tells me that I have more than enough work to do without trying to create more and that I cannot spend any more time on this and that the investigation file I opened is officially closed.

"The strangest thing happened later, though, Grant. I wanted to put some of my notes into the file, so I went to the storage room where the chief said he was taking it. But it wasn't there. The clerk said the chief hadn't given him any file. I went to the chief, and he said the clerk must have been mistaken. He took my notes and told me he would take care of it."

"Lisa, what do you think about Chief Ramirez?"

"I don't know. Sometimes, the chief is uptight. He's always concerned about his budget. He hates to see overtime. Someone probably got after him about his budget."

I wasn't quite sure what to make of this information. I had assumed that Torres ran MS-13 and might have information about Ricky. Now, it seemed that he and, by extension, MS-13 worked for "us" whoever that was. I was confident that I could lean on Torres, but I didn't want to create another Deuce-type disappearance. I wasn't sure where this would lead, but I wanted to know who really controlled MS-13. I needed to frame it so Lisa would help.

"Lisa, I think we may be onto something. Deuce was MS-13, Torres runs MS-13, and it seems someone else controls Torres. We have drugs and a gang that is controlled by someone other than its leader. Maybe Ricky's death is mixed up in this. I know you can't do it officially, but I'd like to know who this woman is. I'll be down there tomorrow. We can cruise some clubs and try to find her. Are you game?"

Lisa was quiet for a long time. I knew she was thinking about the chief and the possible risks to her career. "Okay," she said reluctantly, then, with more conviction, "the chief doesn't run my off-duty social life."

CHAPTER 24

▼

We spent Friday night at Axis, but our mystery lady didn't show. We didn't want to become known there, so on Saturday, we tried a few other clubs and ended up at Sugar Daddy's.

Sugar Daddy's was Scottsdale's newest hot spot for the "finally twenty-one" crowd. The general motif was New Orleans voodoo. A large tree-shaded patio was filled with bar-height tables. Inside, the walls were covered with voodoo memorabilia. There was a long bar and a separate room with three pool tables. Secluded alcoves and minimal lighting created an environment in which a witch doctor would feel at home. It was midnight, and the place was packed. Most of the crowd was dressed in T-shirts, tank tops, and jeans and looked like college students.

Lisa had me dress in a T-shirt, jeans, and an Arizona State University baseball cap. After getting a beer at the outdoor bar, we found an open spot in the corner of the patio where we could see the entrance. Lisa was in blue jeans, a polo shirt, and a long-billed baseball cap with her hair pulled through the strap on the back. In the dim light, the ball caps shaded our faces enough to disguise our age differences.

The purpose of our visit was strictly business; however, it was somewhat depressing that none of the young women took any interest in me. Oh, well, at least they didn't give me that "what is an old dude like you doing here" look.

About 11:30 PM, the woman we had been waiting for appeared at the entrance to the patio. Again, she was really put together. Skin-tight, white tank top and tight black pants about midcalf length. This time, she was with a man and a woman. The woman looked to be about forty and wore jeans and a tank top with a white shirt on top. With highlighted, short, brown hair, she looked like she just stepped off a magazine cover. The man appeared to be in his midtwenties, about six foot four and two hundred thirty pounds with the hard body of a serious weight lifter. His left earlobe sported a small loop earring.

They nodded to the doorman and walked by without being asked for the cover charge. "Lisa," I said, "how about charming the doorman and see if he will tell you who that woman is?"

"You mean, use my feminine charms to extract information from that guy without his knowing it? You sexist pig, you."

"Sexist pigs make the world go round, but I don't hold it against you, gals."

"Oh, shut up. I'll be back in a few minutes. Why don't you go inside and keep an eye on our friend."

I went inside. As I was making my way to the men's room, I saw that the couple had settled into a booth. Our Mexican lady and her girlfriend were sitting very close together and seemed to be holding hands. A very pretty young man approached the table, and the big guy waved him away.

There was an open seat at the inside bar from which I could see the women and "Mr. Muscle" at their table. I ordered a beer. About ten minutes later, Lisa came up beside me, put her arm around my shoulder, and nibbled at my ear while she whispered, "Our lady is Boots Sanchez. Her family owns this place. Let's go back to the station and see what the computer has on her."

We went back to her office, but the computer search came up empty. The next day, I got a call from Lisa. The chief of police had asked her why she had run a computer search on Boots Sanchez. When she had told him, he had put her on indefinite suspension with pay, pending a disciplinary hearing for insubordination. Now, she was really pissed. Before hanging up, her last words were, "Why did I ever listen to you?"

C H A P T E R 25

▼

The seven-hour drive back to Durango gave me plenty of time to think about what I knew and what I didn't know about Ricky's murder.

When I got back to the ranch, I settled down in the library, lit my pipe, got out a pad and pencil, and started making notes:

1. Ricky and Anna Garcia were friends.

2. Anna had a teenaged son named Tomas, who had a drug problem.

3. According to Anna, Ricky had befriended Tomas and had helped him shake the habit. I had no independent verification that Tomas was off drugs. Mothers always wear rose-tinted glasses.

4. All Ricky told Anna was that he was going to look into the drug problem at Scottsdale High. Ricky's best friend in high school died of a drug overdose.

5. Ricky was murdered.

6. Tomas was angry about Ricky's death. He was not depressed. He did not tell Anna that Ricky's death was connected to anything, but he did say it did not pay to mess with Deuce.

7. Tomas died of a drug overdose. The cops thought he did it to himself because he was a user. Anna did not believe that but had no other answer.

8. Deuce was a drug dealer and part of the MS-13 gang. He—or the gang—was connected enough to have Wells & Bunch represent him. He gave up Jorge Torres. Deuce and his grandmother have disappeared.

9. Jorge is the boss of MS-13—a Central American street gang that is dealing drugs.

10. Jorge may be the leader of MS-13, but he seems to be controlled by Boots Sanchez and other, unknown interests. Boots's family owns Sugar Daddy's nightclub.

11. There is an isolated house adjacent to the Tonto National Forest that does not fit with either Jorge or Boots.

12. I have assumed Ricky's death has something to do with drugs and Tomas, but I do not have any connection between events. Ricky's murder could be the result of a random drive-by, the drug scene at Scottsdale High, or something else entirely.

13. While I have been running around, good ol' Detective Dolan is trying to pin Ricky's murder on me, and I have gotten Lisa Gonzales suspended.

Not an auspicious start as a detective. The connection between Jorge and Boots Sanchez intrigued me. According to Deuce, Jorge was his supplier, but I had no independent verification of that. Jorge did not appear to be some hopped-up user, selling to support his habit.

I sat and drew diagrams on my pad and smoked my pipe. Was there another way to connect Deuce and Jorge? Where did Boots Sanchez fit into the drug scene, if at all? Finally, an idea hit me. When Deuce had gotten busted, he lawyered up with Wells & Bunch. Who paid their bill? Could the law firm be the connection? How could I find out? I figured I might as well start with a call to Bill Donovan, general counsel to Tatum.

"Bill, how are you?"

"Doing fine, Grant. To what do I owe the honor of this call?"

"I'm trying to get some information about a law firm in Phoenix called Wells & Bunch. Do you know anything about them?"

"Sure, they are the biggest firm in Phoenix—maybe one hundred fifty lawyers downtown on Central Avenue. We used them on the Baker IPO last year. They did a credible job for a lot less than New York firms."

"Whom did you work with?"

"John Stanley was the partner in charge. There were six or seven others, but I don't recall their names. Why are you interested in Wells & Bunch?"

It would take too long to explain it all to Bill, who didn't need to know what was going on, anyway. "A friend of mine needs a corporate lawyer in Phoenix, and someone recommended Wells & Bunch. He asked me if I could check them out for him."

"We had a good experience with them, and they have an excellent reputation."

"Okay, thanks, Bill, I owe you lunch next time I'm in New York."

Now, I had a way to talk to the lawyers, but I couldn't just call up and ask them why they represented Deuce and who paid his bill. There was a connection between Boots and MS-13 through Torres. Boots referred to "we." Her family owns a nightclub, and drugs are not uncommon at nightclubs. Nightclubs need lawyers. That might work. I called John Stanley.

"This is John Stanley, Mr. Meredith. What can I do for you?"

"Mr. Stanley, I need a business-type lawyer in Phoenix, and Bill Donovan at Tatum & Hallis recommended you."

"I certainly enjoyed working with Bill. What are your specific needs?"

"A partner of mine and I have a bar-nightclub concept that is working well in Denver. We are exploring the possibility of bringing it to the Phoenix area. We'll need legal advice for zoning, real estate, obtaining a liquor license, and other things that go along with a nightclub operation. Do you have any experience in those areas?"

"Personally, no, but one of our partners, Ramon Sanchez, specializes in that area."

"That's great. I'd like to check with one of your nightclub clients if you don't mind—just some due diligence on my part."

"We do not disclose the names of our clients without their permission; however, Ramon's family has a nightclub along with its other business ventures. It's probably best if you talk to him directly. May I transfer you?"

"I've got an appointment, but I'll be sure to call him later. Thanks for your help."

Well, that was interesting. Ten to one, Ramon Sanchez is related to Boots Sanchez.

CHAPTER 26

▼

I had learned to love the Internet; it made so many things so much easier. I fired up the computer, punched in the Arizona Corporation Commission, and tried the name "Sanchez" under corporate filings. Nothing. Not easily discouraged, I tried the Arizona secretary of state filings. Nothing.

I put my feet up on the desk and thought about things. Ramon Sanchez was a big-time lawyer. His family probably owned Sugar Daddy's and, perhaps, other business ventures, but I could find nothing to indicate ownership.

I know there was some kind of connection. Like Lisa, I did not believe in coincidences. Then, I had an idea.

Major investment houses, banks, and financial institutions needed the ability to pull apart complicated business structures. There were United States and foreign corporations, partnerships, trusts, limited liability companies, and other business entities. Often, layers of entities stood between those who really controlled a company and the public filings.

Trying to pull all of this apart was a fairly regular occurrence for these institutions. In a burst of genius, they all joined together to form a private company—Institutional Enterprises—to do all of the research, to maintain databases, and to serve as a clearing house for this sort of information.

Its existence was not public knowledge since one of its main functions was to invade business and personal privacy. When I had been at Tatum, I had heard a rumor that it cost five million dollars a year to belong to Institutional Enterprises and that only a CEO could request information from the company.

I called Rex Lyons for a big favor, and he agreed to try and get me anything that Institutional Enterprises had on the Sanchez family. However, it would take a few days since he had to work through someone else.

The Federal Express package from Institutional Enterprises arrived Saturday morning. I lit my pipe and settled in to read the report:

PREFACE

The following is a "Level A" general background search requested by Tatum & Hallis. No specific transactions with the subject are presently contemplated.

THE FAMILY TREE

(1) Jose Sanchez, 1860–1930
    (2.1) Pablo Sanchez, 1885–1950
    (2.2) Jamie Sanchez, 1890–1961
    (2.3) Fernando Sanchez, 1895–1975
        (3.1) Carlos Sanchez, 1943–
            (4.1) Ramon Sanchez, 1963–
            (4.2) Hector Sanchez, 1965–
            (4.3) Margarita "Boots" Sanchez, 1980–

BRIEF FAMILY HISTORY

Jose Sanchez was a leading businessman in Sonora, Mexico. He was a primary advisor to Pancho Villa during the Mexican Revolution. During the chaos that followed the overthrow of General Dias in 1911, Sanchez was able to amass vast tracts of land in Sonora. It was rumored that when Villa objected to his activities, Sanchez masterminded his assassination in 1919. By the time of Jose Sanchez's death in 1930, the Sanchez family was one of the richest in Mexico. Family interests included land, banks, mines, factories, and the wine and liquor business.

It is also believed that Jose Sanchez was instrumental in the founding of the PRI political party, which controlled Mexican politics until the election of Vicente Fox of the PAN party in 2000.

Jose had three sons: Pablo, Jamie, and Fernando. Pablo devoted himself to protecting the Sanchez family interests through the PRI but never held elective office, Jamie ran the wine and liquor distribution in northern Mexico from the Texas to the Arizona border, and Fernando ran the ranches and the cattle business.

Carlos Sanchez, son of Fernando, is rumored to have utilized the family businesses for smuggling. He is extremely secretive, and there are no known photographs of him. It is rumored that he initially forged a connection with the Colombian drug cartels when the Drug Enforcement Administration (DEA) disrupted the flow of illegal drugs through Florida and the Caribbean. In the 1980s, he expanded the family business in Arizona and, through a myriad of corporations and partnerships, now controls all of the Burger Delight franchises in Arizona and northern Mexico. His three children—Ramon, Hector, and Margarita—were educated in the United States.

Ramon Sanchez is a graduate of Yale University and the University of Southern California law school. He is a corporate lawyer with Wells & Bunch in Phoenix, Arizona, and serves on the management committee. Ramon is married with two children, both of whom seem to spend most of their time in Mexico.

Hector Sanchez is the present governor of the state of Sonora, Mexico, and a major figure in the PAN political party. He is being widely promoted as the next president of Mexico. Hector is twice divorced and has a child from each marriage. He is quite the ladies' man and is often featured in the society pages in Mexico City. He is the public face of the family.

Margarita Sanchez, known as "Boots," has no known employment but seems to be involved in some capacity in the Sanchez nightclub activities in Arizona. She graduated from the University of Arizona. It is rumored that she got her nickname when, after a college love affair ended badly, she and two of her male cousins came upon her ex-boyfriend in Rocky Point, Mexico. The cousins allegedly held the man while Ms. Sanchez, wearing a pair of cowboy boots, kicked him savagely and repeatedly. The rumor says the victim was hospitalized with multiple broken ribs, a shattered nose, a broken jaw, and mangled testicles. Since that time, she has been known as "Boots."

BUSINESS INTERESTS

Through various corporations and partnerships, the Sanchez family owns or controls fifty thousand square miles in northern Mexico. They have the largest cattle operation in Mexico. Cattle are sent to family-controlled feed lots, slaughtered, and exported to the United States. They own La Mirada Packing Corporation, which is the beef supplier to Burger Delight and the largest meat-packing company in the Southwest.

We have, as yet, unconfirmed reports that Sanchez family members and entities controlled by them are acquiring large ranches that run along the United States' side of the border with Mexico.

The Sanchez family owns El Dolce—the largest liquor distributorship in Mexico—and controls La Suerte Company—the third-largest trucking company there. It is estimated that the trucking company and subsidiaries account for 5–7 percent of the trucking activity at the Nogales, Arizona, border crossing. Full implementation of NAFTA is projected to quadruple the size of La Suerte within five years.

We have no reliable means of estimating the net worth of the family.

PROBLEM AREAS

We have no proof, but reliable sources tell us that the Sanchez family has been heavily involved in smuggling since the 1960s and is believed to be in the drug-smuggling business. To our knowledge, there have been no law-enforcement investigations of the family or any of its members.

We have been able to identify Sanchez family members as far down as second cousins. Most are Mexican citizens; however, a significant number, including Ramon Sanchez, are American citizens. The family members live in Mexico and throughout the Southwest United States. As previously noted, the family controls both Mexican and United States' business entities.

We suggest that our members try to avoid doing business with this family. We will be pleased to analyze any specific transactions that are presented to us.

*   *   *   *

The report was fascinating. I got out my pad and added to my notes:

1. My hunch was correct: Ramon and Boots Sanchez are related.

2. "Reliable sources" believe the Sanchez family is involved in smuggling drugs into the United States, but there is no proof.

3. The MS-13 gang sells drugs to students at Scottsdale High. I suspected as much, but Lisa had not been able to prove it.

4. It seems likely that the connection between Jorge and Boots is the selling of drugs. It is possible that the Sanchez family smuggles drugs into the United States and supplies MS-13, but again, there is no proof.

5. The Sanchez family could be smuggling drugs into the United States in its trucks, but there is no proof.

6. If Ricky had been asking the wrong questions about drug smuggling and the Sanchez family, it could have provided the motive for his murder.

7. The Sanchez family is extremely well-connected politically in Mexico.

8. The report from Institutional Enterprises paints a picture of a large family that straddles the U.S./Mexican border like a giant octopus.

CHAPTER 27

▼

I had a good idea about the Sanchez family and drugs but still no connection with Ricky's murder. I had three leads: Ramon, Boots, and Jorge. I was now reasonably certain that Ricky's death had something to do with drugs at Scottsdale High. The most direct link to Ricky was probably Jorge. I headed back to Scottsdale to find Jorge. I didn't call Lisa. She had enough problems.

I found Jorge at Axis. He left about 11:00 PM and went through the drive-through window at the Burger Delight at Hayden and McDowell streets. From there, he went to the Salty Señorita and met two guys in the parking lot. I couldn't get close enough to see what was going on.

After that, he went to the Burger Delight at Indian School and Hayden and got another take-out order at the drive-through window. The next stop was Moustache, a country-western bar on Shea Boulevard. He went inside, and a man came out with him. They went to Jorge's car, and the man walked away with the Burger Delight bag.

His last stop was the Burger Delight in Fountain Hills. Again he went through the drive-through window. From there, he headed down Saguaro Road and pulled into a garage at a house in a Taco Bell-looking subdivision. Five minutes later, the lights in the house went out.

I decided to go back to the last Burger Delight and have a talk with the young man handling the drive-through window when he got off work. While waiting, I took a trip through the take-out window and got a good look at him.

This boy had final-closing duties and was alone when he left the store and went to the lone car parked in the far corner of the lot. I was waiting for him.

"Excuse me, young man; I would like to speak with you for a moment."

"*No hablo Inglés.*" He reached for the door handle of his car.

"Sure you do. What did you give to Jorge Torres?"

"*No hablo Inglés, y no conozco Jorge Torres.*"

This wasn't going anywhere, so I turned him around, put my hands on his shoulders, and squeezed.

"*Por favor, señor, no más.*"

"Speak to me in English."

"Okay, okay, what do you want?"

I eased my grip but left my hands on his shoulders. "What did you give to Jorge Torres?"

"I don't know any Jorge Torres."

I had a hunch. I turned the boy around and removed his wallet from his back pocket. His driver's license said Alex Sanchez. I turned him around and squeezed his shoulders. "Are you related to Boots Sanchez?"

"She is my second cousin." I eased the pressure on his shoulders.

"What did you give Jorge Torres?"

"Nothing. Whatever he ordered."

I squeezed and did not say anything. He tried to squirm out of my grip but no luck. Tears came to his eyes.

"I don't know what was in the bag. He came through and the manager handed me the bag for him, and he handed me a bag for the manager. That is truly all I know."

"Who is the manager?"

"The night manager is my cousin Alex Sanchez."

"How old are you?"

"Seventeen."

"Go home, kid."

Could Burger Delight serve as a pick-up and drop-off point for distributors like Jorge? I headed back to the Boulders for some sleep and to plan my next move.

CHAPTER 28

▼

It was almost noon an hour south of Nogales. Esteban had left the main highway almost thirty minutes earlier and had passed through the security gate onto the Sanchez family ranch. He and his vehicle had been carefully searched by two guards, wearing Mexican army uniforms. Esteban had been working for the Sanchez family since graduating from the University of Texas but had only been to the ranch a few times. He marveled once again at the size of the place. He had been driving at a steady fifty miles an hour along the smooth dirt road. He had seen hundreds of cattle dotting the sparse landscape and some cowboys in the distance on horseback. On three occasions, he passed different jeeps, each with two heavily armed men, who were patrolling the ranch. What he didn't see were the cameras that were randomly placed along the road, feeding pictures directly to security headquarters at the main compound.

Esteban's Range Rover climbed a hill to the compound surrounded by a ten-foot-high wall with wires running along the top; he knew the wires were electrified. He could not see and, in fact, did not know that there were motion sensors and cameras at various strategic places on the walls. He pulled up to a massive, solid-iron gate and was approached by two men in blue blazers, gray slacks, white shirts, and ties. The men had ear pieces in their ears with wires that disappeared under their jackets. Once again, he and the Range Rover were searched. One of the men got behind the wheel, and Esteban climbed into the passenger seat. The iron gate opened, and the security man drove the Range Rover to a covered, landscaped parking area about fifty yards inside the compound. Two Rolls Royces and a Mercedes convertible were parked in the shade.

After parking, Esteban and the security man got into a covered golf cart and drove to the main house, which was about two hundred yards away.

A small man, dressed all in white, met Esteban at the foot of the steps leading to the front door of the largest home he had ever seen. Esteban did not enter the front door; instead, the houseboy led him to the veranda that surrounded the house, around to the right, through French doors, and into a two-story library that opened into the pool area. The view beyond the pool went on for miles. He could see Carlos Sanchez at a table under an awning, enjoying lunch with half a dozen people; two of the people were facing the library and were instantly recognizable: Melina Melindez, a prominent Mexican movie star, and Roberto Salinas, Mexico's newly appointed attorney general—that country's top law-enforcement officer.

Carlos excused himself from his guests and confidently strode toward the library, wearing white slacks, a navy blue, long-sleeve, silk shirt and sandals. The houseboy left the room silently.

"What is so important that you had to interrupt me?" snapped Carols.

Esteban had great difficulty looking directly into Carlos's eyes. Carlos radiated so much power. There had been many times when Esteban thought those eyes looked directly into his soul. He deferentially lowered his head and said, "I think we have identified the gringo who compromised the MS-13 dealer," he said.

"Who is it?" asked Carlos, no longer irritated.

"Grant Meredith. He has a Colorado address."

"What makes you think he is the one?"

"Last night, a gringo grabbed one of our cousins, Alex Sanchez, who works at the Burger Delight in Fountain Hills, Arizona. He wanted to know what was in the bag Alex gave Jorge Torres. Of course, Alex told him he did not know. I am confident that Alex does not know what was in the bag. Alex saw the gringo leave and got the license-plate number of his car.

"This morning, I had Ramon check the license plate. It was a rental car. Juanita hacked into the Hertz computer and determined that the car was rented to Grant Meredith at an address in Durango, Colorado. She also downloaded his picture from the Colorado DMV. The picture and physical description on the driver's license fits the description we got from Deuce. Given the similarity of the approach to Deuce and Alex, I think this must be the same guy."

Saying nothing, Carlos crossed the room to his desk and sat down, leaving Esteban standing. "Esteban, I think you're right. I want you to stop Meredith from poking around in our business, and I want it done quickly."

"You mean, kill him?"

"No, not yet. Do we have anyone in the area?"

"No, the closest is Albuquerque; MS-13 has a substantial presence there."

"Send a couple of them to Colorado and have them locate a friend of Meredith's who can deliver him a message to mind his own business. I don't want the friend hurt, but I want him or her scared enough to deliver a serious message. Once he realizes he has been identified and that he has put his friends in jeopardy, he should go away. If not, I will reevaluate the situation.

"Also get his picture to our border people and add him to our watch list. If this gringo comes to Mexico, I want to know it immediately."

When Esteban left the library, the crow's feet around Carlos's eyes deepened, and the corners of his mouth turned slightly downward. He swiveled his chair around and looked vacantly out the window. The last names were the same; it may be a coincidence but probably not. He was going to monitor developments in this matter very carefully. Carlos stood. By the time he reached the door to the patio, his face was relaxed, and he rejoined his guests with a smile.

CHAPTER 29

▼

Grant had invited Stephanie to the ranch for a long weekend. While Grant went to a local irrigation ditch meeting, Stephanie and Tommy headed for Durango and some shopping. On the way back from Durango, they passed the Billy Goat Saloon.

Stephanie said, "Let's stop for a beer. I've never been in a honky-tonk."

"Miss Stephanie, that ain't no honky-tonk. Locals call it the Bayfield Knife and Gun Club."

"Come on, Tommy, let's go in. You'll protect me."

The Billy Goat Saloon was an old, log building that sat between an auto-repair shop and a mini storage on the main highway. It was a favorite hangout for construction workers, bikers, and Indians in desperate need of another drink. It was no place for a pilgrim. There was a bar, a few tables, a small dance floor, and two pool tables. Tommy and Stephanie went inside and sat at the bar with their backs to the door and a good view of the interior.

Two Mexicans came in and headed for one of the pool tables. They looked like clones of each other. They wore hair nets and tank tops, and tattoos covered their muscular arms.

"What do you think of those two guys?" Stephanie asked in a low voice.

"They don't belong here," said Tommy. "The Mexicans around here are hard-working ranch hands and good family men. Those two look like gangster wannabes. They're probably just passing through."

The two men left the pool table and seemed to be leaving through the front door. Instead, once they were behind Tommy and Stephanie, they turned and moved toward them.

"Raoul, this is a hot momma. We could probably get in her pants for a couple of dollars."

"*Si*, look at those tits."

Neither Tommy nor Stephanie turned around. Tommy slumped off the stool and said, "Be right back. Got to answer nature's call."

"Good thing you're leaving, cowboy. This woman is going out back with us."

Behind the closest man, Tommy reached up with his left hand, grabbed a handful of the man's hair, and pulled his head back sharply. A knife flipped open in Tommy's right hand. He pressed the point into the man's neck, and blood began to drip down his neck.

"Listen up, kid," warned Tommy, "this Spyderco has a serrated edge for cuttin' ropes and such. If you move, it'll sure make a ragged cut in this here artery. It'll make quite a mess."

The Mexican didn't move.

"Oh hell, this is too much trouble." Tommy slammed the man's face into the bar. The man slumped to the floor, blood seeping from his broken nose.

When Tommy had grabbed the first Mexican, the second one had backed off and had just stood there. Stephanie turned on her stool, stood up, and walked deliberately toward him.

"I *am* a hot momma, señor." Stephanie kicked forward and buried the toe of her cowboy boot in the startled man's crotch. He doubled over and fell to the floor.

Two Indians who had been drinking at a corner table came up to Tommy. One of them said, "Not very nice men."

"You got that right," said Tommy. "Do me a favor and put these two out back by the dumpster with the rest of the trash."

As Tommy and Stephanie turned to leave, they saw Grant, leaning casually against the door jamb. He wore black boots, a T-shirt, a cowboy hat, and a smile on his face. "It seems I shouldn't let you two run around loose. That was quite a show," he said.

"How long have you been standing there?" asked Stephanie.

"When I walked in, Tommy had his knife in that poor fellow's neck. That man was ready to come to Jesus. Tommy's been down the river more than a few times. Where did you learn to kick like that?"

"My daddy believed a girl should be able to take care of herself. I can do that."

"Obviously. Let's head for the barn. I wonder where those goons came from." Grant didn't say anything to Tommy or Stephanie, but two out-of-place Mexicans picking them out for harassment made a lot of sense in the context of the

Sanchez family. Fortunately, Stephanie was leaving for New York, Mexico, and South America for a heavy work schedule. Grant thought it was probably better if she were out of the way until he understood if there was a relationship between his inquiries and these goons.

Later that day, Grant packed his large bag and headed back to Scottsdale.

CHAPTER 30

▼

Stephanie couldn't sleep on the plane to New York. Grant Meredith didn't fit in her life, but she couldn't close her eyes without seeing his face.

After graduating from the Sorbonne, Stephanie had contacted her father's old friend, John Walker Wesley III, at the Central Intelligence Agency. She was fluent in French, Spanish, and Italian. She was an Olympic-caliber athlete and a master of small arms. She wanted to fight terrorism. This was what she had trained for since her father's murder.

Three years after joining the CIA—the Agency, as it was called—she had been asked to join the Clandestine Operations Unit. After another three years, John Wesley had come to see her with an offer she couldn't refuse—he wanted her to go undercover. The CIA would set her up as an account executive at a major public-relations firm in New York and provide her with a list of clients, including quite a few in Europe, Mexico, and Latin America.

Stephanie would use the skills learned from her father and the Agency to carry out covert assassinations of terrorists and others deemed critically dangerous to America. Her public-relations job would require business travel and would, thus, provide the cover necessary for her Agency work.

At age twenty-seven, it was what Stephanie had trained for and had been waiting for. Terrorists had killed her mother and had assassinated her father. It was payback time.

The Agency had developed an assassination methodology that assured, as much as possible, her success. She never had more than forty-eight hours notice of a hit. She was never told the identity of her target or why the person had to be eliminated. She had no contact with the target. She was told a time and place for her mission, where she should position herself, and how she would be able to identify the target. That was it. The plan was always to go somewhere shortly before the appointed time, set up, execute, and leave the country within two hours.

Four years later found her with a superficially successful career. She hated the public-relations business. Spin, misrepresentation, outright lies. Everything, people included, lacked substance. During her frequent business trips, she had carried out twenty-three hits. There had been no misses. The killing had no effect on her. She didn't feel good or bad about it. After years of telling herself it was all payback, she didn't believe it any more.

Sinking into depression, she considered visiting the Agency shrink but rejected it. Any sign of mental weakness would result in the end of her career or, at least, reassignment to a desk job.

Stephanie took a month-long vacation and traveled through Brazil, Venezuela, and, finally, Mexico. She visited college friends, who gave her a crash course in American imperialism as they sat in their sumptuous family homes totally aloof from the poverty that surrounded them. They were cynical and rich.

She arrived in Mexico City and, on the spur of the moment, called her old college sex partner, Hector Sanchez. He invited her to a party that very night.

In a penthouse lost in a smoggy cloud of pollution, Stephanie was immersed in a crowd of beautiful people in their late twenties and early thirties, drinking too much champagne, smoking, and arguing politics. America was the villain of the evening. America had an army with responsibility for every part of the globe. It intervened in other countries at will. It toppled governments. If a country didn't go along with what America wanted, it faced economic sanctions. It was somewhat distinct from the Roman Empire, but did the distinctions make a difference? America was crumbling from within. The rich got richer. The barbarians (terrorists) were at the gates, and America did not have the political will to protect itself.

They all agreed that the only way to survive the coming demise of America was with money. With it came power and the ability to protect oneself from the coming chaos.

With the arguments swirling about her in Spanish, Stephanie struggled to follow the conversation, but soon, the champagne made it impossible. She retreated onto the lavishly landscaped balcony with her glass of champagne and stared at the city lights below. An arm gently circled her waist. She turned into an extraordinarily beautiful woman with long, dark hair, who murmured something about boring politics. Stephanie felt her right breast pressing against the woman's left breast, but she didn't pull away. The warm night air, the city lights, the champagne, the woman's perfume, and the warmth of her body were truly intoxicating.

As Stephanie turned to fully face her new companion, she felt a hand on her shoulder, gently pulling her away. It was Hector, who said, "Sister, Stephanie is with me tonight."

She spent the next two weeks with Hector, living the high life in Mexico City and at his villa in Cancun. The sex was like they were back in college. It was an athletic event that left both of them panting, sweating, and satisfied. It was definitely not "love me tender" time.

Stephanie did not see Hector's sister again, and the encounter only came back to her when she couldn't sleep. Hector asked her to stay with him, but she wasn't ready—at least, not yet.

Stephanie had returned to New York fully energized. She had reinvented her life. She was thinking seriously of moving to Mexico where Hector and his friends would welcome her into their circle. Sometimes, she awoke in the middle of the night, smelling perfume that wasn't hers. But Grant Meredith was causing her to rethink everything. Did the relationship have a future? What about her plans? Was he worth it?

CHAPTER 31

▼

Esteban was nervous as he entered La Casona del Patron restaurant in Nogales, Mexico. The attempt to intimidate Grant Meredith had failed. With the clarity of hindsight and the information he now had about Meredith, it was painfully obvious that they had underestimated him. Esteban glanced around the crowded restaurant and made his way down a narrow hallway, past the kitchen and, to what appeared to be a supply closet. He used a key to open the door, which led to a narrow stairway that ascended to the second-floor law office of Juan Mendez. This secret entrance enabled people to enter the law office without being observed.

Carlos Sanchez sat at a conference table in a blue pin-striped business suit, blue shirt, and red tie. To Esteban, Carlos looked like he owned the world. Esteban did not sit down, and Carlos did not offer him a seat. Esteban stood up straight with his hand clasped tightly behind his back in the military parade-rest position.

"Señor Sanchez, I am sorry to report that the men we sent to intimidate Grant Meredith's woman friend failed. They were humiliated by the woman and a broken-down cowboy. The men were beaten and literally thrown out the back door of a saloon. MS-13 has returned these men to Guatemala; there they will be sent back to the army in a very remote region."

Carlos fixed an unblinking stare on Esteban and said nothing. The flat, black eyes had no depth or expression to them. The gaze reminded Esteban of a shark. When the silence became uncomfortable, Esteban rushed on, saying, "Juanita has run a computer background check on this Grant Meredith. He was an investment banker with Tatum & Hallis and was called up as part of the army reserves in the Gulf War.

"This is the interesting part. He never went back to Tatum. He stayed in the army. His military file is classified, and Juanita has been unable to access it. He left the military in 1998 and founded BlackRock USA, which provides ex-military men as so-called civilian contractors. The Felix family hired one of those companies from South Africa to train its security forces a few years ago.

"BlackRock was purchased by a large investment group that seems to be very well-connected politically. Meredith is still on the BlackRock board of directors but lives on a ranch in Durango, Colorado."

Carlos softly drummed his fingers on the tabletop and took a sip of water before responding. "It seems I have underestimated this situation. Is there any indication why he is interested in us?"

"Not yet, but Juanita is continuing her inquiries with our people in Phoenix. Ramon is running down the Tatum angle."

"Good. Be sure Juanita runs him through the database of the DEA's El Paso intelligence center. I want a complete profile on him before we decide how to proceed."

Esteban descended the stairs and left the restaurant, thinking that one of the reasons Carlos was so powerful was that he accepted responsibility for his decisions and did not blame others. The flip side of that characteristic was that he demanded that others take responsibility for *their* actions and decisions.

CHAPTER 32

▼

When I got back to Scottsdale, I was still trying to figure out what to do about the men who harassed Tommy and Stephanie at the Billy Goat Saloon. With some time on my hands, I decided to call Anna Garcia to see if I could stop by and tell her about my conversation with Lisa about Tomas. Perhaps it would give her some closure.

She invited me to come to her home for coffee the next morning. We sat on the small patio behind her house. The backyard had a six-foot wall around it and was beautifully landscaped. It was obvious that someone, probably her, spent a lot of time taking care of it. We enjoyed the warm morning and our coffee, chatting aimlessly; then, we spent about a half hour talking about Tomas and my conversation with Lisa. As I was standing and getting ready to leave, Anna asked if there were any developments in finding Ricky's murderer.

"No, but I've been asking around about Ricky and this Deuce character. A woman named Boots Sanchez keeps coming up. Ever hear of her?"

Anna's face tightened into a disapproving frown. Unknowingly, I had stumbled onto something. "Yes, I have. After Ricky and I stopped dating, one of my friends at the Salty Señorita told me that she saw Ricky with Boots one time. I told Ricky that Boots had a very bad reputation. He brushed it off and told me not to worry. She wasn't his type, he said."

I felt so stunned that I sat back down. This was a direct link between Ricky and the Sanchez family. For a moment, I was speechless. This was so unexpected that I didn't know where to start, so I said the first thing that came to mind.

"Why does Boots have a bad reputation?" I asked, trying not to seem overeager.

"Everyone with relatives in northern Mexico knows the Sanchez family. Their coyotes control illegal border crossings. If you want to come here to work, you pay one of the Sanchez coyotes. It isn't wise to try to cross without their involvement."

Once again, I was stunned. The report from Institutional Enterprises had not mentioned the crossing of illegal Mexicans among the activities of the Sanchez family; however, this activity was apparently common knowledge in Mexico. If it was common knowledge, where was law enforcement?

"What do you mean by 'without their involvement'?" I asked, trying to figure out what was going on.

Anna spoke to me like I was a small child being told to look both ways before crossing the street. "Those who cross with the aid of a Sanchez coyote almost always make it without any problems. It is said that they guarantee crossing. If a person is caught while crossing and is deported back to Mexico, there is no charge for the next attempt.

"I am sure you have read about illegals getting lost in the desert and dying from lack of water or being cooped up in an enclosed truck and dying from lack of air. I have heard that the Sanchez coyotes kidnap other coyotes after they cross into Arizona, leaving their customers to die. Also, truck drivers disappear. They are taken back to Mexico and never heard from again. It is rare that an illegal comes here without Sanchez assistance."

"Anna, how did you learn this?" I asked incredulously.

"It is common knowledge in the Mexican American community but never spoken of elsewhere."

"Why not?"

Anna spoke in an exceptionally patient voice as if I were the slow kid in the class. "Grant, we all have relatives in Mexico. The Sanchez family will not tolerate interference."

"Why hasn't someone gone to Mexican law enforcement?"

Anna took a sip of coffee that had been cold for some time, obviously collecting her thoughts. "I love this country and am grateful for the opportunity to live here, but Americans are so naive. You see the world as you want it to be rather than the way it is. The Sanchez family controls law enforcement. There is little crime in northern Mexico other than smuggling drugs and people into the United States. The few who commit criminal acts are dealt with harshly. We are all safe if we leave the Sanchez family alone. They are the gatekeepers. If you use them to cross the border and then leave them alone, all is well."

If even half of this information were true, Mexico had a shadow government that was, essentially, organized crime. I simply couldn't absorb the implications of Anna's revelations. It was better to get back to Boots and a topic I could handle.

"Where does Boots Sanchez fit into all of this?" I asked quietly.

"Truly, Grant, I do not know. I have heard she has a terrible temper and has killed people, but it is all gossip."

"Do you think Ricky had a relationship with her?"

"All I know is that my friend saw them having dinner once and that Ricky told me not to worry."

I left Anna's with my mind in a whirl. Ricky knew Boots Sanchez. He even had dinner with her. The Sanchez family was into smuggling—big time. It was looking more and more like Ricky got too close to the Sanchez family's illegal activities. My bet was that they were behind his murder. Unfortunately, gossip isn't proof. I decided to shadow Boots for a while and see what turned up.

CHAPTER 33

▼

Sugar Daddy's seemed to be a hangout for Boots, so I got there early and parked where I could see the entrance without being obvious. I had a leisurely dinner at a decent-looking restaurant across the street and settled in about 10:00 PM to watch for Boots.

I sat and watched the kids come and go. The guys all looked the same—T-shirts, jeans, and tennis shoes. The girls wore crop tops. Tall ones, short ones, laughing, yelling, and generally having a good time.

At midnight, Boots and "Mr. Muscle" showed up. They left at closing time, and I followed them to a house half way up the north side of Camelback Mountain off Lincoln Boulevard. "Muscle" dropped Boots off and left. I sat alternately looking up at Boots's house and north at where the night lights of Paradise Valley and Scottsdale twinkled into the distance until they disappeared. This was the prime real estate in the Phoenix area, and Camelback Mountain was some of the most expensive. The headlights of an occasional car further illuminated the streets below.

I watched until the lights went off. This was probably Boots's house, not "Mr. Muscle's." Given the view from up here, she was living well. I decided to leave and pick up the surveillance a little later.

Early the next morning, I was back at her house with a thermos of coffee. About 1:00 PM, I saw her coming out of the garage in a BMW with the top down. I followed her. We headed east on Lincoln, got on Highway 101 going south to Highway 60 east, and then took Interstate 10 toward Tucson. She put the pedal to the metal and settled in at eighty-five miles an hour. Fortunately, there was enough traffic—going almost as fast as she was—that I was able to keep a few cars between us.

She blew through Tucson and headed for Nogales on Interstate 19. Traffic was thinner here, and I hung back as far as possible. The closer we got to Nogales, the more border-patrol trucks I saw, distinctively marked with white and green stripes and lettering. I remembered what Anna had said and figured these guys were wasting their time.

As we came into Nogales, the topography changed. The town on both sides of the border was on a series of hills. From what I could see of the houses on the hills, this area could not be confused with the Hollywood Hills. Boots pulled into one of the many parking lots surrounded by chain-link fence topped with concertina wire. I pulled into the next one. I figured she was headed across the border. Should I follow? Oh hell, I had driven one hundred eighty miles, and it was only 4:00 PM. Why not?

Boots followed the sidewalk to the Dennis DeConcini United States Port of Entry and through one of three full-length turnstiles that every pedestrian entering Mexico legally had to pass through.

Fortunately, I didn't need a passport or any identification to enter Mexico at the Nogales border crossing. There was a free-trade zone that extended about twelve miles into the country. After that, there were checkpoints, and a person needed a passport. Getting back into the United States was another matter, particularly since 9/11.

I pushed through the heavy, silver-metal turnstile and entered Mexico. I saw two men sitting in lawn chairs in the shade of a deep doorway; they seemed to be looking at me quite closely. One of the men lifted a cell phone and said something into it.

It struck me as odd, but before I could give it further thought, I was immersed into Nogales, Sonora. It was a jumble of buildings in all colors of the rainbow. Tourist traps ran into shaded alleyways, and men and women outside all the shops entreated passersby to enter and see their merchandise.

As I moved along, I saw mangy dogs asleep on the sidewalks and little urchins with their hands out. Old women, dressed in big skirts, sat on the sidewalk, creating the appearance that they had no legs. They looked at me with infinite sadness in their eyes. Things changed one block later.

A large poster said the Festival de las Flores was underway. Ten days of celebration. I hustled to follow Boots, but it was becoming increasingly difficult.

Blocked off for the festival, the street was lined with canopies that were printed with beverage names, like, Coke and Tecate. Under the shade of the tents, plastic tables and chairs were filled with revelers. At one end of the street, a band of high-school kids in colorful costumes was playing as loudly as possible upon a stage that had been set up. The only problem was that each band member seemed to be playing a different tune.

A mob of young people in different costumes milled around the stage, waiting for their turn to perform. Young people were parading up and down the street with full-sized, primitive figures on poles.

Tables were full, and the crowd included lots of Americans in tank tops and shorts. The younger ones sported ball caps and tattoos; the older ones wore straw hats and beer bellies. The Americans were already well on their way to hangovers; the Mexicans just seemed to be having a good time. For some reason, it struck me that none of the Mexicans were smoking. Today, Nogales presented a jumble of colors, music, poverty, and life being lived.

Boots was moving along quickly. She went into a stone-faced building; the sign read La Casona del Patrón Restaurant Bar.

As I approached the front door, I was surrounded by a pack of ten dirty little kids, yelling in incomprehensible Spanish and holding out dirty little hands. I couldn't move quickly without knocking over one or two of them, and that would bring me unwanted attention.

I carefully moved through them and entered the door into a hallway. On the right, I saw a dark bar with very high ceilings. Three young women in costumes with banners across their chests were watching a flat-screen TV above the bar; a soccer game was on. The hall led to a door and out into a courtyard with tables arranged under a massive shade tree. The walls enclosing the courtyard were brick covered in plaster, which had been chipping off for years. A huge mural covered the back wall. There, a man on a small stage was playing a guitar.

I moved to the stone bar in the corner and surveyed the crowd. No Boots. To the right of the stage, I saw a sheet-covered opening in the wall that seemed to lead outside. She must have gone that way. I moved to the stage with a dollar in my hand and put it into the musician's tip jar. When I tried to go through the opening, my path was blocked by a Mexican of medium height in a short-sleeved shirt. He had a mechanical right arm. At the end of the arm were what appeared to be clippers.

"*No es possible por usted pasar aquí.*"

Boots was gone, and this guy was not going to let me go past.

I left and headed back toward the border crossing. Just as I was leaving the main street, the urchins surrounded me again, only, this time, there were twenty of them. As I tried to work my way through them, a man approached me, looking like all of the other Mexican men except that he was wearing big, dark sunglasses. He stood outside the circle of urchins and said, "*Silencio*." The pack of urchins was immediately quiet.

"Mr. Meredith, I regret to inform you that it is time for you to leave Nogales. I hope you have enjoyed your visit, because you must not come to Nogales again. You are, of course, welcome to visit Cabo San Lucas, Cancun, or any of our fine resorts, but you are not to come to northern Mexico."

I was stunned. The man obviously had command of this pack of children, but he was not at all threatening, and, in fact, he was smiling. How did he know my name?

"You must have me confused with someone else." I flashed a big smile.

The man stopped smiling, and his tone became hard, totally without emotion. "Mr. Grant Meredith of Durango, Colorado, we are not confused. We picked you up when you crossed the border. We were watching for you. We saw you go into La Casona del Patrón. We kept you from using the courtyard exit. Please look at your chest."

I looked down and saw three red dots from laser sights. This was a very bad situation. I fought the urge to run or to dive to the ground. Truth be told, I was afraid. I had not told anyone where I was going. I was standing in the middle of a small mob of children in a foreign country with three rifles locked on my chest. They could kill me and dispose of the body, and no one would ever know. Anna had said that the Sanchez family controlled law enforcement. I tried to remain expressionless while the sweat trickled from under my arms down my sides.

The man continued in a more affable tone, saying, "You must understand, Mr. Meredith, that we are serious people. I cannot be responsible for your safety if you ignore this warning. We are peaceful unless you refuse to obey us."

A faded, dark blue van with heavily tinted windows pulled up; the man got in it, and it pulled away. The pack of urchins disappeared, and I headed to the border crossing with my tail between my legs. Lisa was right. This was not a game for amateurs.

C H A P T E R 34

The sun was high in the sky outside the exercise room of the Sanchez family ranch when Margarita "Boots" Sanchez finished the treadmill portion of her workout. She was dressed in a stylish exercise outfit that did nothing to hide her jutting breasts, flat stomach, and round derriere. Boots put a white towel around her neck and stepped off the treadmill. She had seen her father's reflection in the mirrored exercise-room wall when he had appeared in the doorway five minutes earlier. Neither of them said anything until she finished her workout.

"Margarita, we need to talk," said Carlos.

Boots dried the sweat off her face with the towel, brushed by him, and said, "Okay, Father, out by the pool, if you don't mind."

Carlos dutifully followed her to the pool, and Boots flopped down on a poolside lounge chair, drying the sweat off her arms and legs. Like most men with a beautiful daughter, Carlos Sanchez had a weak spot for her. He knew he spoiled her and accepted behavior from her that he would not have tolerated for an instant from his sons.

"Margarita, I am very disturbed about this person who followed you. Do you know who he is?"

"No, Father."

"His name is Grant Meredith, brother of the gringo you dallied with. We are doing a background check on him, but regardless of what turns up, he is a problem that will require attention."

Fully aware of her hold on her father, Boots said in a dismissive tone, "This Grant Meredith is not a policeman or associated with the authorities. You should have disposed of him in Nogales."

"Margarita, you must learn that we are not barbarians," said Carlos in exasperation. "We cannot kill someone every time they annoy us."

Boots said nothing. She got up, walked over to the edge of the pool, and dove in with a long, shallow dive. She swam toward the far end of the pool with the relaxed strokes of an accomplished swimmer. Carlos had been dismissed.

Carlos watched Boots swim while he thought. He was sixty-one years old and had been the patron of the family since his father had been assassinated during the war with the Yanez family to control the border. At one time, the Sanchez family had controlled the entire border with the United States. Over time, it had become too much to manage, and Carlos's father had granted "franchises" to other families for the Texas and southern California borders. These families were to pay an annual fee to the Sanchez family for the privilege of doing business at the border.

One of the families, headed by Jamie Yanez, had refused to continue paying what he had called "tribute." Carlos's father had ordered the assassination of Jamie's youngest son as a warning to resume the franchise fee. The murder had had the opposite effect, however. The Yanez family had gone to war, and more than one hundred men and women had died in three months.

Jamie Yanez had called for a meeting to discuss the resumption of the fee. Against the advice of his lieutenants, Carlos's father had gone to the meeting and had been killed by a sniper.

At age forty-two, therefore, Carlos had taken control of the Sanchez family. In retaliation against the Yanez family, he had bribed a schoolmate, who had been in charge of the Mexican army along the southern California border, and his soldiers had stormed the Yanez home, killing Jamie in the battle.

Killing Jamie Yanez had not been enough for Carlos. Within thirty days, under the protection of the army, he had identified and killed every male and female Yanez family member in northern Mexico. Over fifty more people had died.

Nothing about this border war had appeared in the Mexican newspapers. The army and the local police had been bribed by Carlos, things had calmed down, and life had gone back to normal. In this way, the Sanchez family had taken back direct control of the southern California border.

The lesson of the border war was not lost on other criminals. It was one thing to risk one's own life but another to risk that of fathers, mothers, siblings, and cousins. Carlos was too smart to try to control everything. There was plenty of room for others to operate, but he maintained iron-fisted control of smuggling into the United States.

Ramon, his older son, hated violence. He believed in manipulating the system rather than trying to dominate it. If someone tried to smuggle drugs from Mexico into the United States, Ramon would not have them murdered, which was what Carlos would have done. Instead, Ramon would turn them in to the police or the army. That way, the Sanchez family got rid of the problem, and the authorities got credit for doing something about smuggling. Another murder would just cause problems for their friends, Ramon would say. It had taken time, but Carlos had come around to Ramon's way of thinking.

Ramon often pointed out that the family's greatest enemy was a free press. It was easy to control the press on the Mexican side of the border because the family owned the newspapers. The American press was controlled by timing. Do things on Friday so they were not news on Monday when people were paying attention. Move major shipments when the American press was preoccupied with other matters. Keep a low profile during U.S. election years.

Hector, the politician son, had actually been Ramon's teacher. He was a master at accumulating favors from people and gathering information about people that would insure their future cooperation. Mexico's political class, even the so-called populists, had come to respect Hector. Some, with good reason, feared him. To get his way, Hector would destroy an opponent's reputation and his life without blinking an eye. Because of this reputation, Hector seldom had to go beyond a whisper in the ear of a recalcitrant politician, policeman, or army officer. The sting of Hector's rebuke was usually softened with a large envelope stuffed with cash.

Margarita—he hated the nickname, Boots—was his favorite child. She was more like him: smart, dominating, and quick to violence. Because Margarita was a woman, however, Carlos knew that she would never have power in the family. His cousins would not permit it, and even he knew it was time for Ramon's way of operating.

Although Carlos knew that Ramon could devise a way to have the system take care of Grant Meredith, Carlos decided that, this time, he would do it his own way. Carlos had caused this problem, and he had to take care of it.

His people had told him that Margarita was seeing the gringo Ricky Meredith, who had been asking questions about drugs in Scottsdale High School. It had been clear to Carlos that this relationship had to end. When he had confronted Margarita, she had refused. She had said she was falling in love with Ricky and could take care of herself. Carlos had believed that a twenty-five-year-old woman in love, even his daughter, could not be trusted to make an accurate assessment of her man.

Rather than involve his family further in the matter, Carlos had used a contact known only to him and a few others to arrange for the elimination of Ricky Meredith. The murder had been intended to look like a drive-by shooting and, in any event, had not been traceable back to his family. Most importantly, he had deniability with his daughter. Even if she asked questions within the organization, she would not be able to find out that he was behind the murder. She would never understand it had been for her own good and necessary to protect the family.

Now, he had another Meredith on his hands, who had identified his daughter and was following her. Thank God, there was no romance this time. Ramon would want to wait and find a way to have the system eliminate Meredith, but it was Carlos's daughter who was in jeopardy, and that was something he could not tolerate.

Several years ago, as part of the war on drugs, then-President Clinton had sent Special Forces troops to Mexico to train elite units of the Mexican army in drug interdiction and counterterrorism. At the conclusion of the training, about one hundred members of this elite group deserted. They were incredibly violent and absolutely without mercy. Calling themselves the Zetas, they sold themselves to the highest bidder, which, in northern Mexico, was the Sanchez family.

He called for Esteban. "Send one of the Zetas to terminate Grant Meredith. Quickly!"

"It will be done, Señor Sanchez."

CHAPTER 35

▼

Detective Dolan was frustrated beyond endurance. He was investigating a murder, and the Defense Department refused to help him. It was possible that Grant Meredith's personnel file could help him connect Meredith to the murder of Ricky Meredith.

Dolan had contacted his brother-in-law for help. Jerry Drummer was chief deputy to Harry Johnson, Arizona's senior U.S. senator and a member of the Senate Armed Services Committee. Two days earlier, Drummer had called back and had said he would be in Phoenix with the senator and could meet then. He had refused to discuss anything over the phone. They had decided to meet for lunch on Friday.

Dolan and Drummer met at Los Olivos, a noisy Mexican restaurant near the Scottsdale police department. Dolan had never particularly liked his brother-in-law, who had a tendency to be very full of himself. Today was no exception. Between mouthfuls of burrito grande, Drummer gestured at Dolan with his fork and, in a most pompous manner, said, "Dan, I made some discrete calls to my contacts in the Defense Department. Bottom line—there is no way you're getting access to Grant Meredith's file without a presidential order. However, I did get some off-the-record gossip about him."

Dolan hid his disappointment and played to Drummer, using his most deferential tone. "Thanks, Jerry, I really appreciate this. What did you hear?"

"Meredith started with the DIA in the Gulf War and was trained as a foreign-area officer, which is a cultural expert on a particular country. He was inserted into problem areas, sometimes undercover, sometimes not, to gather intelligence for use in formulating battle plans and postwar reconstruction. It is unclear whether he was involved in any assassinations. By the mid-1990s, he was reporting directly to the secretary of defense.

"He was in Iraq, Liberia, Somalia, and Bosnia. He got fed up when the politicians didn't go through with a plan to snatch Slobodan Milosevic, and he quit. It's public information that he started BlackRock USA—the private-army folks—and made a ton of money. They have more three-star generals working for them than the Pentagon does. He's a big hitter and knows a lot of people.

"Look, Dan," said Drummer, filling his fork with burrito, "in my opinion, you're barking up the wrong tree, and it's you who's liable to get pissed on."

Dolan was stunned. He had been thinking Meredith might have been some sort of black-ops guy in need of money to support that fancy ranch of his, but now, he was back at square one. Other than the insurance policy, there was nothing to connect Meredith to his brother's death. Damn!

CHAPTER 36

▼

Dolan had asked me to stop by his office. I would not have gone except he said that it was very important and that he had some new information about Ricky's murder.

"Sit down, Mr. Meredith." Dolan tapped a pack of Camels on his desk, shook one out, looked at it, and tried to put it back in. He dropped the pack and the cigarette on his desk and without looking at me, said, "I asked you to come in because I wanted to give you some good news and some bad news. The good news is that we no longer consider you a suspect in your brother's murder." He rushed on before I could say anything.

"The bad news is that we have no other suspects, no clues, and not much chance of finding his killer. About all we can hope for is if someone facing jail time wants to trade information. It happens, and sometimes the information is useful. To be honest, don't hold your breath." Now, Dolan looked up at me.

It was a relief to hear I was no longer a suspect. I never thought it would go anywhere, but, still, there had been a few nights when Dolan's attitude had kept me awake. What started to bother me was the reality that they had no leads in Ricky's murder. I started to stand, but before I could get out of the chair, Dolan started up again with his tough-cop attitude.

"However, Mr. Meredith, there is still the matter of Deuce and his grandmother. We haven't found any trace of them. I think you may know something about what happened to them."

I sat back down. I wanted to be finished with Dolan. If I stonewalled him, I would still be on his radar screen. I had already told Lisa, so there wasn't anything to lose by telling him what I knew. "I talked to Deuce one time. The guy had been selling drugs to kids at Scottsdale High, and I heard that Ricky had talked to him. Deuce claimed he got his drugs from a guy named Jorge Torres. I had no other contact with him. I never saw or met his grandmother."

Dolan gave me his skeptical-cop look. "Are you telling me you just walked up to Deuce and he identified his supplier?"

"Well, ... not exactly," I said.

Dolan pointed his finger at me and said in a holier-than-thou tone, "This is Scottsdale, Arizona, Meredith, not Iraq. You can't go around torturing citizens."

Dolan must have found out something about my DIA career. That probably explained his changed attitude. I sat back, crossed my legs, and tried to look innocent. "I don't know what you're talking about."

Dolan was on a roll. He stood, walked around his desk, and looked down at me. "Deuce was a scumbag, who belonged in jail, but we have rules, Meredith. A civilized society has rules. Following the rules is what sets us apart from the rest of the world."

I didn't like him looking down at me and pontificating about right and wrong. This guy was starting to really piss me off. I stood and put my right index finger on his chest. "You have rules. People like Deuce don't. That's the problem. Your rules allow the Deuces of the world to run wild. I agree that certain behavior cannot be tolerated in a civilized society, but I'm talking about Deuce's behavior, not mine."

Dolan took a couple of steps backward. I think he was taken aback by the vehemence of my response. "Meredith, he was a nineteen-year-old kid."

I was having none of this bullshit. "That's not the issue, Dolan, and you know it. Deuce and the others are not misguided, otherwise-responsible citizens, who have made an error of judgment. They are evil. They prey on kids and hide behind your rules. In essence, your rules let them destroy children.

"Don't tell me you don't know who the dealers are or couldn't find out from the users in about sixty seconds. If you would go after these people, round them up, and execute them, the supply would dry up. Columbia, Thailand, and Afghanistan could grow all the dope they wanted. It wouldn't do them any good if there were no one to distribute it. Singapore has no drug problem. Do you know why?" I put my hands on the back of my chair. "That, Detective Dolan, is a war on drugs. If you want to win, that's how."

I had been thinking that Ricky's murder was somehow drug related. He had gotten involved in what should have been police business and had gotten murdered for his trouble. If the cops had been doing their job—that is, if the politicians and lawyers had let them—there would not have been a drug problem at the high school, and Ricky would still be alive.

Dolan wouldn't quit. "Meredith, this is the United States of America, not Singapore."

"Okay, then, quit kidding yourself and legalize drugs and regulate them like alcohol. Just let the drugs flow. Survival of the fittest. Users use, and the rest of us work. The catch is that the workers cannot support the users. Let them kill themselves."

Dolan walked behind his desk and sat down, reaching for his cigarette. In a world-weary tone, he said, "The politicians and the religious types will not allow that."

Here, my frustration boiled over, but I had enough control to sit down and calm down. "Look, Dolan, you know as well as I do that they are part of the problem. They talk about 'the children' and then allow drug dealers to prey on their own children. If you want to get rid of drugs, you can get rid of them. If you don't, then legalize them. It's that simple."

Dolan held up his right hand in the peace sign and actually smiled. "Okay, okay, enough. If I take off my cop hat, I don't really disagree with you."

We both seemed to relax. Dolan offered coffee. It didn't seem right to turn down his peace offering, so we went to the break room for a cup and returned to his office. Dolan lit a cigarette and said, "Lisa told me you were asking about Boots Sanchez. Did you find anything?"

Since we seemed to be at peace for the moment, I thought I could use him as a sounding board to try out my ideas; however, I wanted to trade. "What do you know about her?" I asked.

Dolan took a drag on the cigarette, blew the smoke toward the ceiling, took a sip of coffee, and finally said, "We had a sting operation going a few years ago and picked up a couple of dealers, who claimed they got their drugs from her. I assigned a team to dig up some corroborating evidence. Two days later, word came down from above that I was wasting manpower on an insignificant matter, and the men were reassigned. Nothing has come up since. That's all I know. What did you find out?"

"I can't prove anything, but I think this: The Sanchez family smuggles drugs into the United States either in meat shipments or in their other trucking operations. It is distributed to the wholesalers out of Burger Delight drive-ins, and the wholesalers distribute it to the street dealers. Somehow, Ricky got onto this, and I think they had him killed. It wouldn't surprise me if Boots did it. She's a real piece of work."

Dolan sat and smoked and drank some more coffee, obviously thinking about what I had said. Finally, he stood up and said, "You may be onto something, but with no proof, it's going nowhere. There are no other leads, so I'll talk to the chief and see if he wants to follow up on this. If you're right and you keep on with this, you're likely to end up dead."

"Someone might—but it won't be me," I said as I left.

CHAPTER 37

▼

Dan Dolan had been hired by Chief Ramirez five years earlier out of the Chicago police department. Dolan had been looking for sunshine instead of Chicago winters. Over the years, he had been given more or less a free hand by Ramirez in the major case section, except for monthly manpower utilization and budget reviews. Dolan spent most of his time working on securities-fraud cases connected to boiler-room operations, which gravitated to Scottsdale. The Ricky Meredith case was only his second murder case. In Chicago, Dolan had done nothing but murder investigations.

Dolan thought there was real merit to Grant Meredith's scenario. If Meredith was right, it could lead to a solved murder case and a huge drug-smuggling operation. That would be a feather in his cap, to say the least. Dolan considered Ramirez a bean counter, but he could see the potential in this investigation.

Dolan settled into the chair opposite Chief Ramirez and explained the possible Sanchez connection to the Meredith murder and drug smuggling.

"Chief, let me have a couple of detectives to run this down. It's our only real lead on the Meredith murder, and with the possible drug connection, it could be a huge case. I did a lot of this stuff in Chicago and have a feel for what buttons to push. We could get the DEA and the border patrol involved for additional manpower, or we could do it ourselves and show them up. What do you think?"

Ramirez looked at Dolan without speaking. Dolan had expected some resistance based on budgetary constraints, not silence. "Dan, I don't want the feds involved, they will use our resources and take all the credit. I want to think about this for a day or so. If we get involved in an open-ended investigation, it could tie up a lot of people. If you do this, I want it done right. I'll let you know by Monday."

CHAPTER 38

▼

On Sunday afternoons, Dolan liked to relax by going to the movies at Fashion Square. He would usually have lunch in the food court and watch all the pretty, young girls walk by. He and his second wife had divorced before he had left Chicago. He hadn't dated much since coming to Scottsdale. He had fantasized about asking Lisa Gonzales out, but dating within the department could cause problems. What he was really afraid of was being turned down. The Hispanic girls that flooded Fashion Square on the weekends were his favorites; to a Chicago Irishman, there was something erotically exotic about them.

This Sunday, the girl-watching had been great, and he had seen a Jennifer Lopez movie. As he was walking toward his car on the lower level of the parking structure, he fantasized about himself, Lisa Gonzales, and Jennifer Lopez as a threesome on a deserted Mexican beach.

He was startled out of his reverie by two young Hispanic women, who were walking toward him as he reached his car. Both were average height with dark hair and wore short skirts with tight tops that accentuated young, upthrust breasts. They were giggling and laughing and looking in each other's shopping bags.

The women approached him. "Excuse us, sir," said the one in the lead. She stopped about three feet in front of Dolan and smiled. The other was off to his side.

"We are looking for our car but can't find section Blue G. Do you know where that is?"

Dolan reached out and took her gently by the arm, drinking in the fragrance of her perfume and the softness of her skin. They both turned in the direction from which the women had come. He raised his other arm and pointed. "Just over there."

He felt cold metal press against his skull behind his right ear.

Pop. There was virtually no sound as the silenced 22-caliber pistol sent a bullet into his brain. It did not exit his skull, and there was very little blood. Dolan slumped to the cold concrete floor. He landed face up, and the woman with the gun straddled him and placed the pistol in his left eye socket and pulled the trigger. Pop. They grabbed him by the feet and pulled his body between the parked cars.

As they resumed walking down the parking structure, the women both started talking at once. "Listen, listen, Jorge promised he would have really good coke for us. I can't wait. It should be a great party."

CHAPTER 39

▼

I had invited Stephanie to the ranch for a long weekend, and she had flown in Friday morning.

I had carefully planned the weekend, starting with a trail ride. I wasn't sure whether she was an accomplished rider, but I had several horses that were virtually people proof. They took care of the inexperienced rider. A horse that would do that was hard to find, and if you found one, it was part of your stable until it died.

My first clue that I had once again underestimated Stephanie was her manner of dress—well-worn cowboy boots with heels, boot-cut jeans, a denim jacket, and a cowboy hat.

My second clue came when she took the reins from me, grabbed the saddle horn, put her left foot in the stirrup, and lightly swung up and into the saddle. As Tommy was fond of saying, this was no pilgrim.

We headed northwest from the barn, making small talk as we passed through two hay meadows and across an irrigation ditch before we got to the long pasture that ran due west between the trees. As we rode across this mile-long pasture, the elevation gradually rose one thousand feet before we reached some rugged hills.

My final clue that I had underestimated Stephanie came when a flock of birds sprang out of a bush immediately to her left. The horse jumped two quick steps and started to run. Stephanie's only reaction was a gentle tug on the reins and a pat on the horse's neck to calm him down. Horses are flight animals. They run when they're scared; they don't fight. Most novice riders get all upset and often cause a bigger problem when the horse reacts as nature intended.

The path wound among the pine trees, and we continued to climb. After ten minutes, we reached the ridgeline, from which we could see all the way down the Pine River Valley and into New Mexico. The clean, crisp fall air was invigorating.

We dismounted and tied our horses to a tree branch, short and high to keep the horses from stepping over the reins. I offered her a bottle of water, and we sat on a boulder, looking down the valley. Below us, the Pine River wound away toward New Mexico. Above us was the clear, clean Colorado blue sky. On a day like this, one understood perfectly what John Denver meant by "Rocky Mountain high."

"Where did you learn to ride?" I asked Stephanie.

"When I was a kid, my dad insisted I learn to ride. I think he envisioned me in a dressage outfit, riding to a foxhunt in England. I enjoyed riding and, like most young girls, took great pride in my ability to tame the savage beast. I don't get on horseback much anymore, but when I do, I like to see the countryside. I'm not much on riding in circles in an arena."

"If you're game," I said, "we could follow this ridge for a while to a line shack about a mile from here. There's a great view from the porch."

"A line shack?"

"It's left over from the time this place was part of a huge cattle ranch. At various places, quite a ways from the main ranch, the ranchers would build a simple one-room cabin with a stove and a few provisions. If a cowboy got caught out here in a storm, or if it were late in the day, he could put up in the line shack where there was something to eat, and he could keep dry and warm. These days, some of the neighbors use it to camp out with their kids."

"Let's go," she said with enthusiasm.

As we headed toward the line shack, a bank of dark, rain-filled clouds began rolling in from the southwest. It made more sense to continue toward the line shack; we would never make it back to the ranch in time. The wind picked up, and thunder rolled across the valley. We could see lightning flash between the mountain peaks. We loped our horses into the clearing of the line shack and quickly tied them under the old lean-to and raced into the shack as the rain began to fall in earnest.

The shack was made from aspen logs with a metal roof and measured about twenty-by-twenty-feet square. There was a covered porch along the front and a window on either side of the front door. We burst through the door, laughing and shaking the rain from our hats.

Across the room was a fireplace with a stone hearth and chimney. Two sets of bunk beds were placed along the left wall. To the right of the door was a round table with four chairs. Fortunately, the fireplace was set for a fire, and there was more dry wood in a big brass bucket.

As the rain made a deafening sound on the metal roof, I knelt at the fireplace and got a good, hot fire going. I stood and turned. Stephanie pressed against me, took my face in both her hands, and kissed me deeply. As her tongue slipped into my mouth, I could feel my temperature rise. I put my arms around the small of her back and felt her warmth. Her arms went around me and slid down to my buttocks as she pulled my hips into her.

As our kiss ended, I started to say something, but she put her forefinger against my lips. I stood there with my back to the fire as she knelt in front of me, unbuckled my belt, and pulled down my pants and underwear. She took me in her mouth, and my semirigid cock stiffened as her lips moved up and down it.

"Now, I want you now," she said as she shed her clothes. To my surprise, she sat back on the table, spread her legs, and put each foot on a chair. "Come here, cowboy."

I stepped between her legs and entered her. We both looked down and watched our intercourse. Before I could lose all control, she pushed me away, turned, and leaned over the table. I needed no prompting to address the situation, and as I finished, I could see her hands move from flat on the table into tightly clenched fists as she finished with me.

As we stood up, I looked at the bunk and suggested we lie down. I wanted to hold her and enjoy this special moment.

Stephanie shook her head and ran her fingers through her hair. "That was great, Grant. It's stopped raining. Let's head back, and I'll make dinner."

"But—"

"Come on, Grant, get dressed. Let's get going."

On the ride back, she kept up a constant stream of chatter but not about us. I was still trying to figure out what had happened.

We got back to the ranch late that afternoon. As we approached the barn, we heard the boom box blaring "The Stroll," by the Diamonds.

Tommy obviously didn't hear us coming. He was doing "the Stroll" down the barn aisle as he pitched flakes of hay to the horses, singing along with the music. The barn cat was sitting by the tack room door, watching him with complete attention.

Tommy did a pirouette at the far end and saw us as he started back down the aisle. He stopped, walked over, turned off the boom box, and looked at us. He launched a stream of brown tobacco juice at the cat, missed, and said to us,

"Wipe those silly grins of'en yer faces. A man's got to get his exercise, by God. Workin' on my cardio. You ought to try it."

We looked at each other and smiled.

"All right, all right, give me those horses and get out of my barn." He sent another stream of tobacco juice toward the cat. "Go catch some mice, you lazy critter."

CHAPTER 40

▼

That evening, Stephanie and I had cocktails by ourselves on the porch and watched the setting sun dip under light clouds on the western horizon, washing the sky in reddish tones. It was so pleasant; it was hard to imagine a man wanting more.

I grilled halibut while she made a salad. An excellent sauvignon blanc made for a perfect meal. After dinner, we went for a walk and, for the first time, held hands. It felt very strange to have had sex before holding hands. I was still trying to come to grips with our sexual encounter that afternoon. Maybe it was our age difference, or maybe my hormones had slowed down, but I was beyond wanting sex for the sake of sex. I wanted sex to be more than a quick encounter. I wanted it to be part of a relationship. Fifteen years ago, I was a regular horn dog. Maybe it was the army. Who knows? But it bothered me.

After a while, Stephanie and I ended up in the barn. Tommy had left some lights on, and the boom box was playing "You Light Up My Life," by LeAnn Rimes.

I don't know how it happened, but we were slow-dancing in the barn. All eight horses, four on each side, had their heads out, watching us dance. When the song ended, we held each other for a moment, not sure of what to do.

As we left the barn, I saw the Milky Way splattered all across the sky. I put my arm around Stephanie and pulled her to me. She didn't resist but said, "Between you and that saddle, I've had enough for one day."

As we walked to the house, it dawned on me that what was bothering me was my uncertainty as to who was in control here. This had never been an issue before, probably because I thought I was in control of the relationship whether I was or not. Now, the only thing I was sure of was that I certainly had no control over Stephanie.

CHAPTER 41

▼

Early the next evening, Grant was on a BlackRock conference call, so Stephanie wandered out of the ranch house and headed for the barn. She found Tommy there, feeding the horses. The boom box was playing "Rodeo," by Garth Brooks.

"Hey, Tommy, need some help?"

"Miss Stephanie, you could help me quite a bit if you would grab us a couple of beers. I'm just finishin' up here, and some nourishment would be mighty relaxin'."

Tommy and Stephanie settled into two chairs under a worn wooden sign with the words: BEER—SO MUCH MORE THAN JUST A BREAKFAST DRINK.

As the sun sank below the trees on the western horizon, the few drifting clouds were bottom lit with a red glow. Two hawks circled above, looking for dinner.

"Tommy, I have a question," Stephanie said. "When I was at the rodeo that first time, I asked one of the cowboys where to find Grant. The guy tried to hit on me, and when I walked away, he said that I should watch out because Grant had a vicious temper and had killed a man in a bar fight a few years ago. I suppose he was just trying to keep the conversation going, but I can't seem to get it out of my mind. Do you know what he was talking about?"

Tommy spent some time pulling a tin of Skoal out of his back left pocket and putting a pinch between cheek and gum. "It was an accident. This guy took a swing at Grant, caught Grant by surprise, you know, and Grant, he just reacted and hit that ol' boy in the wrong place. It was self-defense. The district attorney said so."

"What about his temper?"

"Ah, Miss Stephanie, he's as gentle as a lamb most times."

"What do you mean 'most times'?"

The barn cat got up and walked around Tommy's legs, rubbing against them. "Well, there was this time that old man Jenkins was marryin' off his last daughter, and he had a big reception up at Sandy's restaurant by the lake. We were sittin' at the bar, watchin' the gals dance and mindin' our own business when this big ol' boy comes up behind Grant and taps him on the shoulder. Grant, he turns around, and this ol' boy says, 'You killed my cousin, and I'm gonna whip your ass.' Now, this ol' boy, he was about six foot tall and maybe two hundred forty pounds, big beer belly, and, sure enough, red-faced drunk. Ol' Grant, he just turns back around on his stool and ignores him. This guy grabs Grant by the shoulder and spins him around. Grant, he just backhands the guy in the crotch, and the guy doubles over. Grant says to him, 'I'm going home; I suggest you do the same.'"

"I see what you mean, Tommy. A fight would have spoiled the wedding reception."

Tommy lifted the cat with his foot, moving it away, and spit a brown stream, hitting the cat in the side. The cat hightailed it out of the barn. Tommy didn't say anything for a while and just sipped his beer.

"That's not all, Miss Stephanie. I ain't never tol' nobody this before, but later that night, that ol' boy and a bunch of his friends showed up here at the ranch all liquored up. Must have been six of 'em that showed up in two trucks. Some of those boys had scrub-oak clubs; one of 'em even had a chain. Surely, those ol' boys thought they were the cat's meow."

"Oh my God, what happened?"

"Well, Grant, he had him some guests that weekend. Not those New York types but a couple of guys he had been in the army with. These guys and Grant, I guess they had worked together when they were overseas. Anyhow, these guys and Grant were all associated with BlackRock USA. Just so you'll know, that's a company that provides ex-military types for everything from bodyguards to corporate security to contract security—private army for hire, actually. Most of the companies doing reconstruction in Iraq are using BlackRock people for security. I hear they get one thousand dollars a day over there, which is a lot of money if you live to spend it. One of the perks is a one-million-dollar life insurance policy.

"Anyway, Miss Stephanie, I'm nigh onto fifty years old, and I've been around bull riders and rough stockmen all my life. Talk about tough. That type of man will climb upon a bull that would just as soon hook you to death as look at you, and the guy will do it with a busted rib and torn shoulder. I can't put my finger on it, but these buddies of Grant's were different. Sure, they were big and strong, but strong guys can be found in any gym. And they weren't the kind that's afraid of nothin'; hell, those kind are too stupid to know when to be afraid. Lots of guys have been combat soldiers. No, these guys had an attitude—not showy or nothin'—just competent. They were warriors, like your first pick for someone to ride the river with you.

"Anyway, that night, Grant walked out of the house toward these ol' boys. Me, I hustled up from the bunkhouse with a shotgun. One of Grant's buddies stepped out of the shadows and put his hand on the shotgun and said, 'Won't be necessary.'"

The barn cat returned and crawled into Tommy's lap. He absent-mindedly stroked the cat. "Well, Miss Stephanie, Grant was standin' there, and those ol' boys were just a hollerin' about what they were gonna do to Grant. Then, Grant's two Ranger buddies stepped out of the dark and into the light behind and on either side of Grant, and the hollerin' stopped. Know anything about vibrations, Miss Stephanie? Well, they were all around, and I believe those ol' boys were seein' the face of the Grim Reaper. I mean, they just stood there, and nobody said nothin'. Then, Grant, he says, 'Leave … now.'

"And they did. They just climbed back inside their pickups and drove out quiet like. So you see, Miss Stephanie, ol' Grant has a handle on his temper. You got nothin' to worry about." Tommy put the cat down.

"Tommy, you really like that cat."

"What? Oh hell, get out of here, cat. Go catch some mice." He launched a stream of brown tobacco juice toward the cat as it sauntered away.

CHAPTER 42

▼

On Sunday morning, Tommy and I were finishing a roping practice session and were leaving the arena on foot, leading our horses. Stephanie had gone on ahead and was in the barn. I stooped to pick up a rock. Suddenly, I heard a clang of metal simultaneously with the sound of a rifle shot. Tommy and I hit the arena sand like our feet had been knocked out from under us. My horse took off like he was heading to town on Saturday night. Tommy's horse just stood there, looking for a blade of grass to worry.

I stayed down and swiveled my head from side to side, covering one hundred eighty degrees. Tommy rotated to face in the opposite direction and did likewise. Off to the right, I saw a brief glint of light off something that could have been a rifle scope. It was on a hill about a quarter of a mile east of the arena.

"Did you see that?" I asked Tommy.

"You bet. Probably sun glinting off a scope. Dumb fuck." Wham! Thud. Sand kicked up about two feet in front of Tommy.

"We'd better do something. This guy won't miss forever," I said.

"Probably not," said Tommy. "Keep your head down. I'll take Loper there and head west and circle around behind him. He'll probably take a shot or two at me. Wait for him to shoot at me. Then, you get to the barn, take care of Miss Stephanie, and come up with a brilliant idea. If he can't hit us lyin' here, I doubt he can hit us movin'."

Before I could say anything, Tommy spat some tobacco juice, jumped up and grabbed his saddle horn with his left hand, and as the horse started to break for the gate, swung his right leg up and over the horse's back. He looked like an Indian in the old cowboy movies as Loper raced away to the west.

Sure enough, the sniper took a shot at Tommy. I dashed for the barn and almost ran into Stephanie, who was crouched by the barn door. She was holding the tack-room forty-five in her hand.

"Listen up, Steph," I said, "I'm going to get the pickup out of the garage and head off east and try to get close to him. Tommy will be coming in from the west. Send an occasional round in his direction so he doesn't head this way."

"Grant, wait—" Too late. I was gone.

A few minutes later, I left the truck by a gully and moved toward the low hill from where the shots had been fired. As I reached the crest of the hill, Loper and Tommy emerged from the woods to the west of the hill. A man's body was draped over the horse behind Tommy, and Tommy was holding a rifle with a telescopic sight.

As they approached, I could see an ear-to-ear grin, splitting Tommy's face. "Dumbest son of a bitch a body ever saw. This señor saw me comin' and just took off runnin'. He kept lookin' back for me and ran smack into a big ol' pine tree. He's out cold."

"The truck's over there, and there's some baling twine in the back," I said.

When we got back to the ranch house, two local sheriff's cars were there. Stephanie had called 9-1-1. We had to turn the guy over to the deputies. There was no chance to make him talk, anyway. I was sure he wouldn't say a word except to call for a lawyer.

After a series of questions we could not answer, the deputies left with the sniper. Tommy, Stephanie, and I stood in the driveway looking at one another. What had once been my personal business now involved them. The incident at the Billy Goat Saloon had been one thing, but attempted murder was quite another.

"Come on, let's get a beer, and I'll tell you what I think is going on."

Tommy knew about Ricky, of course, but nothing else. I had never told Stephanie about Ricky. I'm not sure why, maybe because she was my relief from his murder or maybe because I didn't know her well enough to share such intimate, personal information with her. Regardless, those rifle shots had changed everything. Tommy and Stephanie were involved and had a right to know.

I started with Ricky's murder, and how it had been at a stoplight in Scottsdale in broad daylight. I shared my frustration about the police, whose only clue was a stolen, black Mercedes, and their total lack of progress in finding the murderer. Then, I went through all that I had been doing since his murder. Tommy made a comment or two. Early in my monologue, Stephanie's eyes widened, but from then on, she said nothing.

"That's it," I said. "The only way this makes any sense is the Sanchez family. I'm going to Scottsdale and bring things to a head one way or the other. Tommy, you take care of things here. Stephanie, I'll keep in touch, but until this is resolved, I think it's best if you stay away from me."

I was surprised that Stephanie didn't say very much. She seemed almost in a state of shock. She just nodded a few times. All the way to the airport, we were both lost in our own thoughts. I was thinking about the Sanchez family, and she just looked out the truck window.

I got a sisterly hug and kiss at the airport, and she was gone. As I was driving back to the ranch, I thought about how quiet she had been but dismissed it as a reaction to the shooting. I needed a plan.

CHAPTER 43

▼

It didn't take a veteran detective to conclude that following Boots had struck a sensitive nerve in the Sanchez family. It was one thing to kill another drug dealer and another to go after a civilian. Ricky had been nosing around the Sanchez family. Given their response to me, it made sense to believe that they were behind his death. It made more sense than a random drive-by shooting.

The report from Institutional Enterprises mentioned the Sanchez ranch south of Nogales. A little surveillance there might turn up something.

I called BlackRock headquarters in North Carolina, looking for Luis Hernandez. A former Green Beret master sergeant, Luis had been the senior noncommissioned officer at the army's Joint Readiness Training Center. This small unit had trained the long-range reconnaissance teams for the army. I had personally recruited him to head the BlackRock surveillance teams. He called back within the hour.

"Hello, Major, this is Master Sergeant Hernandez. What can I do for you?" He had been out of the army since 1998, but rank was ingrained in him. I could visualize him through his familiar voice. He was about five foot ten, brown skinned, wiry, and had short, salt-and-pepper hair. He had a scar on his neck where an Afghan mujahideen tried to cut his throat. The miss cost the lunatic his life when Hernandez buried his knife in the inside of the guy's thigh and pulled up hard, severing the artery. He bled out and died in less than a minute.

"Top, I need some help for surveillance on a ranch in Mexico about an hour south of Nogales." "Top" was military shorthand for a master sergeant. I explained that I had a short mission in mind to gather information on a major drug lord.

"Let me get this straight, Major. You want BlackRock to insert you into a one-hundred-square-mile ranch in Mexico that you believe is the headquarters of a major smuggling ring. You believe that it is heavily guarded with state-of-the-art equipment and an unknown number of heavily armed men, who will shoot to kill. You want to get inside the ranch perimeter, approach the main hacienda, and see what turns up. Do I have that right?"

The skeptical tone in Hernandez's voice told me where this conversation was going. "I didn't say it that way, but ... yes, that's right. Just give me the necessary equipment, and I can be dropped into the perimeter at night, bury the parachute, and do the necessary."

"Major Meredith, with all due respect, sir, have you lost your mind? At last count, you are forty-five years old and haven't been in the field for almost ten years. Let's skip over the dispositive facts that you are no longer physically fit for such a demanding mission and that you have no current training. Let's do this by the numbers.

"Number one, advance planning. You have done no advance planning at all. What is the topography, vegetation, and layout of the ranch? How can you rehearse for the mission? You have no timeline for the mission. You are not familiar with our new equipment. You don't know where you will land, so you have no idea how you will get to your objective. It is one hundred square miles. What if you lose your compass and get lost? How will you hide in the daylight? What is the plan for extraction if you are caught or injured?

"Number two, insertion and infiltration. Jumping out of a plane in the middle of the night is not a plan for insertion into the target area. You have not worked with the flight crew, and I assume you are no longer a certified sky diver. How long will it take you to get from the landing to the target and out? You have no idea and, hence, no plan.

"Number three, how are you going to execute the mission? When was the last time you had any field-craft training? What about communication? When was the last time you had any evasion and recovery training?

"Number four, how in the hell are you going to get out of there? What if you are discovered and fired upon? How do we get you out?

"And oh, yes, I almost forgot. What about the Mexican and United States' governments? As you have told us many, many times, we are not mercenaries. We work with governmental permission."

Now, I remembered why I worked so hard to hire Master Sergeant Hernandez. He was a professional inside and out and did not have a deferential bone in his body. "You're right, Top. I may have to do this without any connection to BlackRock."

"Now, I'm seriously worried, Major. We've done some training with the Mexican army for drug interdiction. Half of the men we trained ended up deserting the army and starting their own drug gang. Believe me, I have some idea what these people are like. You aren't James Bond, and what you propose sure as hell isn't a movie. You are completely unprepared, and, in this business, the unprepared die."

"Top, you've forgotten that I used to do this in war-torn countries and am still alive."

"Major, 'used to' is the operative term. To quote an eminent modern philosopher, 'A man's got to know his limitations.' Do you remember what you told me when I joined BlackRock? … Well, I have never forgotten. Rule number one is 'get all our men back alive.' Rule number two is 'never forget rule number one.'"

"All right, Top, I'm slow, but I get your point. I appreciate your candor."

"Major, if you really need this done, we have at least a dozen men who have just returned from Pakistan who have the skills to do this kind of mission, but preparation will take several weeks," said Hernandez in a conciliatory manner.

"No, Top, thanks, but no thanks. It isn't a BlackRock job. I hung up the phone and went for a run to clear my head. I was in shape but not combat shape. Top was right on each account. What was I thinking? The answer was that I hadn't been thinking. Too much time behind a desk. The reality was that Boots was my best, and only, lead.

CHAPTER 44

▼

It was obvious that Boots, given her age and gender, did not run things. Thinking it through, I had three choices: bring in the authorities, question Boots myself, or follow her for a while and see if that turned up something that could link her and her family to drug smuggling, drugs at Scottsdale High, and Ricky's murder. I had a number of dots but needed information to connect them.

The Scottsdale police had jurisdiction over the murder. If I went to Dolan, what could he do? I still didn't know who killed Ricky. In my opinion, the Sanchez family—maybe Boots herself—killed him. But there was no evidence. Given the attitude of the Scottsdale chief of police, this wouldn't go anywhere. The DEA? I had no evidence of drug dealing for them. Deuce had disappeared and was probably dead. I had not seen drugs in the possession of Jorge Torres or Boots. Going to the authorities wouldn't take me anywhere.

I could question Boots myself. Given my methods of persuasion, however, any confession she gave would be inadmissible in court, and I might be the one going to jail. If she didn't murder Ricky, she might know who did, but, then again, she might not. It made no sense that a multigenerational criminal family would confide very much in a twenty-something woman. It was also unlikely that she had enough authority to order a murder. Another minus was that the Sanchez family would quickly know about our question-and-answer session, making my job much more difficult.

I needed more information, and I needed to get it without making waves. Boots was my only lead and my only entrée to the family. Nogales was home to the family. If I could follow Boots there, something might turn up. But I couldn't do it alone. Maybe I could get into Nogales in a disguise with a companion. Maybe Lisa Gonzales could help.

I called Lisa and was stunned to learn about Detective Dolan's murder. Lisa told me that Chief Ramirez had taken personal charge of the investigation since it was the murder of a policeman. There were no witnesses, but the way he was killed, and with a 22-caliber handgun, was typical of a professional hit. The operative theory was that his murder was related to one of the boiler-room operations he was investigating. Lisa said she wasn't particularly friendly with Dolan but had volunteered to work on the investigation. Chief Ramirez had turned her down, she said, using her suspension as the reason.

Lisa and I met for dinner at the Capital Grille. Over a good steak and a bottle of excellent wine, we discussed Dolan's murder. Then, I told her about the fiasco at the Billy Goat Saloon and the attempt to kill me at the ranch. I told her about my visit to Nogales and the confrontation with the Mexican man. Finally, I told her about how I analyzed the situation and about my desire to follow Boots into Nogales.

"Grant, that business in Nogales is frightening. You could have been snatched off the street and killed and nobody would have known what had happened to you." Lisa's concern was genuine. It was nice to have a beautiful woman care about me. Then, her cop attitude took over, and she started to lecture me.

"Grant, for your information, twenty-seven Americans have been kidnapped along the border on the Mexican side in the last six months. Two of them were killed, and eleven are still missing. Last month alone, one hundred Mexicans were reported murdered along the Mexican side. Who knows how many have not been reported?

"The drug dealers and coyotes have automatic weapons and are actually shooting across the border at our border-patrol agents. Last month, there was a report that they were hiring MS-13 gang members to kill border-patrol agents. Did you ever stop to think that maybe you're in over your head? What do you accomplish if you're killed? Think about it."

Lisa painted a persuasive picture of lawlessness, but I was undeterred. "Lisa, I have thought about it. As a matter of fact, it is *all* I think about. I admit it has been amateur hour so far. I admit that I have been very lucky. But the fact remains that, although I'm rusty, part of my job with the DIA was to do just what I propose to do. I'm confident that the Sanchez family is behind Ricky's murder. I just can't prove it, yet. I'm going to find his killer. I owe it to Ricky, and I owe it to myself."

"Men!" exclaimed Lisa in disgust. "There must be something in male genes that causes this overblown sense of machismo."

"Look, Lisa, this isn't about being macho. I'm very confident about who I am. It's who I am that means I'm going to do this. I thought that you and I could get into Nogales if I disguised myself and we looked like tourists."

Lisa didn't say anything; she just got up and excused herself to go to the ladies' room. When she came back, she sat down, put her napkin in her lap, took a sip of wine, and said, "I'll help you and maybe keep you from getting killed—on one condition."

"Sure, what is it?"

"I have an equal say in what we do and how we do it. I have no intention of following you around like a puppy dog."

This wasn't part of my plan. I didn't need a twenty-five-year-old female partner. However, from the look in her eyes and the way she crossed her arms across her chest, it was her way or she wouldn't play.

"Fair enough, partner. What do you think of my plan?"

"It stinks."

"What?"

"It stinks. Everyone going into Mexico on foot at the Nogales Port of Entry passes through the turnstiles. You know they have spotters there. You are isolated as you come out of the turnstile. They are watching for you more than ever. Do you know any Hollywood makeup artists? If your disguise doesn't work, you will be spotted immediately, and we both may be killed. I don't like the odds. If you try to enter in a vehicle, the issue is the same. You want to hide in the trunk? What if they search the vehicle? We could both end up in jail."

"Okay, what's your plan?"

"I have an idea. It's not a plan, yet. I have a friend, Lily Gonzales, who works for the border patrol and is based in Nogales. Last year, she was involved when they discovered a tunnel that ran under the border from a house on the Mexican side to a house on the American side. Get this. The tunnel was twelve hundred feet long and thirteen feet wide and was shored up with wooden beams. There were railcar tracks down the middle, electric lights, and a ventilation system. I have a vague recollection that all kinds of tunnels ran under the border. I think we should talk to her."

"Railroad tracks in a tunnel?" I said incredulously. "That means they must have been moving drugs in mining-type carts under the border. Can you imagine how much product got smuggled into this country with that kind of a setup?"

"A lot more than you can put inside a suppository," Lisa said. "I'll talk to my friend and call you tomorrow."

CHAPTER 45

▼

On the way to Nogales, Lisa told me more about Lily Gonzales, who was known to her friends as "Fast Lily." She was a thirty-five-year-old Mexican American, who had been with the border patrol in Nogales for ten years. Not only did she not go by the book, she seemed not to have even read it. She would have been fired many times except for two reasons: (1) she had a knack for finding out where the coyotes were crossing illegals, which gave her the highest catch record in the district, and (2) more importantly, because she was a Mexican American woman; none of her supervisors wanted to take on the civil-service bureaucracy. The good news was that she had tenure. The bad news was that, under current supervision, she was never going to get promoted.

Lily was a single mother, divorced, with a ten-year-old son. She joined the border patrol after her divorce and never mentioned her ex-husband, who had not been seen for years. When it came to her actions toward men, "bossy" was an understatement. Lily had an attitude. It was her way or the highway. Lisa told me that Lily explained it by saying she just had better ideas. She went through men faster than a movie star—hence, the nickname, Fast Lily.

We met at a Denny's on Sunday morning, and Lisa and I were stunned by what Lily had to say about the Nogales tunnels.

She said that on both sides of the border, much of Nogales was situated on hills and that on both sides, a system of tunnels and canals existed to handle storm drainage. Given the topography, tunnels from both sides of the border emptied into the Nogales Wash—which was on the U.S. side of the border—and then into the Santa Cruz River.

Beneath Nogales, Arizona, the main drainage channel was twenty-five feet wide and twelve feet high, and it ran for a mile and a half. Numerous smaller tunnels connected with the main channel. One of these tunnels actually ran directly underneath the DiConcini Port of Entry. According to Lily, no one knew where all of the storm drains and tunnels were located. These municipal tunnels also served as homes and hideouts for homeless tunnel-kids.

It was fascinating to find out that a municipal tunnel system existed from Mexico into the United States for several miles.

Since 1995, the border patrol and the DEA had discovered thirteen hand-dug, nonmunicipal tunnels that crossed the border. These tunnels ranged from a twenty-five foot, hand-dug tunnel that ran from a wash in Mexico to a dry stream bed on the American side to the twelve-hundred-foot tunnel Lisa had described.

Most of the drug-smuggler tunnels did not attempt to cross the border. They connected with the municipal storm drains. When one of these tunnels was found and plugged, it was unplugged and back in service almost immediately. The tunnels had to be destroyed. But as soon as one was destroyed, another took its place. It was said, not entirely facetiously, that one could not sink a shovel into the ground on the Mexican side without hitting one of these tunnels.

Lily filled us in on the extent of the illegal drug trade. There had been ten billion dollars in drug seizures along the US/Mexican border in 2003. According to the DEA, 70 percent of the cocaine and almost all of the marijuana in the United States entered from Mexico. The Mexican drug trade at the border was controlled by what the DEA called "Gatekeeper Organizations." These organizations used extensive family ties on both sides of the border to transport and distribute illegal drugs.

Lily was a fountain of information. The going rate to smuggle people from Mexico into the United States was one thousand dollars for Mexicans, four thousand dollars for Central Americans, and forty-five thousand dollars for Middle Easterners and Chinese.

All of this was helpful, but what came next was intended to send us home.

"Mexican drug gangs have become the world's number one drug traffickers," Lily said. "They get cocaine from the Columbians and produce their own marijuana and meth. They are very well organized and willingly kill to protect their turf. There are hundreds of drug-related murders in Mexico every year that you never hear about. Neither the Mexicans nor the Americans have committed the resources necessary to deal with what borders on lawlessness.

"The reality is," continued Lily, "that the drug lords own the Mexican government from the president's cabinet to the local policemen. Just a couple of years ago, the Mexican president appointed a military general as the new drug czar, who came to Washington DC and met with Barry McCaffrey. McCaffrey sang his praises and shared all sorts of critical intelligence with him. Well, two weeks later, the drug czar was arrested for corruption. He had been on the take for years. He had put his soldiers, weapons, and airfields at the disposal of one of the cartels. He had used his troops to kill rivals after torturing them on one of his military bases.

"You have no concept of what you're dealing with. Did you know that they use 747s to fly cocaine from Columbia to Mexico? They land the damn planes at military bases down there.

"The drug lords not only use the Zetas," Lily said, "you know, those guys who deserted from the Mexican Special Forces, but now, they are using Guatemalan Special Forces. Those men are trained by our country, take a leave of absence from the Guatemalan army and hire themselves out as enforcers, and then slip back across the border into Guatemala.

"We know all this, but our president won't do anything about it. NAFTA is a sacred cow and the increased traffic at the border has made the smuggling situation uncontrollable." Lily paused to take a sip of her coffee which had grown cold some time ago.

"The Sanchez family is the worst of the world's worst bad guys," Lily continued. "Their people are organized into small, specialized groups, who do not meet or know one another. One group picks up the drugs that are flown or shipped into Mexico and takes the drugs to a rendezvous point. Another group moves the drugs to the border. Another group moves the drugs across the border, and yet another takes the drugs to the distributors. It's like the terrorists—a network of individual cells. If you catch someone with the drugs, there isn't much they can tell you. Bribes to the Mexican police and army are in excess of one million dollars per *week*. You can't find a Mexican politician who will even mention the Sanchez family.

"I know for certain, but can't prove, that they have Americans in their pocket, also. The border patrol and the DEA aren't interested in the Sanchez family. In fact, as far as I know, there has never been a report reaching Washington that mentions the Sanchez family. I am constantly told, 'get me some proof.' They are an extremely powerful political family in Mexico. Bottom line—the family is off limits. My advice to you is to go home. All you can expect to accomplish is to get yourselves killed."

"Lily, I appreciate your concern," I said, "but you have to understand; I think they murdered my brother. The cops are getting nowhere. I can't just let it go."

"Grant, I hope you won't think I'm insensitive, but your brother is dead. Nothing you can do will change that. I can understand you want revenge; that's perfectly normal. But think about this situation. These people would never allow Boots to be involved in a murder. The hit man or woman got a contract from someone they probably had never met before. The person doing the hiring probably got his instructions from an unknown person through a post office box. That person was told who to have killed and how and where to find the money for the job.

"Catching the killer accomplishes what? A primal need for revenge? Are you going to kill the killer? Is that going to give you satisfaction? The killer will not be able to take you up the food chain. If you try to take on the Sanchez family, you will be up against the Mexican police, the army, and the Mexican political system. I don't want to rain on your parade, but the reality is that you can't accomplish anything meaningful."

"What if Boots killed my brother?" I asked in a last-ditch effort to stem the tide of hopelessness.

"These people are not that stupid," Lily replied. "How do you think the Sanchez family has controlled the border for almost a hundred years? Boots may be a loose cannon, so assume she did it. If so, and if you kill her to avenge your brother's death, you will be doing them a favor. I have better things to do than help you kill yourself in a quest that accomplishes nothing. If you want to be macho, go crush beer cans."

Lisa was nodding assent like a bobblehead doll.

I didn't like it, but Fast Lily was right. If Boots did kill Ricky, it was probably because she was a loose cannon in the organization, and, in that sense, they would be glad to be rid of her. Was I trying to accomplish something meaningful or just flailing around, seeking revenge?

"Listen, Grant," said Lily, "I know the tunnels as well as anyone, which isn't all that well. You don't go down there alone. Period. If you go without being armed and run into the wrong people, you will just disappear. If you can give me a reason that makes sense, I can get you across the border through the tunnels, but I won't do it for meaningless revenge."

Lily stood. "I have to take Arthur to the park. Thanks for breakfast."

When we got started up the highway to Phoenix, Lisa finally said something. "I tried to warn you. Lily doesn't pull any punches. I'm sorry if she offended you."

"I shouldn't be offended by the truth. Listening to Lily pull this apart is like taking a cold shower. You may not like it, but you're better off being clean. I need to think things through."

We remained lost in our thoughts all the way back to Phoenix.

CHAPTER 46

▼

I hated to admit it, but Lily was right. What was I trying to accomplish? I wanted revenge for Ricky's murder. To put it bluntly, I wanted to watch his murderer die. If possible, I wanted to do him myself. But what would it accomplish? One less murderer? So what? Ricky would still be dead. Would I feel any better? For a short time, maybe. Why did I continue to pose the issue in terms of myself?

This had to be about Ricky, not about me. What had Ricky been trying to accomplish by nosing around the Sanchez family? He was upset about drugs in Scottsdale High; it undoubtedly brought back memories of his best friend in high school, who had died of a drug overdose. There was no doubt in my mind that my brother had finally found something to do with his life beyond basketball. He had started with Tomas and was going to work to get drugs out of Scottsdale High. This effort had gotten him killed. I had solved that part of what I had set out to do. Ricky didn't care about revenge, he was dead. What Ricky cared about was getting the drugs out of the school.

If I could do something to advance his cause, his death would not be meaningless. This brought me back to the same old problem but, this time, with a good reason to try to solve it. I did not have any proof that Boots or any other member of the Sanchez family was involved with drugs in Scottsdale High. Boots was my key to the Sanchez family.

I called Lisa and explained what I wanted to accomplish by taking on the Sanchez family. I had no illusions that we could bring down a Mexican institution that had been around for a century, but I did hope to finish what Ricky had started, and to do that, I needed information. Lisa listened and said she would think about it and get back to me.

The next day, she called. "I'll help you. For the last three years, I've been beating my head against a wall. Between the ACLU, the courts, the chief's attitude, and the constant lack of funding, I haven't really accomplished anything. A dealer here and there is almost a waste of time. They're replaced immediately by someone who is a little more careful, and, the next time, it is a little harder to catch them. When we do, I don't have to tell you about liberal, hand-wringing judges.

"You absolutely would not believe the type of judges we have here. A couple of months ago, a guy with a drug-dealing record a mile long raped a twelve-year-old girl. The judge said the guy was too small to go to prison and put him on probation. The judge wasn't talking about his private part but about his height and weight. Unbelievable."

"Lisa, I share your frustration," I said. "The government and the courts have abdicated their most fundamental reason for existing; to protect the citizens, particularly the children. Maybe, just maybe, if we work together we can do what we can do, which is deal with Scottsdale High. One step at a time. If we are successful, maybe somewhere else, someone else will try."

Lisa took a deep breath and reverted to cop mode. "What we'll probably get done is end my career in law enforcement, but I've got to try and do something besides collect a paycheck. I'll call Lily and see if she will help."

Lisa called two days later. "Lily's in. We want to meet Sunday morning."

Sunday morning at 9:00 AM found the three of us at a Denny's on Speedway in Tucson. Not surprisingly, Lily had a plan.

Since Lisa was on suspension, she was going to stake out Boots. I was going to camp out in Nogales and wait for a call from Lisa that Boots was heading toward Nogales. I would notify Lily, who would take me under the border to the Mexican side of Nogales. Lisa would follow Boots through the port of entry and use a cell phone to call us with their location. We would rendezvous, and the three of us would take turns keeping Boots in sight. Maybe we would learn something. Most people had a pattern to their lives, and if we learned Boots's pattern, it was likely to be helpful.

I thought about the Mexican man in sunglasses and the red dots on my chest and protested that I didn't want to put the women in harm's way. Their response was twofold: first, they were both trained law-enforcement officers, and second, if I didn't like it, I could take my male-chauvinist tail back to Colorado.

My last question voiced my concern for their safety. "What about weapons?"

Lily responded immediately. "None. Lisa and I are United States' law-enforcement officers. We cannot go armed into Mexico without the approval of the Mexican government. As for you, even if you made it alive to a Mexican jail, there would be little chance you'd get out."

I didn't like this part of the plan, either, even though I understood the reason for it.

We reviewed things for a while and were finished by 11:00 AM.

CHAPTER 47

▼

Ten days later, I was watching Clint Eastwood in *The Unforgiven* for about the tenth time when Lisa called about 4:00 PM. Boots was halfway to Nogales going eighty-five miles an hour with moderate traffic.

I called Lily, and we headed out. Lily took us just east of town and pulled into a gas-station parking lot. We walked behind the station and down a well-worn footpath to the bottom of a sandy wash that was strewn with trash. After fifty yards of trudging in the sand, we walked right up to the concrete opening of a twenty-foot-wide, seven-foot-high tunnel opening. We continued to walk upright toward daylight at the other end of the tunnel, picking our way through the debris. A few minutes later, we exited the tunnel in a sandy wash and walked up the bank on another footpath into Nogales, Mexico. We were on Presidio Street.

It was amazing. It took twenty minutes from the time we entered the tunnel on the United States' side of the border until we were seated on the patio of a bar in Mexico. Our clothes weren't even dirty.

We were halfway through our Tecate beers when Lily's cell phone rang.

"Lily, are you there?"

"Yes."

"Boots went directly to a warehouse down by the truck crossing. It's on Segundo Street, and the sign on the outside is La Suerte Trucking Company. I'll be in the bodega on the north side of the street."

"I know where that is. We're about three minutes away."

As we walked toward the warehouse, I told Lily that I would check the perimeter of the building while she picked a spot on the other side of the building from Lisa.

The two-story warehouse took up the entire block. I saw the front entrance and a loading dock in the rear that ran along the length of the building. On the west side, I saw a roll-up, metal door that covered an opening big enough to accommodate an eighteen wheeler. It was closed. I found a recessed, shaded doorway in what appeared to be an abandoned building about fifty yards from the loading dock.

Nothing happened for an hour. Then, one of the roll-up doors on the loading dock opened, and a woman came out and stood under the light. I used the small binoculars that were on my belt and took a look. She appeared to be about six feet tall and two hundred pounds: solid, not fat. She looked in my direction and scowled. I knew she couldn't see me, but I also knew this was not the kind of woman I wanted to meet in a dark alley.

A dusty, 1950s, four-door Ford pulled up to the dock, and four men got out. Three of them faced outward from the car. They had AK-47s at the ready position. The driver took two boxes of about three feet by two feet in size out of the trunk and struggled to lift them onto the loading dock. With no apparent effort, the woman put them on a dolly and wheeled them into the warehouse. The roll-up door came down, and the men got back inside the car and drove off.

I had a good idea what was in the boxes but no idea what to do about it. Ten minutes later, my cell phone rang. It was Lisa.

"Boots just came out the front door with some guy, and they're heading east. Lily has them in sight, and I'm on the parallel street on this side. You follow parallel on your side."

I headed east along an empty street, trying to stay in the shadows. I had on a long-billed ball cap pulled low, jeans and T-shirt, and well-worn sneakers.

As I walked along, trying to look like I had a destination in mind, I thought about where I was and what I needed to look for.

Three blocks later, Lisa reported that Boots and the man had entered a bar called Negra Señorita. It was a one-story stucco building. I called Lily.

Before either of the women could say anything, I said, "I'll go inside. Lisa, wait out front. Lily, check for a rear entrance. If there is none, join Lisa."

I pulled the brim of my ball cap as low as I could and assumed the unsteady walk of someone with too many drinks under his belt. The door was open. There was no one in the bar except the bartender, a surly looking fellow. There was an open door to a patio in the rear. I went to the bar and slurred, "*Una cervesa Tecate, por favor.*"

Beer in hand, I slumped at a rear table where I had a view of most of the patio and the inside of the empty bar. Dim gas lamps lit the bar and accentuated a layer of oil smoke that drifted near the ceiling, creating an eerie glow. The place smelled of stale beer and cigarettes. Torches on the back patio accentuated the atmosphere.

Boots and two men were sitting at a table on the patio. The men, both in their twenties, had only their heritage in common. One was built like a fireplug with shaggy hair and well-defined muscles. The other was skinny and kept squirming in his chair as if the seat were too hot.

Boots nodded at the big man, and they stood. The skinny guy sat there with his head swiveling around like he was looking for someone, but no one else was on the patio. The big man took a hold of the skinny man's arm and lifted him to his feet.

When they moved through the bar, I slumped at the table and put my head on my folded arms like I was sleeping. They paid no attention to me. I stumbled out the door after them.

The three figures disappeared into the darkness behind the bar. They stopped in the alley, and the big man grabbed the other man and held his arms behind him. A six-inch switchblade knife sprang open in Boots' hand, and she deftly sliced open the small man's shirt, exposing his chest. She traced a line with the knife blade from his throat to his belly button. Blood oozed along the track.

She asked him a question, and he shook his head violently from side to side. She put the blade under his left eye and asked another question. He said something, she nodded, and the knife disappeared. Boots lifted her chin, and the big man moved away into the darkness, dragging the little man with him.

A dark blue van with heavily tinted windows came through the alley from the opposite direction and stopped where Boots was standing. I remembered the van. All doors opened, except for the driver's, and four men got out. The van's interior light was off. One of the men wore night-vision goggles and the other three had rifles with night-vision scopes and handguns on their belts. All had on vests, which I assumed were bullet proof. Boots got into the van, which did a U-turn and drove away.

In profile, I could see that the men wore headsets with microphones. We were in serious trouble. They were too close for me to safely use my cell phone or even to move.

The man with night-vision goggles motioned, and two of the men moved off away from me with him. The other one headed in my direction. I stood completely still in the shadow of the adjoining building. As the man walked past, I stepped behind him and delivered a blow just behind his right ear with the edge of my right hand. I grabbed his rifle as he slumped to the ground. Thank God, the gun hadn't gone off. I checked the safety on the AK-47. It was in the "off" position.

Two things were now obvious: First, I had gotten Lisa and Lily into this, and I had to do whatever was necessary to get them out of it. Second, the sound of an AK-47 would cause all hell to break loose. I kept it anyway.

I didn't know precisely where Lisa and Lily were in relation to the two other men, so the cell phone was useless. Keeping well in the shadows, I moved toward the front of the bar. I saw the three men talking to the bartender on the sidewalk at the bar entrance.

"Ssshh, Grant."

I knew the sound was Lisa and turned to find her standing with Lily in the doorway of the adjacent building.

"Let's get out of here," I said, and we started moving west down the sidewalk and away from the bar. I held the AK-47 with my right hand against my leg. As we approached the end of the building, the big man who had been with Boots came out of the alley fifteen feet in front of us and turned in our direction. His right hand moved to his waist. He shouted something. No choice. I leveled the AK-47 and put a single round through the middle of his chest. We took off running immediately.

As the ringing in our ears subsided, we could hear shouts behind us. There was a burst of AK-47 fire, and the stucco wall beside me shattered, sending shrapnel-like pieces into my back. It felt like I had been stung by a swarm of bees. We skidded left around the corner and out of sight for the moment.

"We're heading away from the border," said Lily, panting. "We've got to cross the street and head north. I know where there is a border-crossing tunnel two blocks north in an abandoned garage. We found it a week ago and have kept it under surveillance on our side. We haven't told the Mexicans, yet."

This was going from bad to worse. The gunshots had not brought anyone outside. In fact, the few lights that had been showing through windows were now out. The sky was full of stars, and a quarter moon shone in the clear sky. There was no other light.

We were the targets in a shooting gallery. Given the night-vision capability of our pursuers, our odds of survival were not that good, but if we waited too long, they would get reinforcements, and the situation would become even worse. There would be no way I could get the women out.

"All right, listen up," I said, "we've got to get across this street to go north. I'm going to move back toward them and do my best to divert their fire. They have night-vision goggles and scopes, so they will be able to see you crossing the street. Keep low and apart, but go together. If you don't, the second to cross won't have a chance."

I did not like this plan, particularly making myself a target. But waiting for help, since none would be coming, was not an option. "Make your break as soon as they fire back at me." I pressed my back against the building and eased around the corner.

The side of the building shattered from rounds from an AK-47. They had seen me immediately. I rolled into the street, up against the curb, and began laying down a field of fire into the darkness on both sides of the street. I used controlled bursts of fire to make the ammunition last. I had no idea what was going on behind me.

The noise was deafening. The street and sidewalk around me were being turned into shrapnel from the exploding AK-47 rounds. The magazine of my AK-47 was empty. I dropped it and ran, crouching across the street. I could feel the little pieces of stone, tearing at my clothes as the rounds riddled the street. I dove to the pavement and started rolling and didn't stop until I was in the alley.

Lily and Lisa were there. Lily was holding Lisa upright.

"She's hit in the right leg and arm. She can't walk. You take her, and let's move." Lily's voice was calm—not a trace of emotion. I picked Lisa up, and we ran north along the sidewalk. I followed Lily as best I could. At the first block, we turned right and caught our breath.

Lily said, "The tunnel is in the next block. Third house on the left. Let's go and hope no one is there."

No sneaking up on the house. We were going full speed. Lily opened the unlocked door. A man rose up from a pallet on the floor where he had been sleeping with a pistol in his hand. Without hesitating, Lily kicked the pistol out of his hand. I unceremoniously dropped Lisa, grabbed the man, spun him around in my grip, grabbed his chin with my right hand, and savagely jerked his head to the right. We heard his neck snap.

We could hear yelling in the street and the pounding of running feet. The tunnel entrance was a dark hole, four feet by four feet, in the middle of the floor. There was no light, and we did not have a flashlight. Without hesitation, Lily dropped into the hole. Her head disappeared. Then, her hands came into view, and she helped me ease Lisa down into the opening as carefully as possible. The initial shock of being shot had worn off, and Lisa groaned softly as Lily helped her to the tunnel floor. I eased myself into the hole.

We were in total blackness, which would have been disorienting except for the fact there was very little room and only one way to move. The dank smell intensified the claustrophobic feeling that the tunnel created. I moved my hand around on the damp earth. The tunnel seemed to be about four feet by four feet. I did not feel any support for the tunnel roof. As we moved away from the opening, it became obvious that there was no ventilation in the tunnel.

"How long is this tunnel?" I asked Lily.

"About seventy-five feet. Keep moving."

We moved farther into the darkness. There was no other choice. Lily led the way, scrambling on her hands and knees. I was on my butt, sliding along backward with my hands under Lisa's armpits, pulling her along. We were about halfway along the tunnel when we heard voices from the Mexican end. Either I was hyperventilating or there wasn't enough oxygen here. It didn't matter which—I was weakening fast.

All they had to do was drop into the tunnel and open fire, and we were dead. I felt Lily's hand pull on my shirt collar. If she hadn't been choking me, it might have helped a bit. Lisa's groans were getting louder as I jerked her along the tunnel, but I could feel her pushing with her good leg. We were picking up the pace. Not much farther now.

Suddenly, there was the whooshing sound of the tunnel collapsing from the Mexican end. Air was forced past us, and my eyes were clogged with dust.

"Pull, Grant! We're almost there!" shouted Lily in my ear. Despite the fact we were in total darkness and the earth was collapsing around us, she seemed remarkably calm. I could hear death coming toward us. I couldn't get any air.

Suddenly, I could feel the angle of Lily's pull on my collar go from horizontal to vertical. My back hit the end of the tunnel, and Lily was pulling me upright. But Lisa and I didn't make it. The earth collapsed around us in a final rush of earth and air. We were buried alive. I was standing with my knees flexed but could not move or breathe. I was still holding onto Lisa. As I was running out of breath, I could feel the dirt being pulled away from my head. Finally, my head was free. Lily was frantically using her hands to pull the earth away from me.

"That won't work," I sputtered, spitting earth. "Look for a shovel or something to dig with," I yelled. I still couldn't move. My legs were starting to tingle.

Lily found a shovel and started to dig.

"Careful, you don't want to hit Lisa in the head with the shovel," I said.

"Shut up! She won't care," said Lily.

After a minute of superhuman effort, Lily had dug down deep enough that I could pull myself free. I pulled the shovel from Lily's hands and dug with all the power in me.

Lily dropped to her knees and scooped frantically with her hands to uncover Lisa's head. Lisa was now buried up to her neck in the damp earth. She wasn't breathing. Lily lay flat and hung over the side of the tunnel opening and tried to blow air into Lisa's mouth. I put my finger on Lisa's carotid artery. There was no pulse.

"It's no use, Lily. She's gone." Lily ignored me and kept blowing air into Lisa's mouth. I tapped her on the shoulder. "She's gone, Lily." Lily continued to ignore me. I tried to gently pull her up, but she wrenched herself free and continued to try to breathe life into her friend. She kept at it for another minute, and I just stood by helplessly and watched.

Reality finally seeped in, and Lily pulled herself up to her knees. Her head dropped into her hands, and she started to sob—deep, painful, soul-wrenching sobs. There was the kind of agony that came from physical pain. That, I was familiar with. But I had never seen someone with their entire soul in agony. I wanted to help but had no idea how.

I knelt next to Lily and put my arm around her shoulders. She didn't even notice. Silent tears streamed down my face, creasing the dirt. What had I done to these good people? What was wrong with me? The words of Master Sergeant Hernandez reverberated inside my head, "In this business, the unprepared die."

What I had done was just as stupid as trying a night drop into the Sanchez ranch. I hadn't planned for getting caught in Mexico, and I certainly hadn't planned for being confronted by four thugs, carrying AK-47s. The thought that the women had forced their way on this expedition did not help. I allowed it. I was the leader, and I was responsible. I had failed at rule number one of long-range surveillance. I had not brought all of my people back alive. There was no excuse for what I had done. It was a mistake I could not fix, and one that would haunt me the rest of my life.

After awhile Lily, her eyes now dry, stood, and I stood and faced her.

"She never hurt anyone," said Lily.

There was nothing I could say. I tried to hold her, but she pushed my arms away, turned, and walked out of the building.

Lisa was buried three days later on a beautiful, sunny day in Scottsdale Memorial Cemetery. Along with her family and several hundred civilians, there were uniformed contingents from the Scottsdale police department, the border patrol, and all of the other Phoenix-area police departments.

CHAPTER 48

▼

Stephanie's body jerked as if she had unexpectedly stepped off a curb. Her plane had just lifted off from the Durango airport on the way to Denver and then to New York. She had been in a trance-like state ever since Grant had left her at the airport. She had no memory of passing through security, boarding the plane, or taking her seat. Mercifully, no one sat in the seat next to her.

She was sure she had killed Grant's brother. There could not have been two such killings in broad daylight at a stoplight in Scottsdale, Arizona. The CIA had ordered her to kill him. She knew something wasn't right, but she did it anyway. Now, it appeared that Hector's family was trying to kill Grant because he was trying to find out who killed his brother. How screwed up could things get? Stephanie had killed the brother of her American lover. The family of her Mexican lover was trying to kill her American lover. And it seemed likely that the family of her Mexican lover was involved in the CIA's decision to kill her American lover's brother.

The only thing that was not totally confusing was that her job was clearly in jeopardy. In fact, she could end up in prison.

It looked like Denver below. How long had she been sitting here, staring out the window? What did her father say about complex problems? It was senior-year calculus, and it was driving her nuts. Most complex problems, her father had told her, were a series of interrelated, less-complicated problems. You just had to break the problem down into its component parts and get started. The hardest part was just getting started.

From her point of view, this was all about her. Something seemed wrong from the start about the hit on Ricky Meredith. Why did the CIA order the hit on

Ricky? Two possibilities existed: First, the CIA thought his death was in the national interest. If that were the case, there would be no problem for her. Second, the Sanchez family got the CIA to order the hit on Ricky. This scenario would not be a matter of national interest but of corruption. If it were corruption, she was in big trouble if her boss cleaned house and denied giving her the order. She knew that to protect herself on the hit, she needed to be sure her boss would back her up. That was step one.

Why was the Sanchez family trying to kill Grant or, at least, stop him from investigating the hit? Were they involved in selling drugs to high-school students? Were they involved in the hit on Ricky?

Now, what about Hector Sanchez? The Sanchez family in question must be his family. To what extent, if any, was he involved? She wondered if she should contact Hector. If so, should she call him or go to Mexico? What if he were involved? If so, how would she feel about him? That answer depended on the nature of the involvement. It was one thing if only his family members were criminals and quite another if he were involved. Stephanie wondered how much she loved Hector. Actually, she wondered if she loved him at all. She had to find out if Hector were involved.

What about Grant? How did she really feel about him? What if he found out that she killed Ricky? Would there be any future with him? How could he have a relationship with his brother's killer? Stephanie thought that maybe she should just dump him and hope he didn't find out. But if he did find out, or if she were to tell him, what would he do to her?

What if she just resigned from the CIA and went into hiding? No, that wasn't the answer. She did not want to live that way. Now, she thought, this mess was getting organized. She would deal with the CIA first. If it were a righteous hit, her only problem would be her love life. There was no use spending a lot of time on how to cover her ass until she found out if the hit were righteous.

When Stephanie got back to New York, she called her CIA contact, Truman Knobly, and arranged a meeting the next day in Washington. They met at the Lincoln Memorial and walked around the reflecting pool. Knobly was a tall, thin man with brown, slicked-back hair and an out-of-season tan that did not hide the broken capillaries on his cheeks. His bloodshot, brown eyes peered out from under eyebrows that grew together over his nose.

Stephanie did not waste any time. "Truman, you had me hit a man in Scottsdale about three months ago. Why?"

"Now, Stephanie, you know I can't tell you that. You're not cleared for the information," said Knobly in a condescending manner.

Stephanie put her hand firmly on his chest. It was clear she was deadly serious. "You're going to have to tell me something, Knobly. I accidentally met the brother of this man, and when he mentioned how his brother died, it was obvious that I was the killer. He told me about his brother, and it is inconceivable to me that he was a terrorist. I demand an explanation, and I want it now."

Knobly hadn't risen to a GS-17 in the CIA by being shy. He calmly took hold of Stephanie's wrist and gently removed her hand from his chest. Looking directly into her eyes, with his most sincere look, he quietly and firmly said, "Stephanie, I can assure you that Richard Meredith was a direct threat to the security of the United States. There was no mistake; however, you must appreciate the fact that we have rules. The rules were explained to you before you came on board. I can show you the Acknowledgement of Disclosure and Acceptance of Terms that you signed. You are going to have to live by the rules."

Stephanie was a trained assassin and not easily intimidated. She crossed her arms under her breasts and said in an equally quiet and firm voice, "Listen to me, Truman. Grant Meredith is stirring up some serious trouble. He thinks some Mexican family named Sanchez killed his brother or had him killed. I want to know what's going on."

Knobly gently reached out and took her arm. "Come, Stephanie. We can't keep standing here. We'll draw attention to ourselves." They continued walking around the reflecting pool.

"Stephanie, let me take care of Meredith. I promise you, in a short while, he will be out of the picture. Trust me."

Stephanie stopped and turned to face Knobly. "Just how do you think you can accomplish that? By killing him?"

"No no, don't be silly. Come on, keep walking. The CIA doesn't kill American citizens. Well, Ricky Meredith was an exception. Look, just trust me. With a little misdirection, we can have Grant Meredith believing it really was a drive-by shooting."

"Okay," said Stephanie, sighing and not trusting him one bit, "but this is no good for me anymore. I'm just burned out. I just don't have the will to do this anymore."

Knobly didn't say anything as they continued walking. He was obviously considering what she had said, so Stephanie kept quiet and walked along beside him. Finally, he said, "I can fix it for you, but I need something in return."

"What do you want?"

"I must ask you, as a personal favor to me, to do one more job. Do it, and we will give Meredith some gangbanger as his brother's killer, and you are out of the CIA without any problems."

Stephanie hesitated, and they walked some more. After almost a full minute, she sighed, stopped, turned to face him, and said "Okay, I'll do it, but I don't want any excuses. If you don't keep your word—"

"Stephanie, don't even go there. You have my word that this will be your last assignment for the Agency, and we will be out of your life forever. You'll receive your assignment in the regular way."

Stephanie drove slowly back to her hotel. Something was very strange here. Ricky was messing with a criminal Mexican family, and the CIA ordered a hit on him. Correction—all she knew was that Knobly ordered the hit. What if he were in the Sanchez family's pocket and they used him and the CIA to get rid of their problem?

C H A P T E R 49

▼

Truman Knobly eagerly trotted back to his government-issued sedan. He had the solution to this unexpected mess. It was brilliant. He crossed the Fourteenth Street Bridge and took the GW Parkway exit, heading for CIA headquarters in Langley, Virginia. He was back in the building in thirty minutes, practically jogging down the linoleum-tiled hallway on the fourth floor to his office.

He rushed past his secretary and told her to get Jack Lehman, the head of Intra-Agency Security, up here to his office ASAP. Knobly's office befitted a GS-17. It was twenty feet by twenty feet in size and carpeted. It had a large wooden desk, a matching computer credenza, and secure file cabinets. A leather sofa and two leather guest chairs rounded out the furniture. The office was not quite big enough to handle a coffee table with the sofa. Offices of that size were reserved for the political appointees.

Jack Lehman was there in less than five minutes. He was short and fat, and his big belly hung over his belt. His bald head glistened with sweat. Knobly knew that Lehman, like many short men, had a huge ego, which he intended to play to the hilt.

Knobly shook Lehman's hand and grasped his elbow with his other hand a la Bill Clinton. "Thanks for coming so quickly, Jack. I've got a job that I can't trust anyone but you to accomplish. This is the kind of situation for which your department was created."

Lehman practically preened at the compliment. Most people ignored this short, fat gnome. Lehman puffed out his chest, sucked in his gut, and said with pride, "I'll help you anyway I can, Truman."

"Thanks, Jack. I knew I could count on you. We have an out-of-control agent on our hands. She is dangerously unstable and may leave the country. We must act quickly."

"Can do, Truman. What's the problem?"

"I can't tell you, Jack, other than to identify her and give you the time and place she can be intercepted. You know we must work on a need-to-know basis—Agency rules and all that."

Lehman could not hide his disappointment, but he had a long career of following orders. "All right, who, where, and when?"

"It is a woman by the name of Stephanie Chambers. I will have the time and place tomorrow. Send two of your best men. She is very capable and will, undoubtedly, be well armed. Take her by surprise, and get rid of the body."

"Will do."

Lehman left the office, and Knobly turned to the window with a small, satisfied smile that tugged at the corners of his mouth. This was one of his best ideas ever—even if he did say so himself.

CHAPTER 50

▼

The letter was in Stephanie's post office box at Grand Central Station the next day:

> The subject will be at the Phoenician Resort in Scottsdale on the fifteenth. Subject will be in room number 303. You check in after 5:00 PM on the fourteenth. There will be a reservation for "Rachel Smith," driver's license, airline ticket, and credit card enclosed. You will be in room number 356, which will be directly across the courtyard from room 303. From your window, you will have a clear view of the door to room 303. On the fifteenth, between 7:00 AM and 7:30 AM, subject will exit room.

On the fourteenth at 5:30 PM, a taxi pulled up to the front of the Phoenician Resort. A tall woman with flowing red hair under a large straw hat and big Jackie O sunglasses got out. She also wore stylish thin cotton gloves. The bellman picked up her single suitcase. The woman approached the front desk.

"I'm Rachel Smith. You have a reservation for me?"

"Yes, it is prepaid for tonight only. You will be in room number 356."

As soon as the bellman left, Stephanie took off the hat, red wig, and sunglasses and opened the suitcase. She removed the white gloves and put on thin surgical gloves. Wrapped in a quilted blanket inside the suitcase was a Russian 7.62mm Dragunov sniper rifle. She took the rifle to the window and opened the sheer curtain. After putting the rifle to her shoulder, she looked through the telescopic sight and zeroed in on the door to room number 303, which was forty yards across the courtyard. She put the crosshairs on the room number, inhaled, relaxed, and squeezed the trigger. Click. The rifle dry-fired. Stephanie wrapped the rifle in the blanket and put it under the bed.

She called room service and ordered dinner. Forty-five minutes later she heard a knock on the door. "Room service."

"I just got out of the shower. Please put the tray on the table. The ten dollars is yours." Stephanie unlocked the door and stepped into the bathroom, closing the door.

She was in bed by 10:00 PM but couldn't sleep. Her thoughts kept coming back to Grant Meredith. She liked him; maybe she was in love with him. But what could she say to him? Hello, I killed your brother. Sorry about that; it was a mistake. Don't worry about it. I love you.

Grant would start asking questions to which she had no answers. Knobly said he would take care of Grant. Did that mean ... kill him? Did she care? Of course, she cared. Knobly gave the order to kill Ricky, but she had no proof. It was strictly she said/he said. The CIA would deny it regardless of whether it was right or wrong. The Agency could not be involved inside the United States. There had to be a way to get Knobly to take the fall for this.

She kept tossing and turning, twisting the sheets that had pulled loose from the foot of the bed. Stephanie got up and tucked the sheets in. Back in bed, her thoughts turned to Hector. Was she in love with him? Did she want to live in Mexico and be a politician's mistress? Did she want to be his wife? Would he marry her? Did she want to marry him?

At about 4:00 AM, she decided that a relationship with Grant would never work. Even if he could get over the fact that she had killed his brother, it would be a constant reminder of a life she wanted to forget. After five minutes of flopping around on the bed, she wasn't sure any more. Could love conquer all? She tossed and turned until 6:00 AM when the alarm brought an end to her torment.

By 6:30 AM, she had pushed the desk near the window, sat down with the rifle on a tripod, and sited on room 303. She marked on the window where the bullet would pass and stuck a suction cup in the middle of the area. She then took out a glass cutter, cut a hole in the glass around the suction cup, and removed the glass.

At 6:55 AM, she turned up the volume on the television, settled in the chair with the sight focused on room 303, and waited. Ten minutes later, the door opened, and a man in a black baseball cap and sweatshirt opened the door and stepped out. The logo on both the cap and the sweatshirt was a white paw print with some lettering above it. Stephanie zeroed in on the man's head, took a deep breath, and held it.

It was Grant! Stephanie was so startled that she pulled her head sharply up, and the rifle went off. Between the silencer and the noise from the television, the shot made no sound.

CHAPTER 51

▼

I heard a noise behind me like wood splintering, and I turned. I saw a hole the size of a quarter in the door to my room. I dropped as if a drill sergeant had ordered me to give him twenty push-ups, and I surveyed the rooms across from me. Directly across the courtyard, I spotted a room window with a small hole in the middle of it. I could see a figure moving behind the window. I got up in a crouch and then headed for the stairwell. Maybe I could catch the son of a bitch. He was probably heading for an exit from the building or into the garage.

CHAPTER 52

▼

Stephanie saw Grant look behind himself and drop to the floor. At that point, her years of training took over. She set the rifle down, stood up, turned, and walked out the door. She was dressed in a baggy jogging suit, running shoes, and a long-billed ball cap. Her dark hair was tucked under the cap. At first glance, one could not tell whether she were a man or a woman. After racing down four flights of stairs, she opened the door to the underground parking garage. She headed toward a silver Toyota Camry midway through the garage.

Stephanie's peripheral vision took in two men, walking casually in the general direction of the Toyota from opposite directions. They both wore loose-fitting Hawaiian shirts that were not tucked in. Alarm bells went off in Stephanie's head; both of the men's right hands were obscured from view along their right thighs. If she tried to retrace her steps, she would have to turn her back on them. Not a good idea.

CHAPTER 53

▼

I had to guess where the sniper would go. He couldn't stay in the room or even in the hotel. Trying to leave the Phoenician on foot would draw attention, and a hasty exit through the front door to a cab or a waiting car would draw too much attention. Exit by car from the garage was the most likely choice.

I ran down the stairs and stopped at the door to the garage. I slowly opened it, knelt down, and put one eye around the door.

Fifty feet in front of me, a man in a baggy jogging suit stopped and looked down at his feet. Then, he knelt to tie a shoe lace. To my absolute astonishment, he removed a Glock subcompact pistol from a holster on his left ankle and stood with the pistol cradled in both hands. I saw two men in Hawaiian shirts, moving quickly in his direction with guns up. The man in the jogging suit immediately pointed at the man on the right and fired. The Hawaiian-shirted man fell over backward.

The man in the jogging suit then whirled toward the second Hawaiian-shirted man. Too late. The Hawaiian-shirted man fired. The man in the jogging suit's left arm went slack; yet, he turned toward the left, pointed the pistol with his right hand, and fired. The bullet pierced the middle of the Hawaiian-shirted man's throat, and the man fell behind a new Mercedes.

The man in the jogging suit moved quickly toward the Toyota. I slipped through the door and moved silently toward him. He was preoccupied by look-ing at his left arm and didn't hear me. As he reached for the car-door handle, I caught him. My left arm went around his neck and into a choke hold while my right hand ripped the gun from his hand.

In almost simultaneous movements, the man stomped on my foot, thrust his hips back against mine, brought his hips forward, and drove the back of his right fist into my balls. As the pain reached my brain, he pivoted off his right foot and used his left leg to sweep me off my feet.

I hit the floor, and my head cracked against the concrete. I saw stars—millions of stars.

CHAPTER 54

▼

Where was I? I was in the back seat of a moving car. As I stirred, the car stopped, and a blurry face appeared above me.

"Stay still. I'll be right back and explain things," said a familiar voice.

As the world came into focus, I realized that I was in a parking structure. I tried to sit up, and it was too much. The world went black again. No stars this time. I groaned and slowly opened my eyes. The blurry face appeared and slowly came into focus.

"My God, Stephanie. What the hell!"

"Just relax. You banged your head pretty good, and I've got to bandage my arm. You'll live."

My head felt as if a small man were breaking concrete inside there with a sledge hammer. I blinked and rubbed my eyes, and the world started to come back into focus. My thoughts were in a whirl. What happened to the men in the garage? Where was I? How did I get here? Where did Stephanie come from? Stephanie was taping a bandage on her arm. As she pulled on a new sweat shirt, I asked, "What happened to you? What's going on?"

"Just relax and take it easy, Grant. One thing at a time. I picked up a flesh wound. No big deal. The bullet just cut a groove in my upper arm. A camping store in the mall had some first-aid supplies. Now, come with me, and I'll explain everything."

She helped me from the car, hooked her arm through mine, and led me from the car into Fashion Square Mall. As we walked, my vision cleared, and the small man inside my head switched from a sledge hammer to a regular hammer.

Stephanie settled me into a quiet corner of Starbucks and went to get us some coffee. By the time she got back, I had organized my thoughts and was ready for answers. "You're the man I grabbed in the garage, aren't you?"

With a wry smile, Stephanie replied, "Yes, but as you well know, I'm a woman."

"Where did you learn those self-defense moves? I'm still not sure what you did to me," I asked in amazement.

Stephanie took a sip of coffee, sighed, and reached out and put her hand on top of mine in a conciliatory gesture. "Grant, I'm asking you to listen to what I have to say without interrupting. When I'm done, I will answer all of your questions, but I need you to listen to what I have to say first."

I looked into her green eyes and saw sadness there. Her expression told me she was going to deliver bad news. I nodded tentatively and waited for her to begin.

She took a deep breath and began, "I've worked for the CIA since graduating from college. The Agency set me up in the public-relations business. I have clients all over the world, and I travel extensively on business. That is a perfect cover for my Agency work."

She paused, took another sip of coffee, looked out the window, and then looked directly into my eyes. "I've been what's called a 'wet-work specialist.' I've killed whomever my handler told me to kill. I was never given a reason for the hit, but I understood they were terrorists or connected to terrorists. I had to sign some paperwork when I started that said I agreed I would never be told why a particular hit was necessary, just that it was required in the best interests of the security of our country. All I got was a description and a time and a place where the mark would appear. The rest was up to me.

"Over the years, I have assassinated twenty-three people without questioning orders. Most of the time, but not always, I could figure out from reading the papers why they were targeted. We were in an undeclared war against terrorism long before 9/11. I have no regrets about twenty-two of them. But I do have a problem with the last one and with today. The last one has caused me more pain than anything else in my life."

I sat quietly, listening and sipping coffee from time to time. I didn't take my eyes off her. Her voice was strong and direct until the very end. Then, it broke a little. I was not surprised that the CIA assassinated people. But Stephanie as an assassin? Well, that thought was having trouble finding a home. As she paused to take a sip of coffee, I asked, "Are you finished?"

She squeezed my hand and said, "Not yet. That was the easy part. Let me finish before you say anything. I am going to hurt you. I want you to understand that I would give my life to have kept it from happening, but I can't. Acting on orders from the CIA, I killed Ricky." She rushed on without taking a breath. "I didn't realize it until that day at the ranch when you described how Ricky was killed. It blindsided me. I couldn't say anything then. I didn't know what to do."

This was unimaginable. I heard the words, but they didn't register. I pulled my hand from under Stephanie's and sat back, staring at her.

Stephanie rushed on before I could say anything. "When you told me about Ricky the other day, it was the first time I knew. I flew to Washington and asked for an explanation. They wouldn't tell me anything about why his execution was ordered. I told my handler that I was through with the CIA. He asked me to do one last job. He hinted that if I didn't do the job, the Agency might cause me problems and that if I did, they would assure a smooth transition. I agreed. My God, Grant. It was you! I had no idea. I knew the hotel room number and the time the mark would exit the room, but that was all. When I saw it was you, I jerked up in such surprise that the rifle went off. I left the room and went directly to the parking garage where I had a car. I have no idea who those two men were. I wish I could forfeit my life for Ricky's, but I can't. I'll do whatever you ask me to do. I know there is nothing I can do to make this up to you, but I'll do whatever I can. I know you can never forgive me, and I'll live with that forever."

I just sat there. This woman had just said she had killed, no, had murdered my brother. Equally unbelievable was her claim that the CIA had ordered her to do it. Her confession turned my world upside down. Ricky, Tomas, Deuce, Jorge, the Sanchez family, drug smuggling—none of this fit with Stephanie killing Ricky on orders from the CIA.

I forced myself to focus on Stephanie. I saw the pain in her eyes and the anguish etched in her face. I could accept that she hadn't tried to kill me. Christ, the bullet hit the door three feet behind where I had been standing. The nature of the miss was consistent with her story. But the rest of it? There would be no reason for her to lie about killing Ricky or about working for the CIA. But I could not accept that the CIA had ordered Ricky killed. The Agency had no authority to do such a thing. At least, I thought they hadn't. Also, those men in the garage—who were they? Stephanie was looking at me, waiting, I had to say something.

"Stephanie, I just don't know what to think or do right now. At the moment, I have more questions than answers."

Stephanie said nothing and waited. Her hands were folded on the table in front of her, and her knuckles were white. When she saw me looking at her hands, she put them in her lap.

"Look," I said, "let's try to answer some of the questions and see where that takes us." Stephanie nodded tentatively.

"Who is your handler at the CIA?"

Stephanie hesitated for only a moment. "Truman Knobly."

"Do you have any other contacts at the CIA?"

"Only John Wesley. I've been on the outside so long that I don't know anyone else there."

"Does Wesley know what you've been up to?"

"I don't know. He encouraged me to go outside, but I haven't seen or spoken to him since. The Agency had to have deniability."

"Knobly set up the hit on me and Ricky?"

"Yes."

"You told Knobly you were quitting?"

"Yes."

"He asked you to do one last job and sent you here?"

"Yes."

"Did you tell anyone you were going to Scottsdale or staying at the Phoenician Resort?"

"No."

As we went through this series of questions, I watched Stephanie's expression become quizzical, then intense. After she answered the last question, realization flooded her features.

I had been working on the assumption that Ricky had been killed because he had been nosing around in Sanchez family business. I believed the Sanchez family had tried to keep me from looking into their business and had tried to kill me at the ranch and in Nogales. Yet, the CIA had sent Stephanie to kill Ricky and to kill me. There had to be some connection between the CIA and the Sanchez family. I think Stephanie and I both realized this at the same time, but we sat there, lost in our own thoughts.

CHAPTER 55

▼

Stephanie thought about the early years. She had been able to read about the people she had killed in the newspapers. It hadn't taken a genius to figure out how their demise had benefited the United States. However, things had become much less clear in the last few years. Before Ricky, three of the last six hits had been Mexican politicians. Ernesto Ruffo had been the chief of police in Nuevo Laredo. Armando Noriega had been the attorney general of Mexico, and Juan Maria, the mayor of Nogales.

Before his death, Noriega had fired the entire elite antidrug-intelligence unit of the national police, publicly stating that corruption was so extensive it was impossible to fix. The deaths of the other two had not made the U.S. papers. When she had asked Knobly about it, he dismissed her, saying all Mexican politicians were corrupt.

Since she couldn't understand why people who seemed to be trying to deal with corruption should be killed, she had put it out of her mind and had trusted in the CIA. After all, the Agency knew more about what was going on than she did. The CIA had so much information that wasn't available to her. She just didn't have the information to second-guess Agency decisions.

In any event, it was her job to follow orders. The military and, by analogy, the CIA, could not function if every decision had to be justified to subordinates. She could not imagine a world where an order given in a war had to be justified to the lowliest private. Could you imagine a basic-training course given to nineteen-year-olds entitled How to Evaluate Whether You Have Been Given a Lawful Order? Or better yet, The Applicability of the Fourth Geneva Convention Protocols to Terrorists (The Need to Act Humanely Toward Someone Who Has Dedicated His Life to Killing You)?

She had thought about all this before when she had been ordered to make the hit on Ricky inside the United States and had come to the conclusion that, in the final analysis, you had to rely on your superiors.

CHAPTER 56

▼

I broke the silence by telling Stephanie what had happened in Nogales and about the death of Lisa Gonzales. I also said, "There must be a connection of some sort between the Sanchez family and the CIA. There are just too many coincidences."

Stephanie spent another half hour telling me about the deaths of the Mexican politicians and Knobly's curt rejection of her inquiries.

I stood and took Stephanie by the arm. "There's an Internet terminal in the corner. Fire it up, and I'll get us some more coffee. I think we need to do a little research." Two hours and two cups of coffee later, we had scoured the Internet for information about the Mexican/U.S. illegal-drug trade. We sat looking at the notes Stephanie had made on a sheet of paper:

1. Mexicans assumed major role in drug trafficking for Colombians when Florida became too hot. United States spends sixty billion dollars a year on illegal drugs. Over half of the cocaine and most of the marijuana comes across the Mexican/U.S. border.

2. Corruption is widespread on both sides of the border.

3. Violence is extreme.

4. Mexican cartels have recruited U.S. street gangs and middle-class, Mexican American youths for assassinations in the United States.

5. Law-enforcement personnel in the United States are increasingly becoming targets for violence.

"Are you thinking what I'm thinking?" I asked.

"If you're thinking that it's possible that drug-money corruption has found its way into the CIA, then I am."

"Stephanie, do you realize that if someone in the CIA is on the take, you may have been turned into an assassin for the Sanchez family?"

"Please don't belabor the obvious. Let's find a pay phone; I want to set a meeting with Knobly."

We found a phone booth, and Stephanie called the number she had been given for emergencies. This was a damn emergency.

"This number is no longer in service," said the recorded voice.

Stephanie stood there for a moment, unable to move.

"What happened?" I asked.

"I'm cut off from the Agency. I knew this was possible if something went wrong overseas, but I never thought it could happen here in the States. Grant, I don't know what to think right now."

As we walked across the mall toward the exit, the voice of Neil Diamond sang about it supposedly never raining in California.

I headed back to the Phoenician Resort, and Stephanie checked into the Four Seasons and began making calls.

CHAPTER 57

▼

When I got back to the Phoenician Resort, the BlackRock board meeting that I was there to attend was concluding. The other board members told me about the double homicide in the parking garage. The police had made no public statements.

I asked Wally Richards, the former CIA director, to join me for a drink. We settled into leather wing chairs in a secluded corner of the empty bar. Wally ordered a gin and tonic. When I asked for a club soda with lime, Wally raised his bushy, light gray eyebrows. "What's wrong? I've never see you turn down an expense-account drink."

I leaned forward with my forearms on my thighs and said quietly, "I have a major problem, and I have to ask you for some help."

Failing to pick up on my seriousness, Wally grinned and said, "I'll do what I can, but I must warn you that despite being seventy-five years old, I don't know anything about women."

"I wish it were that simple. Wally, I need you to check something out for me at the CIA—something that involves current operations."

The grin faded, and the jovial Wally Richards was all business. "Tell me what you want checked out and why."

"I think the killings in the garage may have been related to the CIA in some way. There is a guy in the CIA named Truman Knobly, who is the controller for an outside wet-work specialist named Stephanie Chambers. I saw what happened in the garage. Those men tried to kill Chambers, and she shot them. She was wounded in the process."

Wally sat silently and seemed to be turning things over in his mind. His eyes left mine and focused on some faraway place.

"I won't ask what you were doing in the garage or how you know about CIA personnel. I probably don't want to know, at least, not now. I remember Knobly. Another damn Yalie. He was a real womanizer in those days."

My eyes bored into Wally's. "Chambers killed my brother on orders from Knobly," I said. "Besides the fact that it was my brother, it was a CIA hit inside the borders of the United States. The only conceivable way to justify that is terrorism, and my brother was not a terrorist. To top it off, Knobly ordered Chambers to kill me."

Wally was visibly stunned; then, his look turned skeptical. "How do you know this Chambers woman killed your brother and tried to kill you?"

"She told me."

"How do you know she works for the CIA?"

"She told me." I could see where this was going, but I knew better than to interrupt Wally. He was a consummate, professional spy boss, who was in his element. His questioning continued at a rapid-fire pace.

"When did she tell you?"

"After the shootings in the garage."

"You mean, after you saw what happened in the garage?"

"Yes."

"This was after she tried to kill you?"

"Yes."

"Rather than run to you to see if you were all right, this Chambers woman went directly to the parking garage?"

"Yes."

"Why do you believe her?"

"Because I trust her."

"That's all?"

"And … I think I'm in love with her."

Wally's previously expressionless face turned incredulous. His voice rose three octaves and matched his expression before he caught himself. "You're in love with the woman who murdered your brother?"

There it was—square in my face. She had murdered Ricky, my brother. She had told me only after she had tried to kill me and had killed the two men in the garage. Even if I accepted her explanation for all of the killing, she had killed Ricky. Maybe it had been a mistake, but she had undoubtedly killed my brother.

"Wally, your point is valid. I admit that I don't know what to think and that I may be wrong to believe her, but the larger issue is CIA corruption."

Wally took a sip of his drink before responding, saying, "Grant, I have no confidence in this Chambers woman's story. It's too pat, and it came at the wrong time."

"I appreciate the timing, but there's more to it. When my brother was murdered, he was looking into a Mexican family that is involved in drug smuggling. When I started to retrace his steps, looking for his killer, they tried to kill me. I think the genesis of all of this is illegal-drug smuggling. If I'm right, this Sanchez family has corrupted someone in the CIA and, maybe, more than one."

Wally was still skeptical. "What if you are only half right? Let's assume that someone in the CIA has been corrupted by drug money. Perhaps the corruptee is your Ms. Chambers. Perhaps she is lying to you to save her backside. Would that be so surprising?"

There was no point in arguing with him. I needed to shift his focus away from Stephanie and back to the CIA—play on his patriotism. "Probably not. Look, Wally, if I had all the answers, I wouldn't have to ask you to check things out. You're right. I don't know how this will turn out. If the CIA has been corrupted, the president needs to deal with it immediately. If you won't do it for me, do it for the CIA. If Stephanie is a liar or some kind of rogue agent, so be it. I'll turn her in myself."

I had hit the right button. In a resigned voice, Wally said, "I'll make some calls. If there is nothing there, no harm, no foul. If there is ... well, let's wait and see. I'll meet you in the lobby in an hour."

Wally Richards stood and walked away with purposeful strides and a ramrod-straight back.

CHAPTER 58

▼

John Walker Wesley III lived in McLean Virginia, not far from CIA headquarters at Langley. He had been born on the Upper East Side of Manhattan in 1930 to an immensely wealthy family. He was too young to serve in World War II, but after graduating from Yale, he had served as a second lieutenant in the Korean "Conflict." The "conflict" ended, and he had exited the service with his life and the Silver Star. He was recruited to join the other Yalies at the CIA and had been there his entire career.

Wes, as his friends called him, rose to the head of Clandestine Operations, which was a civil-service position, and had been there for twenty years. Every director of the CIA with whom he had served had looked to him to get the information they needed without running afoul of the politicians in Congress. He succeeded more than he failed and always stayed under the congressional radar.

He was at home Saturday morning, trying to make some sense of Friday's events. General Tony Chambers had been one of his best friends. He had known his daughter, Stephanie, all her life. He had welcomed her into the CIA and had carefully monitored her career even after she went outside. Although he was reluctant to have her involved in wet work, he knew she had the skills to be outstanding. The CIA and the country needed someone who wasn't a psychopath to do that kind of work.

He had Knobly's report, and he didn't know what to think. According to Knobly, Stephanie had become a rogue agent in the pay of a Mexican drug lord. She had killed a man in Scottsdale, Arizona, named Richard Meredith. The hit had no CIA purpose and had to be related to Mexican drug smuggling. Knobly had sent two agents to apprehend her, and she had killed them. She was on the run, and the FBI had been brought in to find her.

This made no sense. Stephanie wasn't rich, but as far as he knew, she had enough money for her lifestyle. She was an army brat. Army brats sometimes had problems, but wanting to be in the jet set was not one of them. He thought he knew her until now. She had no children, no husband and, as far as he knew, no lover. He simply could not find any motivation for her to kill for a drug cartel. He was startled out of his reverie by the ring of his home telephone.

"Mr. Wesley, this is Stephanie."

"My God, girl!" exclaimed Wesley. "What is going on? I can't believe what I have been told about you!"

Stephanie forced herself to keep her tone calm and professional. "I don't know what you've been told, but I need to talk with you privately as soon as possible."

Wesley's momentary lapse into emotion disappeared immediately. "Stephanie, I think it would be best if you just turned yourself in to the Agency."

"Why, because I didn't finish the Grant Meredith assignment?" snapped Stephanie.

"No." Wesley's voice was ice cold. "I don't know anything about that. According to reports, you have killed two CIA agents, and there is speculation that you have been co-opted by a Mexican drug cartel."

"What!" exclaimed Stephanie, all pretext of professionalism gone.

Wesley's voice softened, but only a little. "Stephanie, two of our agents were killed in the parking garage at the Phoenician Resort in Scottsdale. I have a report that you did it. You need to turn yourself in so that this can be straightened out before things get worse."

Stephanie's surprise quickly gave way to understanding of what Knobly had tried to do. She kills Grant, and they kill her as a rogue agent. End of story. The Sanchez family wins again, and business goes on as usual. If she couldn't turn this around, well, she had to turn it around.

In her most sincere voice, she said, "Mr. Wesley, I will turn myself in after I have a chance to meet with you. I would like to bring a friend, Grant Meredith. I believe there is a problem in the Agency, and it isn't me. Can we meet at your home tomorrow morning?"

Wesley went for it although reluctantly. "All right, I'll be here, writing a report on this conversation. If you are not here by noon, I will assume you have changed your mind. It would be logical for you to assume that there is a search underway for you."

"Thank you, sir, I will see you tomorrow."

CHAPTER 59

▼

I was sitting in a remote corner of the vast lobby of the Phoenician Resort when Wally Richards found me. The look on Wally's face told me he was not bringing helpful news.

"I spoke to the director, who knows nothing about what happened here. He has only been on the job a few months. He checked with Clandestine Operations. Knobly has filed a report that Chambers is a rogue agent, working for Mexican drug lords. She killed two agents who tried to apprehend her, and there is an all points bulletin out for her. I shared with him your theory about Knobly, and he said he would have someone look into it. Your Ms. Chambers is in deep trouble. My suggestion is that she turn herself in and cooperate with a complete investigation."

This was a terrible development. Knobly had preempted Stephanie. Instead of Stephanie turning him in and protecting herself, she had been turned into a fugitive. He had to warn her as soon as possible. I stood and held out my hand to Wally. "I appreciate your efforts. I'll talk to Stephanie and pass on your advice. Thanks again."

Back in my room, I tried unsuccessfully to reach Stephanie. Maybe a thorough vetting of Knobly would turn up something, but then again, maybe it wouldn't. I needed to do something drastic to turn things around. I needed to strike back at the Sanchez family. The stakes were high. Boots was small potatoes. Ramon Sanchez—the big-shot corporate lawyer—that was it. I decided to shake his tree and see if I could make something happen.

CHAPTER 60

▼

Wells & Bunch occupied the top three floors of the tallest building in downtown Phoenix. I stepped off the elevator on the top floor and thought I was back in New York at Tatum & Hallis. The reception area had floor-to-ceiling windows that looked north up Central Avenue. There was original art on the walls, enhanced by specially designed lighting. An elegantly dressed woman of about fifty with short, blond hair and a single strand of pearls sat behind a reception desk with only one phone on it. Obviously, the phones were answered somewhere else. As I approached the desk, she stood to meet me.

"May I help you, sir?" she asked in an upper-crust English accent.

"Grant Meredith to see Ramon Sanchez. I have an appointment."

"Good afternoon, Mr. Meredith. We were expecting you. Have a seat, and I'll let Mr. Sanchez know you're here. May I offer you something to drink? Coffee or bottled water perhaps?"

"No, thank you, I'm fine," I said even though I was far from fine.

I went into the waiting area behind her desk and selected a comfortable leather chair with its back to the bank of windows. Just as I was settling in with the *Wall Street Journal*, a Hispanic woman approached and asked me to follow her. We went through double solid-mahogany doors down a long corridor and through another set of double doors into what seemed to be a suite of offices separate from the rest of the firm.

This suite had its own sitting area; exquisite Oriental rugs graced the marble floor. Each of the offices had its door closed. Through the glass interior wall, I admired an impressive view north along Central Avenue. In the middle of the north wall, I noticed a very large office, in which sat a man, talking on the telephone. I assumed the man to be Ramon Sanchez.

"Mr. Meredith, if you would step over here for a moment, please," said my escort. I stood in front of a full-length screen, and the woman pushed a button. "Please turn around." I did so, not sure what was going on. "Thank you, Mr. Meredith. Now, if you would be so kind as to leave your cell phone, fountain pen, and keys with me, I will return them when you leave."

"What?"

"Security, Mr. Meredith. Since 9/11, we have to be so careful. I'm sorry, but these are Mr. Sanchez's rules, and I have my orders."

I gave her what she wanted and was ushered into the office of Ramon Sanchez. He stood immediately and came around his desk with his hand out to greet me. He was about six feet tall and one hundred sixty pounds on a trim frame with wavy black hair, glistening with mousse. He wore a dark blue Armani suit; a brilliant white shirt; a red, patterned Hermes tie; and black Gucci loafers. This man knew how to dress.

"Good afternoon, Mr. Meredith. I have looked forward to meeting you. Would you like some coffee?"

I shook his hand and declined the coffee. The woman left, and the door closed behind her with a hiss.

"Please, let us sit over here."

Ramon led me to a corner of the room where two leather wing chairs and a sofa surrounded a glass coffee table. We settled into the wing chairs opposite one another. He casually crossed his legs, tugging gently at the crease in his trousers. Ramon Sanchez was perfectly at ease.

"Mr. Meredith, please forgive the security procedures. I am sure you understand. Now, what can I do for you?"

"You know why I'm here."

"Actually, Mr. Meredith, I do not. I know who you are, of course. I know you have caused some difficulty for my lovely sister and seem to be of some concern to my father. But I do not know why you are here."

I had planned to confront him, shake him up, and, hopefully, cause him to do or say something that would help Stephanie. I was thrown off balance because, rather than playing dumb, he started off being candid. Well, let's see him be candid with this. "It's very simple, Mr. Sanchez. I'm here to find out who in your family ordered the assassination of my brother."

Ramon ignored my accusation, leaned forward, and opened a burl-wood humidor on the coffee table. He held it out to me and said, "Cigar, Mr. Meredith? They are Cuba's finest."

I waived the humidor away and stared at him. He shrugged and said in an agreeable voice, as if we were discussing the weather, "A most regrettable incident. I understand your concern, but I am afraid that I cannot answer that question."

What a pompous asshole. "I think you could if you were properly motivated."

Ramon selected a cigar and snipped off the end with the silver cutter that was on the coffee table. While he was doing this, he didn't look at me. He focused on the cigar. "Oh, please, Mr. Meredith. Threats of violence are so pedestrian. Please look outside."

I looked into the reception area and saw two uniformed policemen, drinking coffee and laughing with Ramon's assistant.

"I wanted to make sure our conversation was peaceful, so I called Chief Ramirez, and he sent those men to chaperone our conversation. The police chief and I are quite close." He paused to light his cigar without asking me if I minded breathing his smoke. Once the cigar was properly lit, he continued, saying, "I am sure you know that I am past president of the Maricopa County Bar Association and president-elect of the Arizona Bar Association. However, you probably did not know that Chief Ramirez is my second cousin."

Now, I was really irritated. If I thought he was pompous before, now I thought he was absolutely arrogant. "Listen, Sanchez, the cops can't be with you 24/7, and I'm not concerned with a few bodyguards."

Ramon took a drag of his cigar and exhaled toward the ceiling; an exhaust fan sucked the smoke out of the room. "Very true, Mr. Meredith. I am well aware of your accomplishments. Perhaps you will be kind enough to indulge me while I explain things to you."

His tone had not been the least bit threatening. He sounded more like a parent trying to explain something to a recalcitrant teenager. When I said nothing, he sat there, patiently looking at me, smoking his cigar, and waiting. Watching him, I was reminded of a cat, waiting outside a hole for the mouse to appear. I had planned to catch him off guard and to rattle him into making a mistake. It wasn't working. I was beginning to wonder if I were the mouse. I shrugged, and he began.

"It is unfortunate that your country does not understand Mexico. You insist upon seeing the situation only from your perspective. If you will permit me a brief history lesson, it will help you begin to understand things.

"After the Mexican Revolution, there was nothing but chaos, particularly in the countryside. The various presidents were virtually powerless. In order to stay in office, they came to an informal understanding with the local officials. The federal government was not going to interfere in local activities, legal or illegal. In return, the local government, military, and police would be loyal to the government. Among other things, smuggling was a very profitable business, and local officials needed money. My family and others supplied it. By the mid 1930s, we controlled the government, the police, and the military. We have never been stingy helping our friends, and we have all shared in the profits."

I was having a hard time sitting still, and it was time to try again to rattle him. I interrupted, saying, "You're just a bunch of thugs, running drugs. You're drug lords—just common criminals."

Ramon took a long pull off his cigar and exhaled the smoke. He continued in a patient voice, "Please, Mr. Meredith, are you really so naive as to think that a bunch of thugs, running so-called cartels in various cities, are in control? These men are enforcers, and they are very good at it, but do you really think a man, like, Arellano Felix has the ability to run such an organization? Now, if you please. Let me continue."

I was the one who was getting thrown off balance, so I decided to keep quiet and see if he would say anything useful.

"Now that you have some history, it is time for some basic economics. Do you know that Mexico is your second-largest trading partner?" When I didn't answer, he continued, saying, "Do you know which of our exports to your country has the largest dollar volume?" This time he didn't wait for me to answer. "It is not oil or agriculture, my friend. It is illegal drugs. There are more dollars involved in illegal drugs than in our top two exports combined."

Despite myself, the man was engaging, and I could not help but become interested in what he was saying.

Ramon continued by saying, "My family has been involved in cross-border politics and business for over one hundred years. Our extended family on both sides of the border numbers in the thousands. Over the years, we have made certain that all members of our family have had an opportunity, please excuse the expression, 'to be all they can be.' You could kill me and there would literally be ten people trained to take my place overnight. We spend more time planning for management succession than General Electric does.

"Take a trip along the border with Mexico. It is virtually wide open. Your local ranchers are afraid. Your government's piddling efforts at protecting your border are totally ineffectual. The local ranchers have given up. If the ranchers try to protect their land and families, your government arrests them and puts them in jail. That is bizarre, even to me. Your government is more concerned about illegal immigrants than about your own citizens.

"The ranchers are trying to sell the ranches that run along the border, but no one will buy them. No one, that is, except us. Soon, we will own both sides of the border, and it will become completely irrelevant."

Ramon was really warming to his subject. His cigar was lifeless in his hand. "Do you know that the South Orient Railroad, which the state of Texas purchased in 2001, has been leased for forty years to Grupo Nuevo? Do you know who controls Grupo Nuevo? We do. The South Orient Railroad provides daily passenger-train and freight service between Mexico and the United States. Do you know that Mexico has built the four-lane La Entrada al Pacifico Highway from the deep-water port city of Topolobampo, Mexico, to Presidio, Texas, which will then intersect with I-10, I-20, and I-40? This route will save up to four shipping days for goods moving between the Pacific Rim countries and Texas. The truck traffic will be enormous. The point is, you do not and cannot control the border with Mexico."

Now, he gestured with his cigar. "Look at the population statistics for Texas, New Mexico, Arizona, and California. The Mexican population is growing exponentially. The traditional white population is already a minority. Your public schools conduct classes in Spanish. You people are asleep. Mexico is retaking the Southwest, which your country stole from us, without firing a shot. Forget the Alamo. Soon we will be electing the politicians."

Ramon was charismatic. He was a believer, and I was completely caught up in his lecture. He stopped to relight his cigar and to take a puff before resuming. I could not think of anything to say.

Putting his cigar in the ashtray, he leaned forward and continued. "You make no effort to assimilate the Mexican population. In fact, you completely discourage the precise thing that made your country work. Now, you celebrate diversity. What a stupid notion. Just look around the world. In large part, your company, BlackRock, exists because people around the world celebrate diversity by killing each other.

"As for drugs, your police need a search warrant to look for tunnels along the border. You passed NAFTA, and any fool with enough supply can get drugs into this country. Do you know the statistics? Of course not. Well, it is my business to know these things, so let me tell you. Fewer than 5 percent of the vehicles coming into your country from Mexico are searched. Last year, ten million private vehicles, nine million pedestrians, and three hundred thousand commercial trucks entered Arizona from Mexico. The reality is that we could have an excellent business without the participation of border guards, but with their participation, we lose less than 1 percent.

"The United States Supreme Court has finally opened your borders to full implementation of NAFTA. Within the year, the commercial-truck traffic at the border will triple. You are no more prepared to deal with that than you are with President Bush's ill-fated guest-worker program."

Ramon picked up his cigar, sat back in his chair, and crossed his legs. "I thank you for listening to this because there is a point to it. There is no war on drugs. That is political cover for a hopeless situation. You cannot stop the flow of a product that your people want. You learned nothing from Prohibition. The only way to reduce the flow of illegal drugs into your country is to reduce the demand. And you do not have the political will to do that. Make possession and use of illegal drugs a capital crime? You will never do that even though within a year, that would put an end to the drug problem. Legalize all drugs? It will never happen."

Ramon's voice lost its emotion and changed from professorial to hard and cold. The change came without warning; it was like being slapped in the face. "Your brother's death was unfortunate; however, neither of us can bring him back. It is time to move on. In fact, you must move on."

Now, it was my turn. I leaned forward, looked him directly in the eye, and pointed at him. "I will find out who ordered the murder of my brother. I know you are smuggling drugs into this country, and I know you are providing them to dealers who sell to school kids. Before I am finished with you, you will need a lawyer, probably this whole firm, to save your ass."

Ramon wasn't fazed. He held my gaze with dead black eyes. I had seen eyes like that before, mostly in the Middle East, in the heads of men who had ordered the deaths of thousands of their countrymen. His voice seemed to come from a tomb. "Let me explain what can happen if you persist in annoying my family and interfering in our business. You must understand that Mao Tse Tung had it terribly wrong; power does not flow from the barrel of a gun. Power is the ability to manipulate people and the system to achieve a predetermined result.

"I completely understand BlackRock USA. It is a private army for hire, and you control it. Most Americans are unaware of its existence and the extent of your international activities. You claim to be businessmen licensed by the State Department to provide security services. Please consider this possibility: Very young girls from Bosnia, Iraq, and Columbia file suit against BlackRock and you in federal courts in New York, Miami, and Los Angeles alleging that your 'security contractors' used them as sex slaves and then sold them to others. These allegations would be very popular in the press.

"This type of publicity would quickly lead inquiring reporters to reveal on the front pages of newspapers all across the county that BlackRock is a private army and that you are, in essence, a warlord right here in the middle of the good ol' USA. I am sure you can imagine the field day the politicians would have with you and your company. There are more ex-generals in your organization than are on active duty in the Pentagon. One might even speculate that you are planning a coup. This would all be very bad and very easy to achieve.

"We have family in most of the news organizations in the country. Think of someone like Geraldo Rivera on prime time with this story. Bill O'Reilly and the others could not leave it alone. You should know that our family and its businesses are very large contributors to both the Republican and Democratic parties, but it would take you a lifetime to figure out how that is done. Last week, I had dinner with the chairman of the Senate Armed Services Committee and discussed the funding of his reelection campaign.

"Now, Mr. Meredith, I know full well that you are an intelligent and accomplished man, but there are things you need to understand. For many years, members of my extended family have worked for and with the DEA and the border patrol. It would be child's play to have a cache of illegal drugs found on your ranch or in the BlackRock compound, which I think is now six thousand acres. Such a discovery could easily trigger claims of racketeering. The DEA and the Justice Department would seize all of your assets and take over BlackRock. All of this is legal and can be done without a trial or any finding of guilt.

"We are owed many favors, and, in the atmosphere that could be created in the press, our friends would jump at the chance of enhancing their political reputations. They would think we had done them a favor. All of this could happen to you within forty-eight hours, Mr. Meredith. You would lose everything and find yourself alone. One would not be surprised if a man under such enormous pressure committed suicide.

"I realize that this is harsh and undoubtedly frustrating to you. But the fact is that you and your little army are helpless against us. You may win a small battle here and there, but you have no chance to win the war. You should take some comfort in the fact that my sister has returned to Mexico and will stay there. That is your victory. If you fail to realize that and continue to bother us, well, that would create an unpalatable situation for us, and we would have to act accordingly."

Ramon stood and announced peremptorily, "Now, you will have to excuse me. I have a very busy day. Ms. Martinez will show you out."

I left Wells & Bunch deep in thought. I had shaken the tree, and a bunch of snakes had dropped on me.

CHAPTER 61

▼

Stephanie and I were the only passengers on a BlackRock-owned Gulfstream jet on the way to Washington DC for the meeting with John Wesley. BlackRock had bought the used jet from General Electric a year ago, and it had been in the air over two hundred days since then. Stephanie and I sat across from each other in sumptuous leather seats with a two-foot-wide table between us, containing the remnants of the KFC takeout dinner we had picked up on the way to the airport.

"What are you going to tell Wesley? It's your word against Knobly's," I asked her.

"He has known me my entire life. I think he'll believe me."

"Stephanie, I don't want to be a killjoy, but we are going to need something more than that. The decisions won't be made by Wesley alone. Other people, whom you don't know, will be involved."

"Knobly and I can both take lie-detector tests."

"You can, but it won't be dispositive. Didn't you take the training session on how to fool a lie detector?"

"OK, you're probably right," she said in an exhausted voice.

Stephanie cleared away the remnants of our dinner, and we moved to two seats across the aisle that reclined flat. Mercifully, we slept until the plane went into final descent for landing.

We were met by a car and driver from BlackRock, who took us to Wesley's house. We were no closer to dealing with the conundrum of she said/he said.

John Walker Wesley III himself met us at the front door of his massive colonial home that looked like a replica of Tara in *Gone with the Wind*. Wesley was of average height and build. He was wearing a smoking jacket from the 1940s. He obviously did not buy this house on his CIA salary. The immense entry foyer and massive staircase, leading to the second floor, could have served as Tara in the movie. Wesley hugged Stephanie like a long-lost daughter and shook my hand firmly before ushering us into his study, which was to the right of the front door.

The room was cozy, about twenty feet by twenty feet with floor-to-ceiling bookcases on the three inside walls. The shelves were filled with books except for two areas on each wall that had been cut out for paintings. Surprisingly, the discretely lit paintings were abstract works, as opposed to the usual hunting scenes or Impressionist paintings. A modest-size desk was placed perpendicular to the window, facing the front door. Stephanie and I sat on the plaid sofa, and Wesley took the side chair.

Stephanie and I told him all that had happened.

"Sanchez virtually admitted that his family was responsible for Ricky's death," I said. "If that's so, Knobly must be on their payroll."

"Very true," said Wesley, "but the problem is that you can't prove what he said. You and Stephanie have a personal relationship, and one could say you would do whatever you could to save her."

Stephanie and I looked at one another with a sense of hopelessness. Wesley sat silently. Finally, Stephanie broke the silence. "Well, if it's me versus Knobly, I will just have to take my chances that I will be believed and that the truth will come out. Where do you want me to turn myself in?"

I put my hand on her knee and spoke intensely, "Look, Stephanie, let me work on this. Maybe I can get to Knobly. I can't let you disappear into a black hole at the CIA. Mr. Wesley, surely there must be something I can do to help. Maybe the Agency can run a through-check on Knobly and see if anything turns up."

Wesley nodded. "You both would be surprised at what the CIA and our government can do if they put their minds to it. In the last twenty-four hours, we have done deep background checks and interviews on Knobly and Stephanie."

Stephanie and I looked at each other with surprise. Why hadn't Wesley told us that at the beginning? Had Knobly checked out? Had he done more to frame Stephanie? Before we could say anything, Wesley held up his hand to silence us.

"Information is just that—information. It may lead to the truth, or it may not. You will have to excuse me, Stephanie, but I am an old spy. I wanted to see how you reacted and what you would decide to do if I couldn't help you. The CIA should conduct security reviews of its personnel on a frequent basis; however, that takes money, and the last director chose not to spend the money to update background checks on senior personnel who had been with the Agency for more than ten years. We now see that the failure to do that has had its own cost. Stephanie checked out just like her profile. The blank was romantic entanglements." Wesley nodded at Grant. "Mr. Meredith here filled in that blank. Knobly, on the other hand, quickly became an open book with a bad ending.

"Because of 9/11, we now keep a record of all people who purchase airplane tickets with cash. Once a month, Knobly had been traveling with a woman to Barbados for a long weekend. The plane tickets had been purchased with cash. He recently purchased a house in Montgomery County for three hundred thousand dollars. He had forty-five thousand dollars in a savings account and obtained a loan for two hundred fifty-five thousand dollars. No big deal except that houses in his new neighborhood were going for eight hundred fifty thousand dollars and up. We interviewed the seller at 2:00 AM this morning, and with a grant of immunity, he admitted receiving five hundred fifty thousand dollars in cash from Knobly. The seller avoided capital-gains taxes on the sale, and Knobly used hidden cash.

"We checked with his credit-card companies and found that he often made payments with money orders or cashier's checks. We could find no inheritance or any other source of the cash."

Stephanie stood up abruptly and said, "That seals it. Bring him in, and let's find out what he knows."

Wesley motioned her to sit down. "We sent a squad of agents to his house at 6:00 AM this morning. He was in bed with his throat slit. The house was ransacked, and it appeared a television and some personal items were missing. In the abstract, it looks like a burglary gone bad. I very much doubt that, but, in any event, he's dead."

"How long had he been dead?" I asked.

"We don't have the final answer, but the preliminary finding puts his death at Friday morning around 5:00 AM."

I thought for a moment. "That means he was dead before I met with Sanchez."

Wesley said, "Exactly so. It seems these people are not fools."

As we left Wesley's house, Stephanie and I said little. After a while, the silence became uncomfortable. Neither of us mentioned Ricky. Finally, Stephanie broke the silence. "I'd better stay here for a few days and wrap things up with the CIA."

"Yeah, well, I've got some thinking to do about a number of things. Ramon Sanchez bugs the hell out of me."

"Why?"

"Because he may be right, and I just can't accept that."

"What are you going to do?"

"I don't know, yet." I asked the driver to drop her off at the Willard Hotel where she had reserved a room.

We didn't kiss good-bye.

CHAPTER 62

▼

The board room of the Plaza Group at 425 Park Avenue was exquisitely furnished. The west wall of windows looked down on Park Avenue. A fourteenth-century tapestry towered over a credenza that held a silver coffee service. Twelve leather chairs surrounded the polished-mahogany conference table. The Plaza Group was a private merchant bank that had extensive holdings in the defense industry.

Today was not a Plaza Group board meeting. Seated around the table with me were five people, who were listening intently. After being introduced by John Walker Wesley III, I had been speaking to the group for thirty minutes, explaining the Sanchez drug connection. I concluded by saying, "It is clear to me that the DEA should move against those Sanchez-family assets here in the United States. Mr. Wesley has been able to confirm that the businesses on the list are controlled by the Sanchez family and are likely to be involved in the distribution of illegal drugs in the Southwest."

I sat down.

All eyes turned to Arnold B. Dobben, chief of staff to the president of the United States. Dobben wore a rumpled suit and what looked like a wash-and-wear, white, button-down shirt with a dull tie. The dark circles under his eyes revealed evidence of the grueling pace at the White House. He looked around the table, gauging how the other meeting participants were reacting to my presentation. Although nondescript looking, Dobben was rightly considered to be the power behind the president and a political genius. He ran his hand through his thinning brown hair and began.

"Mr. Meredith," Dobben said, "I would like to express the gratitude of the president for uncovering the existence of the Sanchez family's role in the illegal-drug trade. I have discussed this matter with the president, and we would like to do something about it. However, there are very serious political and diplomatic considerations that involve our relationship with Mexico. Three administrations have worked to implement NAFTA. As you point out, Mexico is our second-largest trading partner, and the Sanchez family is, at minimum, very well-connected politically. It may be that they are the de facto government of Mexico. At this time, Mexico needs all of the political stability it can get. It may well be in the national interest to accept their role in the drug trade. Even if we could get rid of them, someone else would take their place. Put another way, better the devil we know than one we don't."

Robert Samuels, former director of the DEA spoke next. He was a former major general in the army and looked the part—short, gray hair without a part and ramrod-straight posture. He had left the DEA to run unsuccessfully for the Senate from Virginia. He had become a FOX News analyst and an author. Dobben had insisted he be included since the administration might need a spin doctor in the media on this issue.

"Arnold is making sense. We have to look at the reality of the situation. Our paramount concern should be trade with Mexico. After five years as director of the DEA, I became convinced that the only way to deal with illegal drugs in a meaningful way was to legalize them. If the demand is there, someone will fill it. Why risk disrupting our relationship with Mexico over drug smuggling? We could cause a great deal of harm while, at best, putting a short-term crimp in some of the drug trade."

Lillian R. Harris, a short, grandmotherly looking woman, who reminded me of the female M in the James Bond movies, was the current DEA director. She interrupted Samuels by saying, "Bob, we have to engage these smugglers. They spread corruption like the plague. Our intelligence estimates that in Sonora, the cartel spreads around bribes of one million dollars a week. Increasingly, we are finding that our agents are on the take. Many of our agents along the Mexican border are Mexican Americans. They have family on both sides of the border. We need them to help us, but the potential for corruption is always there. All they have to do is look the other way at the right time. If the field personnel come to the conclusion that the DEA isn't really trying to stop the trade, the corruption will escalate, possibly out of control."

Homer Johnson cleared his throat, and everyone turned in his direction. Johnson, a Republican, had served part of one term as president. At six foot two with a full head of salt-and-pepper hair, the elegantly dressed former president was an articulate, no-nonsense businessman. He had stymied the Washington press corps because he told the truth about what he was trying to accomplish and why it was in the best interest of the nation. He was always respectful of those who disagreed but was merciless in his logical response to stupid ideas and questions. He was not afraid to say that he wasn't sure whether a policy would work to accomplish what he intended. He was not afraid to say that reasonable people could support a different policy. Where he was always rock solid was in his belief that he had been elected to decide between competing policies and to move forward with something. He had been well on his way to dealing with the Social Security problem when his wife was diagnosed with cancer.

He had resigned from the presidency to spend his time with her. In his resignation speech, he had said that the vice president was more than qualified to serve out his term and that the nation had many fine men and women who could serve as president. On the other hand, his wife had only one husband and one life. Even the most jaded Washington hand had nothing but respect for the former president.

"I agree with Arnold that, in the big picture, the most important thing is trade with Mexico—unless it is your child who becomes addicted to drugs. I also agree with Bob that we do not have the political will to stop the illegal-drug trade and that we should legalize drugs and regulate them like alcohol. Finally, I emphatically agree with Lillian that corruption of our law-enforcement personnel is a major problem. Now, I know I sound like a politician, trying to be on all sides of every issue, but there is no easy answer to what I perceive as a menace.

"In my opinion, we have to rely on the Sanchez family, or whoever really runs Mexico, to have some common sense. They have no reason to believe they can run wild in the United States. They are survivors and will learn to adapt to whatever we throw at them. I hold no illusions that we can stamp out the drug trade, but we have to, at least, try to stop drug smuggling. I suggest that the DEA move against the Arizona businesses that have been identified. If the extent of the Sanchez wealth is what you say, it will inconvenience them but will probably be considered a cost of doing business."

Lillian Harris spoke up, saying, "I'm concerned about that meat-packing plant. Our intelligence informs me that the place is like a fortress. Frankly, my people are good, but they don't have the type of training to take down a facility like that. It simply isn't a SWAT team mission. A lot of people could be killed, or we could end up in a Waco-like stalemate. The press would be all over us."

I looked at Homer Johnson, who smiled and nodded.

I said, "Ms. Harris, dealing with a situation like that is exactly what BlackRock can do better than anyone else in the world outside the organized military. The DEA can hire us as contractors. We will take the facility and turn it over to the DEA."

Harris looked at Dobben. "Excellent idea," said Dobben enthusiastically. "If things don't go smoothly, we have deniability, and, God forbid, if we lose any-one, there won't be the publicity and institutional hand-wringing that would come if we used conventional law enforcement. I'll speak to the president. I'm sure he will approve the raids."

CHAPTER 63

▼

The *Tucson Times*, April 1, 2006, page one:

"The Drug Enforcement Agency swooped down on La Mirada Packing Corporation yesterday in a predawn raid that netted over five thousand pounds of cocaine with a street value of eighty million dollars. Twenty people were arrested, and a substantial number of automatic weapons were confiscated. La Mirada is the largest meat-packing company in the Southwest. Authorities are searching for Arturo Sanchez, president of La Mirada."

*   *   *   *

The *Phoenix Gazette*, April 1, 2006, page one:

"DEA agents, assisted by over two hundred law-enforcement officers, drawn from around Arizona, raided one hundred Burger Delight restaurants in metropolitan Phoenix and Tucson yesterday. The simultaneous raids uncovered over one thousand pounds of cocaine with a street value of sixteen million dollars. So far, there have been no arrests. A spokesman for the U.S. attorney general stated that the restaurants served as distribution centers for the largest illegal-drug operation in the Southwest. Twenty attorneys and investigators from the FBI are untangling the maze of corporations, partnerships, and other entities involved in the ownership of the restaurants in an effort to determine if there is common ownership. Arrests are expected to start occurring shortly."

*   *   *   *

The *Phoenix Gazette*, April 1, 2006, second section, page five:

"Fire broke out on the twentieth floor of 100 Central Avenue yesterday. Quick action by the Phoenix High-Rise Fire Response Team and a state-of-the art fire suppression system prevented the fire from spreading beyond a suite of offices on the north side of the twentieth floor. A spokesman for the law firm stated that all client files and records, other than those in the fire-damaged area, were safe. The extent of the client files maintained in the fire-damaged area was presently unknown. Fire investigators have tentatively concluded that the fire was started by an incendiary device in the office of Ramon Sanchez. Mr. Sanchez's whereabouts are presently unknown. Telephone calls to his home have not been answered. A security guard observed a small helicopter briefly touching down on the building roof shortly before the fire. It has not been determined whether the incident was related."

*   *   *   *

The *Raleigh Observer*, May 5, 2006, page five:

"Three Mexican nationals were killed in a hail of gunfire last night at the BlackRock USA training facility seventy miles east of Raleigh. The men were challenged by a BlackRock patrol and opened fire. Early accounts indicate several thousand rounds of ammunition were consumed in the firefight, which only lasted a few minutes. Authorities found two duffle bags with the dead men. One bag contained fifty pounds of cocaine, and the other contained seventy-five pounds of marijuana. It is not known what the dead men were doing at the BlackRock compound or why they had the drugs. BlackRock had no comment."

*   *   *   *

The *Scottsdale Tribune*, September 29, 2006:

"A larger-than-life-size bronze statue in memory of Scottsdale policewoman Lisa Gonzales was dedicated yesterday with speeches by various Scottsdale officials. The ten-foot-high statue was donated by BlackRock, USA, and bears the inscription:

Lisa Gonzales
1980–2006
She gave her life for our school to be drug free.

Spokesmen for the Greater Phoenix chapter of the ACLU joined the Scottsdale chief of police and the chief judge of the Maricopa County superior court in announcing a four-point program to combat drug use in the high school, which would serve as a pilot program for the entire state: (1) random, unannounced drug tests for all Scottsdale High students; (2) random, unannounced locker searches; (3) regular police patrols to ensure that non-students were not on campus without approval; and (4) a mandatory drug-education program. In a related event, Black-Rock USA announced that Lily Gonzales had resigned from the U.S. Border Patrol and had been appointed vice president for Latin American relations."

*   *   *   *

The *Washington Journal*, December 1, 2006, page three:

"Senior Judge Robert Q. Larson dismissed with prejudice three lawsuits accusing BlackRock USA contractors of engaging in black-market trading of young girls allegedly sold as sex slaves. The cases, originally filed in Miami, Houston, and Los Angeles federal courts were consolidated before Judge Larson for disposition. In a move that took observers by surprise, Judge Larson read from a prepared decision that scathingly rejected every allegation in the complaints as being without justification or as outright fabrications. Using his powers under FRCP 11, Judge Larson sanctioned the three lawyers who brought the cases—Jamie Sanchez of Los Angeles, John Lopez of Miami, and Eduardo Hidalgo of Houston—one million dollars each and reported each of them to their respective states' bar associations for potential discipline."

*   *   *   *

The *Washington Journal*, December 24, 2006, page seven:

"In unprecedented simultaneous decisions, the bar associations of Florida, Texas, and California disbarred John Lopez, Eduardo Hidalgo, and Jamie Sanchez from the practice of law in their respective states and referred the cases to local authorities to consider criminal fraud charges against the men."

*   *   *   *

The *Phoenix Gazette*, December 27, 2006, page ten:

"Wells & Bunch announced that Juanita Sanchez-Yanez has joined the firm as head of its cross-border trade practice. Ms. Sanchez-Yanez was formerly with the firm of Jones, Johnson & Girth in Tucson. According to sources at the firm, she will fill the gap in the firm caused by the unexplained disappearance of Ramon Sanchez."

*   *   *   *

Center for Public Accountability Report: Private Military Contractors and the Revolving Door, April 2006:

BlackRock USA was established by ex-Army Ranger Grant Meredith after leaving military service in 1998. Funding was provided by a small group of venture-capital investors assembled by the legendary Rex Lyons. The business plan for BlackRock was to provide security services and military assistance to the United States military and foreign countries under licenses issued by the State Department.

In a 1998 interview, the only one ever granted, Meredith said BlackRock was intended to capitalize on the need for private military services caused by the end of the Cold War and the downsizing of military forces by the super powers. These events combined to unleash a surplus of weapons and military personnel on the open market at a time when third-world countries were in chaos and the U.S. military was in the middle of a massive outsourcing program.

In 2001, BlackRock USA was acquired by Integrated Security Services, a private company based in Washington DC, which provides security services to private clients, including foreign governments. It also trains military and police personnel. Integrated Security Services lists the following individuals on its board of directors:

- John Eikenberry, director of the Defense Intelligence Agency in the Carter administration

- General (Retired) Arnold J. Schwartz, head of the Joint Chiefs of Staff from 1992–1998

- Wallace W. Richards, director of the CIA in the H. W. Bush administration

- Thomas D. Dillon, former secretary of the navy and member of the board before resigning to become assistant director of the Department of Homeland Security

Integrated Security Services is owned by the Plaza Group, a private merchant bank also headquartered in Washington DC. Its partners include the following:

- Homer A. Johnson, former president of the United States

- James A. Brown, former secretary of state

- Lawrence A. Kammerer, former secretary of defense

BlackRock was recently awarded a one-year, one-billion-dollar contract to provide security for oil fields in the kingdom of Saudi Arabia as well as for the Saudi royal family.

CHAPTER 64

▼

Almost a year had passed since the Lisa Gonzales ceremonies when the phone rang in the Meredith ranch bunkhouse. Tommy picked it up.

"Tommy, this is Stephanie Chambers. How are you?"

There was a brief silence before he slowly answered, "Why, Miss Stephanie, I'm alive, so I'm just fine. Is there something I can do for you?"

Stephanie could tell Tommy didn't want to talk to her, so she skipped the pleasantries and went directly to the purpose of the call. "I assume Grant told you that I was responsible for Ricky's death."

"No, he didn't. What he said was that you killed Ricky on orders from your crooked CIA boss. He didn't say nothin' about you being responsible."

"How is Grant? I'm afraid to call him. I'm sure he would just as soon forget about me."

"Well, Miss Stephanie, he's alive, same as me, but he isn't much fun these days. He mopes around a lot. We haven't been to a rodeo since I can remember. If you ask me, which you did, I think he would like to forget about you but is havin' some serious trouble doin' so."

"Do you think he would want to see me again?"

"Frankly, I don't know. He sure needs somethin', but I ain't quite sure what."

"Thanks for your time, Tommy. I would appreciate it if you wouldn't mention to Grant that I called."

"No problem."

C H A P T E R 65

▼

I was sitting just inside the south end of the barn, mending a broken bridle. The boom box played LeAnn Rimes's "How Do I Live".

Maybe I should call Stephanie? How? I didn't even know where she was.

Tommy came rushing up to me, breathless. "Grant, you won't believe it. I was watching the news. There was this press conference in Washington about a new multiagency cross-border plan to stop drug smuggling. The president introduced Hector Sanchez, the Mexican president-elect, and, by God in heaven, Miss Stephanie was standin' right next to Sanchez with a big smile on her face."

▼

The best fiction is often extensively researched and based on fact.

THE FOLLOWING MATERIAL IS NOT FICTION.

1995

Statement by:	Thomas A. Constantine, DEA Administrator
Before the:	U.S. Senate Foreign Relations Committee
Regarding:	International Drug Trafficking Organizations in Mexico
Date:	August 8, 1995

During the early 1980's, most of the Colombian cocaine entered the United States through South Florida by way of the Caribbean. But, traffickers were forced to find new routes when U.S. drug agencies increased enforcement action in the Caribbean and South Florida. The Colombian drug lords naturally turned to the trafficking groups in Mexico which had what they were looking for, proximity to the United States, a 2,000 mile expanse of border offering unlimited smuggling possibilities, and an already established drug trafficking infrastructure that stood ready to serve their needs.

The drug trafficking organizations easily adapted their operations to include cocaine trafficking, and by the mid-80's, were well-established and reliable transporters of Colombian cocaine. Delegating cocaine transportation to the traffickers in Mexico was a tactical decision on the part of the Cali mafia. With the transportation assistance of these traffickers, the cocaine barons could now move larger bulk quantities through Mexico which would have been logistically impossible to move by any other means. By turning the riskiest part of the cocaine distribution cycle (the transportation) over to these traffickers, the Cali mafia could turn its attention to other aspects of their cocaine enterprise. This drug trafficking partnership has become one of both convenience and profit.

Mr. Chairman, in a few years down the road, I believe it's entirely possible that these newly emerging groups could rise to an equal (or superior) footing with the Cali mafia. If this happens, life as we know it in both the United States and Mexico will change dramatically. They care little for the devastating impact they have on the people of Mexico and the United States. They are international criminal elements that must be dealt with.

1996

The *Washington Post*, July 30, 1996:

One year ago the Mexican government dispatched newly recruited federal agent Ricardo Cordero Ontiveros to the northwestern border city of Tijuana to head an intelligence unit created to hunt down the leader of one of the nation's most powerful drug cartels.

Cordero never got closer to the notorious Arellano Felix brothers than a photograph. Instead, Cordero said he discovered that the Mexican government's top crime-fighting organization was so corrupt that his own colleagues were escorting massive shipments of drugs to the U.S. border, serving as bodyguards of drug traffickers and misusing U.S. anti-drug funds....

A U.S. federal law enforcement official familiar with Cordero's work supported many of the details of his charges, including allegations that senior law enforcement authorities thwarted Cordero and his intelligence team's attempts to investigate the drug cartel. A spokeswoman for the U.S. Drug Enforcement Administration in Washington said the agency would not comment.

1997

Statement by: Thomas A. Constantine, Administrator DEA
Before the: U.S. Senate Caucus on International Narcotics Control

Regarding: SWB Corruption
Date: May 14, 1997

The power and influence of traditional Organized Crime groups pale in comparison to the sophisticated, wealthy syndicates who control the drug trade today in the Western Hemisphere. For the first time in our history, organized crime in the United States is controlled by individuals who reside outside our borders. These mob leaders of today are the Rodriguez-Orejuela brothers in Columbia and Amado Carrillo-Fuentes, Miguel Caro-Quintero and the Arrellano-Felix Brothers in Mexico. They are far wealthier and more influential than their predecessors, which make them a more dangerous and difficult adversary to attack.

It is essential that we understand that the power and influence of these syndicate bosses are not just felt in their countries and along our borders but extends all along the seamless continuum of the drug trade. Our central enforcement strategy against these international syndicates is to attack the communication systems of the command and control functions as well as the leadership of their organizations. Referred to as the Southwest Border Strategy, it has provided a clearly defined picture of the way in which these organizations conduct their business. One thing has become perfectly clear; their influence does not stop at the Southwest border but extends into virtually every city and town in the United States as they dominate the cocaine, heroin, marijuana, and methamphetamine trade in our country. The corruption that we are concerned with here today does not stop in San Diego, Nogales, and Brownsville, but extends its tentacles everywhere these organizations distribute their poison. As their wealth and power increase, often exponentially, so does their ability to corrupt. Our Southwest Border Strategy may well be better named the Western Hemisphere strategy, for wherever we face this enemy we see corruption, intimidation and violence the tools of the organized criminal....

... Unfortunately, both the violence and the corruption that are attendant to the drug trade in Mexico are spilling across the border into the United States....

... They have also aggressively recruited and established a cadre of assassins on both sides of the border to carry out their orders.

The *Washington Post*, November 2, 1997:

> Traffickers often hid drugs in shipments of food, such as fish or produce, that would spoil if they were stopped and thoroughly searched. "Much of the time you're dealing with perishables, and unless we have specific information (that drugs are on the load), the priority is business and trade," said a federal official who, like many others, complained that NAFTA's mandate of unfettered commerce has hampered drug interdiction efforts....

> "In El Paso in 1996, we had 4,545,657 pedestrian crossings [into the United States], 594,434 commercial vehicles and 16,247,097 private vehicles, for a total of 46,881,381 people," said Tom Kennedy head of the DEA there. "With that kind of volume, forget corruption. Simple math shows that if you run enough across, the odds are in your favor." ...

> "The border is absolutely overwhelmed with numbers—people, vehicles, modes of transportation," said a DEA intelligence analyst. "Even though conventional wisdom says it is the riskiest choke point in the hemispheric drug pipeline," he said, "it may be that the border is the easiest part of the whole business." ...

> The Mexican drug groups also learned valuable lessons from their Italian Mafia and Colombian cartel counterparts on how to thwart law enforcement. The Mexican groups are usually organized around family ties to prevent infiltration by informants, and they are compartmentalized to protect the leaders and to ensure that if one cell of their group is dismantled, the entire business is not destroyed.

2001

DEA Drug Intelligence Brief, Mexico-Country Profile, January 2001:

> Mexican organizations now have a major share of the wholesale cocaine market in the United States, directly controlling the wholesale distribution of cocaine throughout the western and mid-western portions of the United States. Chicago and Los Angeles are the primary command and control centers for Mexican Drug trafficking organizations in the United States. In addition, over the past several years, Mexican groups have worked towards establishing themselves in the eastern United States as transporters for Colombian organizations. In some cases, Mexican transportation organizations are now transporting shipments from Mexico all the way to New York....

Since l997, there has been a notable escalation in the level of drug-related violence in Mexico.… From late l999 to early 2000 the targets of assassination have had increasingly higher profiles, as evidenced by the brutal execution in April 2000 of Jose Luis Patino Moreno, Director General for the FEADS Public Ministry, who had been tasked with targeting the AFO [a drug organization], and two of his colleagues outside Tijuana.

2002

DEA Drug Intelligence Brief, Mexico: Country Brief, July 2002:

Multisource reporting indicates that Mexican drug traffickers continue to devise clandestine, underground routes to smuggle drugs across the Southwest border. An increase in drug seizures in the Nogales, Sonora, area during March 2001, led Mexican counterdrug officials to discover that a complex drainage system running underground between the cities of Nogales Sonora, and Nogales, Arizona, was used to smuggle drugs and illegal aliens into the United States. In February 2002, a 1,200 foot tunnel was discovered by U.S. federal agents on a ranch in the community of Tierra Del Sol, approximately 70 miles east of San Diego, California. The tunnel opening in Mexico was located on a ranch at the outskirts of Tecate, about 200 feet from the border fence. This tunnel is believed to be among one of the longest and most sophisticated tunnels ever encountered by law enforcement authorities on the U.S.-Mexican Southwest border. The tunnel had been framed with wooden planks, and rail tracks had been installed to transport large quantities of drugs in carts. The tunnel was also equipped with electric lighting and a ventilation system.…

The precise number of drug-related murders in Mexico is difficult to estimate but drug-related violence accounts for hundreds of murders each year. Typically, drug-related violence in Mexico is centered on retaliatory killings of individual traffickers. However, murders of Mexican law enforcement officials, journalists, lawyers, politicians and innocent citizens are prevalent. Violence by MDTOs [Mexican Drug Trafficking Organizations] persists with relative impunity because of law enforcement corruption, a scarcity of resources to properly investigate these crimes, and a lack of resolve due to the threat of retaliation.

Many narco-assassinations in Mexico take place using high-powered assault weapons such as AK-47s and AR-15s. These weapons are often used during high-profile drive-by shootings and during other executions. Other victims are sometimes kidnapped and then murdered; their remains are dumped along the sides of roads or in isolated desert areas. In addition, heinous acts of torture often precede drug-related murders; the victims may have been severely beaten, burned, or have had their body parts severed.

2003

Excerpts of Statement by:	James A. Woolley, Assistant Special Agent in Charge, Tucson District Office, DEA
Before the:	U.S. House of Representatives, Government Reform Subcommittee
Regarding:	Criminal Justice, Drug Policy and Human Resources
Date:	March 10, 2003

The unique character of the SoLilyn/Arizona border creates an important tier of "gatekeeper" organizations along this border with corridors through Yuma, Lukeville, Nogales, Naco, and Douglas. These "gatekeepers" are smuggling organizations that specialize in exploiting their areas for the sole purpose of getting drugs across the border and into the Tucson or Phoenix areas. The "gatekeepers" are characterized as generational local families extended across the SoLilyn/Arizona border communities. They have used these generational ties to leverage even more corruption, create a transportation infrastructure. They maintain an intelligence apparatus along the border specifically targeting the Ports of Entry. These "Gatekeepers" have constructed and maintained tunnel systems under the border, engineered increasingly sophisticated vehicle traps, and they have successfully co-opted (or simply stolen from) car rental companies to supply rental sport utility vehicles for smuggling purposes....

Mexican drug groups have become the world's pre-eminent drug traffickers, and they tend to be characterized by organizational complexity and a high propensity for violence....

Drug trafficking organizations operating along the Arizona/Mexico Border continue to be one of the greatest threats to communities across this nation. The power and influence of these organizations is pervasive, and continues to expand to new markets across the United States.

2004

The *Charlotte Observer*, January 30, 2004:

> Ciudad Juarez, Mexico—Authorities questioned 13 state police Thursday about drug trafficking and the murders of at least 11 people, feeding fears that officers in this border city take part in the crime they should be fighting.

> The officers were detained Wednesday. Their commander and three fellow officers were being sought.

> A state police spokesman acknowledged officials have been unable to clean up the force despite firing about 300 officers in the past two years. Thousands of other local, state, and federal lawmen in Mexico have been dismissed in recent years.

BBC News, April 13, 2004:

> Federal police have taken over security in central Mexico's Morelos state after a governor dismissed its entire police force. The state's 552 policemen were sacked after the arrest of two top officers for allegedly protecting a drug gang…. Prosecutors say planes ferrying cocaine from Colombia were allowed to land at an airport in Morelos State's capital, Curenavaca. They further allege that consignments of cocaine would leave the airport in police vehicles, before being sold.

The *Washington Post*, June 21, 2004:

> Matamoros, Mexico—Luis Alberto Guerrero was no ordinary outlaw. He wore a grenade around his neck.

> When his body was found last month in this border town across from Brownsville, Tex., state police said his signature grenade was still dangling over his bloody chest….

> The unknown assailants who fired more than 100 bullets into Guerrero's silver Jeep on May 10 outside the popular Wild West dance hall also killed three teenage girls, leaving five corpses and two live explosives a mile from the U.S. border and shining a new spotlight on Mexico's most unusual criminal organization, known as the Zetas.

> The Zetas are former Mexican army commandos who were trained to capture drug traffickers but joined them instead, around the end of the 1990s.

Armed with AR-15 and AK-47 assault rifles, the 15 or so Zetas currently at large are considered the number one security threat on this busy stretch of the border.

The *Los Angeles Times*, October 10, 2004:

In broad daylight at a shopping center where dozens of people were emerging from a movie theater, at least 10 assassins fired 500 large-caliber rounds at drug trafficker Rodolfo Carrillo Fuentes and his entourage Sept. 11....

There have been more that 300 drug-related killings in Sinaloa since early 1999. Criminals are often indistinguishable from police: One of Carrillo Fuentes's bodyguards, wounded in the shooting, turned out to be a moonlighting State Police commander.

2005

The *Wall Street Journal*, January 24, 2005, page A17:

A dangerous new phase in Mexico's prolonged war against drug traffickers has broken out as a government crackdown has been met by a deadly response, raising fears of wider instability.

The clash, which began when the government learned jailed drug kingpins were running their businesses from a maximum-security prison, is a major challenge to President Vicente Fox and threatens one of his administration's few successes. Since he took power in 2000, several leading crime bosses have been killed or captured—a record surpassing that of the country's former ruling party, which was widely viewed as having been corrupted by drug money during its 70 years in power.

The latest sign of trouble came when the bodies of six executed employees of a federal prison were discovered outside the prison grounds late last week. The government interpreted the killings as retaliation by drug bosses, because they occurred just days after officials transferred several traffickers from the country's La Palma prison to a site in Matamoros, near the Texas border.

"This is a direct challenge to our power," Mr. Fox said in a statement, later telling Mexican television he would wage "the mother of all battles" against drug traffickers....

The discovery of how easily traffickers continue to operate even after incarceration underscores how difficult it is for Mexico—the major transit point for cocaine from South America to the U.S. market and a supplier in its own right of marijuana and methamphetamines—to uproot the illegal-drug trade.

The *Washington Post*, January 28, 2005, Page A21:

A U.S. State Department warning to American citizens about a "deteriorating security situation" on the U.S.-Mexican border provoked an angry response Thursday from Mexican officials, who called it unfair. They pointed out that the United States, as the world's largest consumer of illegal drugs, shares blame in a recent spate of drug-related killings and kidnappings, some of which involved U.S. citizens....

In Washington, State Department spokesman Richard Boucher told reporters Thursday that 27 Americans had been kidnapped in the last six months on the Mexican side of the border. Two were killed and 11 remain missing....

U.S. law enforcement officials have said that while some of the 27 U.S. citizens were innocent victims, more were involved in the drug trade. They also said they were frustrated that the abductions were being treated as a local problem in which more experienced Mexican federal officials could not intervene.

An FBI official, who spoke on condition of anonymity, said there had been no progress on these cases, despite considerable evidence and witnesses in some instances.

The *Dallas Morning News*, June 6, 2005:

The dead include university students, assembly-plant workers, farm hands, businessmen, journalists, money couriers, drug gang henchmen, and dozens of police officers.

At least 550 people have lost their lives in drug-related executions in Mexico so far this year....

Among the latest: A police commander assassinated in Nuevo Laredo early Thursday. Enrique Cardenas Saldana was gunned down in front of his

9-year old daughter. He was the sixth police office—the fourth commander killed in the border city this year.

The *New York Times*, August 17, 2005:

Citing a surge of smuggling and violence along the border, the governors of Arizona and New Mexico have issued state of emergency declarations in recent days.

The *Seattle Post-Intelligencer*, November 5, 2005:

In 2003, Mexican traffickers supplied 77 percent of the cocaine that entered the United States. Last year, it was 92 percent, Anthony Placido, the top DEA intelligence official, told a congressional panel in June. The other 8 percent moved through the Caribbean.

Mexican gangs also dominate the growing methamphetamine trade, producing 53 percent of the drugs on the market in "super-labs" in Mexico.... Much of the rest is made in clandestine labs in California, also run by Mexican gangs, U.S. officials say.

And as has been the case for nearly 100 years, Mexico is the biggest marijuana supplier to the U.S. and produces nearly half the heroin consumed north of the border, behind only Colombia.

The Associated Press, November 16, 2005:

Guatemala's top anti-drug investigator, his deputy, and another senior official were indicted here Wednesday on charges they conspired to import and distribute cocaine in the United States.

The *Wall Street Journal*, by Mary Anastasia O'Grady, August 26, 2005:

A fertile mix of incentives—high demand for cocaine "up north," the prohibition against buying and using, and U.S. insistence on interdiction—has pushed lucrative trafficking operations off traditional routes and onto paths that pass through places like this [rural Guatemala]. Locals here say that everybody and his uncle is getting into "transporting," and they're all getting rich.

One thing the "war" [on drugs]—with its $40 billion per year price tag—is not doing is reducing the supply of cocaine in the U.S. so that prices go up. In their recent book titled *An Analytic Assessment of U.S. Drug Policy* (AEI

Press), ... reported that "adjusted for inflation, cocaine prices have fallen by more than half since l980, despite much greater enforcement efforts." ...

There's a message here for Washington. To end drug abuse, discourage demand. The war against supply, with its huge monetary, social and political costs, is nothing more than a jobs program.

2006

Statement by: Karen P. Tandy, Administrator DEA
Before the: U.S. Senate Foreign Relations Committee Subcommittees
Regarding: International Economic Policy, Export and Trade Promotion
                    and Western Hemisphere, Peace Corps and Narcotics Affairs
Date: June 21, 2006

Methamphetamine poses a unique and significant threat to the United States. Methamphetamine is unique in that it is a synthetic drug, it is not dependent of cultivation of a crop, its production requires no specialized skill or training, and its precursor chemicals have historically been easy to obtain and inexpensive to purchase. These factors have contributed to meth-amphetamine's rapid sweep across our nation....

Most of the methamphetamine consumed in the United States is produced by Mexico-based and California-based Mexican traffickers.... These same Mexican criminal organizations control most mid-level and retail metham-phetamine distribution in the Pacific, Southwest, and west-central regions of the United States, as well as much of the distribution in the Great Lakes and Southeast regions.

BBC News, Mexico City, October 6, 2006:

The entire police force in the Mexican city of Tijuana is to be investigated on suspicion of being involved in drug trafficking and organized crime. In an unprecedented move, the authorities say it is the only way to clean up the force.

A Line in the Sand: Confronting the Threat at the Southwest Border
House Committee on Homeland Security
Subcommittee on Investigations
page 4
October 17, 2006

"Mexican drug cartels operating along the Southwest border are more sophisticated and dangerous than any other organized criminal enterprise. The Mexican cartels, and the smuggling rings and gangs they leverage, wield substantial control over the routes into the United States and pose substantial challenges to U.S. law enforcement to secure the Southwest border. The cartels operate along the border with military grade weapons, technology and intelligence and their own respective paramilitary enforcers.

In addition, human smugglers coordinate with the drug cartels, paying a fee to use the cartels' safe smuggling routes into the United States. There are also indications the cartels maybe moving to diversity their criminal enterprises to include the increasingly lucrative human smuggling trade.

Moreover, U.S. law enforcement has established that there is increasing coordination between Mexican drug cartels, human smuggling networks and U.S.-based gangs. The cartels use street and prison gangs located in the United States as their distribution networks. In the United States, the gang members operate as surrogates and enforcers for the cartels."

Statement by:	Karen P. Tandy, Administrator DEA
Before the:	U. S. House of Representatives Committee on Appropriations, Subcommittee for the Departments of Commerce, Justice, the Judiciary and Related Agencies
Date:	March 24, 2004

Americans spend approximately $65 Billion per year on illicit drugs.

978-0-595-85153-9
0-595-85153-3

Printed in the United States
71390LV00004B/40-69